The cellar stairs were steep and dark. Bella wanted to refuse to go down them, but a dreadful fascination forced her on.

In the guttering light of two candles, Bella saw Noah towering in the dank room, his black tousled hair all but touching the ceiling.

The room was damp and chilly enough, but what made Bella freeze with horror was a box that the wavering light showed. A long narrow box made out of rough planks of wood. An identical one lay beside it.

They were coffins. . . .

DOROTHY EDEN

Ravenscroft

A FAWCETT CREST BOOK
Fawcett Publications, Inc., Greenwich, Conn.

A Fawcett Crest Book reprinted by arrangement with
Coward-McCann, Inc.

Printed in the United States of America

Ravenscroft

1

IT HAD BEGUN TO SNOW BEFORE the London coach rumbled down the narrow Windsor streets. Bella and Lally thankfully climbed aboard.

Bella had said the only thing for them to do was to go on to London. If they were set down in Piccadilly, which Papa had always said was the hub of the universe, they could surely find inexpensive lodgings for a few days until they had obtained employment.

What else was there to do? Papa's cousin, to whom he had said they must go (he remembered her as always warm-hearted and generous although he hadn't seen her for a long time), had left the small narrow Windsor house, one of a row towered over by the great castle. She had been employed as one of the laundry-maids doing the fine linen from the castle. Her work was reputed to be exquisite. She had been entrusted with the shifts and starched petticoats of the little princesses, and sometimes Queen Victoria's underwear as well. Papa had been sure that she could find work for Lally, who was a good needlewoman, and perhaps for Bella, too, although Bella was not particularly accomplished at any one task. She was too much of a dreamer, her head filled with the novels of Mr. Dickens and Mr. Thackeray.

But the stranger living in Cousin Sarah's house said that Cousin Sarah had got the rheumatism so badly that she could no longer do her work. She had moved back to Ireland, where she had lived as a child.

So Bella and Lally, in one sentence, had lost their anticipated home. They could scarcely cross the sea to Ireland to search for Cousin Sarah.

Lally was inclined to be tearful, and blamed Papa for his lack of foresight.

"Why couldn't he have written to her? Why couldn't he have made sure it would be all right?"

"Because he didn't know he was dying," Bella said tartly, the pain turning in her heart again. Papa had known he was dying. As a doctor, he couldn't not have known his condition, Bella realized that now. But he had wanted to protect his daughters from the knowledge. So he had behaved in his usual noisy careless way, going on his rounds, ignoring the pain in his chest, until, just a week ago today, he had dropped dead on one of his patient's doorsteps.

Later, going through his meager possessions, Bella had found the envelope containing the five sovereigns—Papa had been improvident, spendthrift, fond of his rum and whisky, and never sparing of his time for poor patients who could pay him nothing—so this money represented his entire savings. With the money was a letter telling Bella and Lally to keep the sovereigns and not use them to pay his debts—the few pieces of furniture in their cottage could be used for that. And to go at once to Cousin Sarah who was now their only living relative.

"He did what he could," Bella said stormily. She had to be angry, or she would weep, like Lally, and what was the good of that? She had wept all the tears she would ever weep over the dead when Mama and their two little brothers had died of the cholera seven years ago, and Papa, who blamed himself for bringing home the infection, had begun to stop too frequently at the Horse and Hounds for his rum.

"Anyway," she went on, "Papa knew we were grown women and able to do something for ourselves."

Lally was nineteen, but didn't feel particularly grown, certainly not as much as Bella did at eighteen.

"Like going to London alone?" she asked with trepidation.

Bella drew her shawl more closely round her. The flecks of snow had begun to fall and it was very cold, much too cold to be uncertain where they would find a roof for their heads and a warm bed. But she was impatient, as usual, with Lally's timidity.

"Whatever can happen to us if we mind our own business? I'll ask the coachman if he knows of suitable lodgings. Or there may be a passenger who can help us. For goodness sake come, Lally, and don't look so miserable."

"I'm hungry," said Lally.

"Well, so am I. But we're not going to die of hunger before we reach London."

"And cold." But Lally's tears were more from fright than physical misery. She took after their mother, a gentle girl with large innocent blue eyes, a mouth given to trembling, and masses of fine fair hair. Bella had the hazel black-lashed

8

eyes of her father, curious eyes that turned golden when she was excited or agitated. They were her best feature, for her face was pale and three-cornered, and her black hair so heavy that it constantly fell down. She also had her father's quick temper and impetuous romantic nature. When her eyes flashed stormily she no longer looked a child. Lally, although older, had always leaned on her.

It turned out that she was right once more, for before they reached London there was a passenger on the coach who could help them.

At Twickenham the old gentleman, who had stared at the two girls with unabashed curiosity, got out, and a woman, elderly, but with youthful plump pink cheeks and large pebble-grey eyes, perfectly round, like an owl's, got in. She settled herself fussily, shaking the snow off her shawl and demanding that her basket be put on the seat beside her since it contained a dozen new-laid eggs and some fresh farm butter.

Then, seeing that her companions were decently dressed young girls, she beamed upon them in the most friendly manner.

"What a nasty cold evening, my dears. Home and a good fire is the best place. And the kettle on for a nice cup of tea. My son Noah will be seeing to that for me. If he hasn't gone gadding, of course. Young men do so like to gad. I've been visiting my sister for the day. To get a breath of country air, though it was very sharp air today, I must say. We're in for a cold spell. I pity the poor folk without a roof over their heads this night. And plenty of those there'll be. You only have to walk down Fleet Street and along the Embankment to see them, poor creatures. Little children, too. The fate of poor people is monstrous. There ought to be questions in Parliament. Noah and I say that time and again."

Lally nudged Bella. Bella scarcely needed to be nudged. She was well aware of the heaven-sent opportunity. This garrulous cosy little woman was exactly the way one had imagined Cousin Sarah.

But before she could speak their talkative companion made it doubly easy for her. Rocking gently to the motion of the coach, the plump little woman said in her soft voice,

"And you two sweet creatures? How do you come to be travelling alone? Or is that not my business? Noah always says I'm far too prying. But there. I'm interested in human nature. Human nature is my great study."

She fell silent, her round eyes watching the girls, waiting their reply.

Bella said, "Our father died. We're on our way to London to find employment. My sister Eulalie is very clever at needlework, and I—"

The woman leaned across to tap her with a small dimpled hand.

"No need to tell me, my dear. I can see that you would be capable at anything. You have a fine open look. Not cringing. I can't bear cringing servile young ladies. That is your upbringing, perhaps?"

"Our father kept us to our studies."

"Ah, so you can read and write. Then you can be a governess in a fine house. And your sister a milliner, or a dressmaker. You have nothing to worry about, my dears. And so healthy." The last words were said in a reflective murmur.

Bella put her chin up. She had never found it easy to ask for help.

"But we hardly know how to set about finding positions. We know nobody."

"Nobody?"

"No. The cousin we went to see in Windsor had moved. Papa didn't know. So we have no one."

Lally's lip trembled. The old lady noticed this. She pursed her little mouth and said, "Tch! Tch! Tch!" sympathetically.

"Lodgings?" she asked presently.

"We shall find some. We have money. Though if you live near Piccadilly, Mrs.—"

"Proudfoot."

"Mrs. Proudfoot. This is my sister Eulalie, and I'm Isabella McBride. If you knew of respectable lodgings near Piccadilly, Mrs. Proudfoot, we'd be very grateful."

"I live in Seven Dials. I have a smallish house. It's near the market. Covent Garden market. My son works there. He unloads cargoes of fruit from the ships coming up the river, oranges and the like from the Indies and the East, and brings them to the market. He works hard. He's a good lad. He keeps his old mother in comfort. Mind you, it's not an elegant street, and the house is smallish. Smallish but not too small. There's the attic room empty. You'd be welcome to it for a night or two until you get yourselves permanently settled. Mind you—" she silenced Bella, as Bella began to exclaim gratefully, "—I'd have to make a small charge just to keep my son happy. He has such a head for business, you see.

Say a shilling a night, and a good hot meal. As for looking for lodgings, I'd say be wary, very wary. Two sweet unprotected young creatures like you. You've still to learn the wicked world, my dears. So if you're interested there's the room upstairs and a good double bed, and I'd be happy thinking I'd helped someone in need."

She clicked her tongue again as she saw Lally now weeping in earnest.

"She has too much sensibility, that one. She must grow tougher. Or find a husband to protect her, of course." Mrs. Proudfoot chuckled pleasurably. "There should be no trouble about that. Such bonny young things, both of you. Any man would be lucky to get you. I'm a widow myself. But I have my good son, Noah. He takes after his father. Strong. Black-haired. A fine young man."

It was now quite dark outside. Flakes of snow spattered on the windows of the coach. They were coming into London, for the road was lit patchily by the flaring yellow of gas lamps. There were rows of houses, low, and huddled together, and sometimes an open space with trees or bushes, as black, in the dusk, as the unknown Noah. Bella didn't know why she had had a sudden shiver of aversion about Noah. But that was purely unreasonable, and the sort of thing much more likely to happen to Lally than herself. Noah was a good son, with a head for business, and his mother was an angel in disguise.

As soon as she could interrupt the gentle monologue that was going on beneath the nodding bonnet, Bella expressed her gratitude.

"How can we thank you, Mrs. Proudfoot? We'd be so grateful to accept your offer of a room until we find positions."

"Why, isn't that nice!" Mrs. Proudfoot gave a beaming smile, disclosing the only defect in her pleasant appearance, broken and blackened teeth. It quite altered her appearance, and for one moment she seemed to be someone entirely different from the placid kind-hearted person she was. But in a moment that queer impression left Bella and she listened to Mrs. Proudfoot assuring herself and Lally that there was no need for them to be hasty about finding positions.

"Young girls can be led astray. Things are not always as they appear on the surface. Why, I heard of a sweet young creature of sixteen thinking she was going as personal maid to a lady of the aristocracy, and finding herself meant only to amuse the son of the house. And he a monster." Mrs.

Proudfoot's bonnet, a gay little affair trimmed with a bunch of red cherries, nodded vigorously. "There's traps and traps for the innocent and the unwary. So I hope and pray you young ladies will allow me to be of assistance. I have acquaintances in various positions able to give advice. For instance, my great friend, Mrs. Jennings, has a sister who is housekeeper to Lord and Lady Massingham, and all of fashionable London passes through the doors of that house. I heard her mention only the other day some rich family that was looking for a governess. Who knows, we might be able to place you both in the same house, seeing you're such devoted sisters."

At that, Lally was able to speak at last.

"Oh, Mrs. Proudfoot, that would be kind."

"I can't believe how fortunate it was that we should meet you," Bella added.

Mrs. Proudfoot smiled gently, this time not parting her lips to disclose the offending teeth.

"Heaven sent me, my dears. Heaven helps the innocent."

They alighted from the coach at the stop in Piccadilly. Mrs. Proudfoot said it was but a step to her house, not far enough to take a cab.

The snow had already turned to slush beneath the hundreds of feet of passers-by, and the crowding vehicles, omnibuses, cabs, tradesmen's drays and wheelbarrows. The noise was bewildering: horses snorting and stamping, drivers' shouting, a newsboy yelling something about a great battle with the Russians at Balaclava, a skeleton-thin boy feverishly turning a barrel organ, and a ragged old woman urging passersby in a stentorian voice, to buy her bonny heather brought all the way from the moors of Scotland by the fast Scottish express.

The gas lamps flared down on this extraordinary noisy hectic scene. Lally clutched at Bella, and Bella, giving a fleeting thought to the quiet Buckinghamshire village which they had left only that morning, resolutely followed the surprisingly nimble figure of Mrs. Proudfoot.

"Hold up your skirts, my dears," said that lady over her shoulder. "The mud's worse than ever, what with the snow and all. Keep close to me. We'll be home in a jiffy and ready for a nice cup of tea."

Lally thought the journey down darker and narrower streets and bad-smelling alleys a nightmare, but Bella was already exhilarated and excited by the strangeness of it all.

12

She responded to new situations from which Lally, in her timidity, shrank. The bad smells, the anonymous figures huddling in doorways, sudden scurrying forms and unrepeatable shouted words of abuse, were all part of London. The same as the great houses and parks and theatres such as they would see in the next few days. They were actually going to be lodged near the wonderful Covent Garden Opera House, which all the famous singers of the world visited. She had read about it, with its chandeliers and grand staircase, and red plush. One day, she and Lally would go there to hear a performance. She didn't know how this would be achieved, but struggling through the evil-smelling mud after Mrs. Proudfoot's bunchy, nimble figure, she knew without doubt that somehow such a thing would happen. They would wear low-cut satin dresses and jewels, and everyone would look at them, the two beautiful sisters, one fair and one dark ... And the man who escorted them (there was only one man in Bella's dream) would be greatly envied ...

"H-ss-t! Out of my way!"

The vicious hiss cut like a whiplash across Bella's dream. She jumped aside as a man pushing a barrow loaded with an unidentifiable mass of junk pushed by, spattering her with mud. For a moment she was as weak as Lally, tears springing to her eyes at her abrupt descent to reality. The hiss seemed to ring in her ears as, cold and hungry and now with filthy skirts and shoes, she plodded down the mean streets, with Lally's panicky grip on one arm, and Mrs. Proudfoot steering ahead indomitably.

But once within Mrs. Proudfoot's cosy parlour Bella's momentary depression vanished and even Lally's tears dried.

In the well-blacked, shining grate there was a glowing fire. A kettle sang on the hob. Two wooden rocking chairs were drawn up on the multi-coloured rag rug in front of the fire. There was a dresser, well-stocked with platters and tankards, and a table laid for tea. The red plush curtains were drawn across the window making the room as cosy as could be. It was possible to forget at once the cold muddy streets outside the front door. Here was warmth and comfort and safety.

Mrs. Proudfoot saw the girls' expressions and nodded happily.

"You see, my dears. I spoke the truth. The kettle boiling and a good fire, and upstairs a warm bed." She rubbed her little plump hands, and held them out to the blaze. "Would

13

you like to see your room at once, and take off your wet shoes? I'll take you up and show you where the water closet is. Oh, yes, this isn't a grand house but that comfort I insisted on having installed. I don't hold with ladies having to go to outdoor privies in all weathers. Now don't be long upstairs. When you come down tea will be ready and Noah will be home."

Upstairs, alone with Bella, Lally found her tongue.

"Oh, Bella, isn't this wonderful! I think Mamma and Papa must be watching over us, don't you? Look, a real feather bed!" She bounced on the bed excitedly. "And everything so spotless. See, we have our own washstand, and there's water in the jug. Mrs. Proudfoot must always be prepared for guests."

"Lodgers," said Bella. She was glad they were being independent and paying for their lodgings. For all Mrs. Proudfoot's kindness, she was a stranger and one couldn't accept too much generosity from strangers. At least, one might wonder why it was offered . . .

But there was nothing to make her uneasy here. The room was scrupulously clean, which was probably a rare thing in this neighbourhood, and their welcome couldn't have been more genuine had it been from the missing Cousin Sarah. Lally was right, Mrs. Proudfoot had been heaven-sent.

"Perhaps she's looking for a wife for Noah," she said reflectively.

Lally looked startled.

"Do you suppose—oh, but she couldn't be. Noah sounds the kind of young man to find his own wife. To tell the truth, I'm a little scared of him."

"You're scared of everybody," Bella said, not wanting to admit that she herself had had that strange moment of apprehension about Noah. Strong, black-haired, Mrs. Proudfoot had said. "And I shouldn't think there are many nice young women in these parts. Or didn't you have your eyes open as we came along?"

Lally shivered, nodding.

"Yes, I did. I kept thinking, supposing we had been alone in these streets. It is true that London's no place for unprotected girls. And that makes it so much more fortunate that we're here. Oh dear, do I look too awful? My nose always gets red from crying. Shall I change my gown, Bella? The skirt is dreadfully muddied. It wouldn't take a minute to unpack. I could put on the blue—"

14

"For Noah?" Bella teased. "I thought you were so scared of him."

Lally's pretty chin went up.

"Oh, Bella, you know that I can't bear not to be neat and tidy. I must wash my face and brush my hair. Oh, do look at the sweet little mirror. Bring the candle closer so that I can see. I declare, my hair is a ruin—oh, what was that?"

Her flushed face with its tangled mop of fine fair hair vanished like a ghost from the tilted mirror as she shot round.

"What was what?" To her annoyance, Bella's heart had jumped and her voice was no more than a whisper.

"I thought I heard someone moaning."

"I expect you did. In the street." Bella went and flung up the window and leaned out. "This is a horrid street," she declared vigorously, finding relief in indignation. "I had thought the centre of London would be so grand. But this! It smells of bad fish, and worse. And look, the snow's black with soot almost before it settles. What a good thing we're safe indoors. But we won't stay in these parts long, Lally. We'll get into a grand house with a hundred rooms, and staircases, and a conservatory with orange trees—"

"You're sure it was in the street?"

"What? That noise? Of course!"

"I thought for a minute it came from just under us." Lally stood uncertainly, her eyes enormous. Then she made herself laugh. "I suppose it's because I'm tired and hungry, but I'm as jumpy as a cat. Isn't it silly of me, when Mrs. Proudfoot is so kind. Help me pin up my hair, Bella, so we can go down."

Bella twisted her sister's hair deftly and impatiently.

"If you're going to be so helpless, how will you ever get a position? You need a lady's maid yourself." The brush became still in Bella's hands. "But wouldn't it be fun if we did have one? Or one each."

"Now who's dreaming? A lady's maid! Us!"

"Why not? Things happen. Or if they don't you can make them. Look at how we're here safe for the night."

"Yes, I know, but this is very different from those grand houses you're dreaming about. You read too many books. Papa always said so. But I do admit it's nice to dream."

For a moment the girls stared at each other, caught up in their faith and optimism. Then suddenly Lally shivered. "O-oh, I'm cold! Don't let's be parted, Bella, wherever we go to work. I'd so hate to be parted."

"My dears! My dears!" That was Mrs. Proudfoot calling

15

up the stairs. "Come on down. Supper's ready and Noah's home."

The tall young man dominated the room. His head with its thatch of coarse tousled black hair was only an inch or two from the ceiling. He had very broad shoulders and great hands that rested loosely on his hips. His cheeks were reddened to a holly brightness, perhaps by the cold wind off the river or perhaps simply by the health that flowed through his strong body. But his eyes, small and intense, were blacker than anything Bella had ever seen. Black and piercing beneath heavy brows. His loosely hanging hands and his negligent attitude were simply a pose. He was summing up the two girls with the most acute awareness.

"These are the young ladies, Noah," Mrs. Proudfoot said with her warm enthusiasm. "Miss Eulalie McBride and Miss Isabella McBride. Fancy two such innocent creatures abroad on a night like this. Didn't I do right to bring them home?"

Noah began to grin broadly, showing large white teeth. "Quite a find, eh, Ma?"

Mrs. Proudfoot turned to the girls to share her delight. "Now isn't that a clever way Noah has of talking? Quite a find. As if you are both jewels. Now sit down, my dears. Tottie, Tottie! The eggs! The bread and butter!"

A girl came hurrying in from the kitchen laden with a crock of eggs and a plate piled high with thick slices of bread and butter. Hungry as she was, Bella noticed Tottie before she was aware of the food. Her shock at Noah's size now turned to a new feeling of uneasiness. In an old brown dress, terribly shabby, with her wispy hair hanging round the white wedge of her face, Tottie looked no more than twelve years old. She had a dull daft look. Her hands were covered in chilblains. In contrast to Mrs. Proudfoot's plump cosiness and Noah's radiant health, she was like a starved cat, all eyes and bones.

She put her burden on the table, clattering the eggs as if she were terrified.

But Mrs. Proudfoot said quite kindly, "That's a good girl, Tottie. You've counted right this time. How would you like to boil another egg for yourself?"

The child stared as if she hadn't heard correctly. Her mouth fell open in disbelief.

"Well, off you go and do it. Nobody starves in this house."

Mrs. Proudfoot flapped her hands and Tottie fled like a scared chicken.

"There's no use expecting any sense out of her," Mrs. Proudfoot explained. "She's dumb, poor soul, and I rather think half-witted as well. We've only just found her, haven't we, Noah. She was living all alone like a little rat in an old shed. Noah brought her home. We've not had time to dress her decently yet. Indeed, if Miss Eulalie's as good with her needle as she says, she may help me make the poor child a gown."

"Oh, *yes*, Mrs. Proudfoot," said Lally eagerly.

"Don't call me Mrs. Proudfoot, call me Aunt Aggie. All my girls do."

"All your girls?" Bella asked.

"Bless me, my dears, you aren't the only ones I've helped. Are they, Noah?"

Noah gave his gleaming smile.

"But they're prettier than Tottie, Ma. You had a better find than me."

"Oh, pshaw, Noah! None of your making sheep's eyes. The girls are only here for a day or two until they find positions. I'm going to send word to Mrs. Jennings tomorrow. She'll know of something, I'll be bound."

Bella knew she should have been grateful and happy for Mrs. Proudfoot's plans. But all she could think of was trying to avoid Noah's sharp black stare. He never stopped staring. He had no manners at all. Bella found herself wondering how poor little Tottie, crouching in the darkness of the tumble-down shed, had felt when she had been dragged into the light by that great hand that was now carelessly cracking an eggshell. Perhaps that was when she had been struck dumb . . .

After supper Mrs. Proudfoot, who liked to be called Aunt Aggie, sat in her rocking chair knitting. She had put on steel-rimmed spectacles, and through them her eyes were magnified until they seemed to Bella, who by now was sleep-dazed, like perfectly round grey moons. Her needles clicked and she sometimes pursed her little pink mouth and said "Tch! Tch!" reflectively. She had stopped talking and Bella had no idea at all what her thoughts were.

Noah had gone out. Bella didn't wonder what his errand was. She was only thankful he was gone. She tried not to think about him at all, because if she did she would imagine him searching derelict houses and sheds for more starved little girls.

But it was only her tiredness and the strangeness of the long day that was making her so foolishly imaginative.

At last it was Lally's head that fell forward on her chest. She jerked it up, exclaiming in confusion, "I'm sorry, Aunt Aggie! I dozed off."

Mrs. Proudfoot started up.

"Oh, my poor dear! There you are tired out and I hadn't noticed. You must go straight upstairs, both of you. Come, I'll light your candles myself."

She preceded them up the stairs, carrying the flickering candle. The girls stumbled after her, scarcely able to see their way, the frail light obscured by Mrs. Proudfoot who, with her wide skirts, completely filled the narrow stairs. The first time they had mounted the stairs they had been too intent on where they were going to notice the first landing, and now it was too dark to see what doors led into what rooms.

In the attic room Mrs. Proudfoot lit two candles on the dressing table, and made a great fuss of turning down the bed and untying the pretty blue ribbon bows of the curtains so that the night was shut out. Then she stood in her dark gown with its snowy kerchief and smiled her goodnight.

"You must sleep soundly, my dears. Tomorrow, as I said, we'll begin planning your future. I am sure Noah will have some notions. He was very taken with you. Especially Miss Eulalie. I noticed him looking at her pretty face."

"Aunt Aggie!" Lally gasped.

The old lady chuckled, showing her shocking teeth. In the flickering light, her mouth was a dark hole, her pale eyes swallowed into the pale blur of her face. For a moment Bella had another of her disconcerting impressions—that Mrs. Proudfoot had a gargoyle head, open-mouthed and staring.

"Isn't it nice to be admired by a strong young man? But there, I won't tease. Sleep well. And don't be alarmed if you hear strange noises in the night. You little country dears. You're not accustomed to the goings-on in a city street. Such goings-on. They don't bear listening to. But you'll be safe here, my little loves."

As soon as she had gone Bella sprang to the door and shut it, then wedged a chair under the knob.

Lally watched her, open-mouthed.

"Whatever's come over you, Bella? Surely you're not afraid of Noah. Not with Aunt Aggie—"

"Don't call her Aunt Aggie!" Bella said.

"But she asked us to. Everyone does, she said. You heard her."

"Who is everyone?"

"Why—girls like us, I suppose. She said she often helps girls. She must keep this room just for them, I mean with the ribbons on the curtains and that darling mirror. And this bed. Oh, this lovely bed! I can't wait to get into it. I shall sleep like a log."

"I shan't close my eyes," said Bella.

"Bella, whatever has come over you? You weren't like this before supper."

She hadn't seen Noah then, nor Tottie. Where did Tottie sleep? In a dark cupboard in the kitchen, curled up in her rags? Out of sight of Noah? Surely, if she had been in the house only a day, there would have been time for Aunt Aggie (now even she was thinking of Mrs. Proudfoot as Aunt Aggie!) to find some warmer tidier clothing for her. But she had had a freshly-laid egg for her supper. She wasn't being starved any longer. And if she were really as frightened as she looked she could run away, couldn't she? Even in the snow. Cold was better than terror. So it must be only that Mrs. Proudfoot hadn't yet had time to wash her hair and dress her decently.

Lally in her nightgown, with her hair let down, was climbing into bed.

"Do hurry, Bella. Blow out the candles and let's get some sleep. I didn't like Noah either, if the truth must be told. But we might not need to see him again. I expect he goes to work before dawn, and by night we might have positions to go to ourselves. Anyway, Aunt Aggie isn't entirely philanthropic. She's getting a shilling a night from us. So we aren't in her debt."

It was unusual for Lally to be the one who was calm and sensible. Bella was suddenly ashamed of her wild imagination, and began to undress quickly.

"I expect you're right, Lally. Anyway, it's only for tonight. Tomorrow we'll go out ourselves and see what can be done. It will be stopped snowing by then."

"Aunt Aggie must have found positions for those other girls," Lally murmured sleepily.

"Yes, she must. And we're in London at last. It's really very exciting. Think of all the famous people perhaps not a mile from here. Think of the great houses and the lights. Anything can happen to us now we're not in a little village any longer."

Lally was pleased to hear the familiar optimism in Bella's voice.

"There you are, dreaming as usual. Well, perhaps your dreams will come true. Perhaps you will live in a great house."

"You, too, Lally."

But when the candles were blown out the girls clung to each other in the feather bed, tense and listening, until sheer weariness overcame them and they slept.

Because they slept so soundly, the shriek that awakened them seemed doubly shocking.

2

AS BELLA HAD SURMISED, NOT A mile away, indeed less than half a mile, there were many famous people, and they in their turn were watched over by portraits of more departed famous.

Beside a richly glowing fire in the Garrick Club, Guy Raven was entertaining his old friend, Doctor Bushey.

"Some more brandy, Daniel?"

"I will. It's excellent. It'll keep the cold out on my way home."

"I'll give you a lift."

"No, no, I prefer to walk. You fellows in carriages never see life."

"Life? What sort?"

"My dear Guy, don't raise your eyebrows like that. Not your sort of life, I grant you. It has nothing to do with smart gambling dens or restaurants or ballrooms. Or boudoirs. It bears no relation to your invented diversions."

"Invented? That's the right word at least, even if the following one hardly fits my case. I seldom feel diverted!"

Doctor Bushey's shrewd eyes were almost lost beneath the luxuriating grey lichen of his eyebrows.

"Now look here, Guy, you've indulged in enough self-pity. That's what it is, no matter what you like to call it."

Guy shrugged. "You're talking of my behaviour? I put no labels on it. My mother calls it licentious. She thinks because I no longer have a wife I also no longer have physical desires. I agree that what I do isn't related to love. But if a

20

pretty woman's willing—who the devil cares about my reputation?"

"Don't misjudge your mother, Guy. She wants you to marry again. And rightly."

The young man leaned back with an exasperated sigh.

"Not you, too, Daniel. So Ravenscroft needs an heir. So I tie myself to some eager young virgin and produce one. Isn't that as licentious as sleeping with a whore? And what the devil would I talk to this young woman about for the rest of my life? Damn it, Daniel, marriage might have been invented to regularize having children, but no one said it should be a prison." His eyes went dark. "And it would be a prison for me with anyone but Caroline."

Doctor Bushey regarded his host, a young man in his late twenties, handsome with his high-browed face, his lazy blue eyes that could turn to steel, and too often did, his cool hard mouth, his air of dandyism. It was becoming difficult to remember the Guy Raven of two and three years ago, passionately in love with his delicate young wife. There had been no boredom in his eyes then. A great deal of enthusiasm for the son he hoped for, but most of all that unashamed tenderness for Caroline.

Of course Guy would be thirty on his next birthday. All this cynicism and impatience had been in him and would have come out one day, but it would have been levelled intelligently only against hypocrisies and the smug social values he hated.

Now, alone, and, Daniel guessed, appallingly lonely, he was simply letting himself go. He did need to marry again. But who? In spite of his wealth and looks the more timid eligible young women were being frightened off him—or their mothers were. He could be unforgivably rude and deliberately shocking. And the purely ambitious woman who would have been a match for him he scorned. Besides, as in a slightly drunken moment he confided to Daniel, young women were romantic and wanted some vestige of a heart. His was in the grave with Caroline and the dead baby.

But perhaps his recent plans for a political career—as another diversion?—would save him. He was standing for his own constituency in Hertfordshire, and so far was bringing a surprising amount of energy and enthusiasm to his campaign. Although that, Doctor Bushey knew, had a good deal to do with his opponent, Sir Henry Shields, being a man whom Guy disliked and despised. He could be a devilish hater, another tendency Caroline might have softened. Surely there must be some other young woman in the world who could care for this unpredictable exasperating brilliant reckless young man who was so good at making enemies.

Doctor Bushey firmly believed in the balance of good and evil. A hater could also be a lover.

After the silence that had fallen between them Doctor Bushey thought it discreet to change the subject.

"Have you decided yet on what issue you're going to fight this election?"

Guy grinned, and looked suddenly much younger.

"Chiefly the desire to do down my opponent who's a smug-faced hypocrite. He leads his wife and his five daughters to church every Sunday, and on Monday starves his employees, and uses children, babies, in his mills."

"He's a powerful man, Guy. He has the press on his side."

"I'm not frightened of the press. They could use cleaner ink, too. But of course you're right again, Daniel. Once I've trampled Sir Henry in the dust I've got to build something on top of him. There's the defence policy, of course. This expensive and exceedingly bloody and, in my opinion, quite useless war in the Crimea. There's the Irish question. There's income tax. It'll have to go up, not down."

"And there are the poor," said Doctor Bushey.

"Unpopular."

"I didn't think you were concerned with popularity. And you mentioned yourself the children in Shields' mills. Do they have to be used only as a weapon against him? He isn't the only guilty one. The whole country's guilty. Why don't you fight their cause generally?"

Guy smiled lazily at his companion's earnestness.

"You're not on an election platform, Daniel."

"Sometimes I'd like to be. Look here, come with me to one of the Ragged Schools one day. You might think, or make your constituents think, how washing facilities could be introduced into the tumbledown shed where the schools are held. Then, when the children come off the streets from selling matches or running three miles behind a cab in the hope of earning twopence for carrying baggage, or any of the other devious occupations they pursue to fill their bellies, we might be able to wash a bit of the filth off them. And perhaps even give them a bowl of hot soup to encourage their learning of the alphabet."

"What else?" said Guy, very quietly.

"Well, there are the young women, girls, mere children, forced on to the streets either by drunken parents or because they have no parents. I won't try to describe their lives, unless they're rescued pretty young. Have you noticed Betsey at my house, by the way? But of course you have. You've an eye for a pretty girl. Would you believe that two years ago she was in a brothel in Waterloo Road? She got typhoid and was thrown out into the street to die. Someone picked her up and took her to the fever hospital in Islington. I found her there. So now her story has ended happily. But for one Betsey there are hundreds less fortunate. Innocents . . . Come, Guy, there's a cause worth fighting for. Get this city cleaned up. Crush these monsters who exploit the unfortunate."

"You're on your hobby horse, Daniel."

"I'm giving you a cause."

"I admit I'm interested. Now convince me. This girl, Betsey, for instance—she's now clean and well-fed, but hasn't that experience perverted her?"

"Untouched!" Doctor Bushey declared heatedly. "Untouched! A child can have an inherent innocence that saves it. Not all, of course. But if they have, they seem to overcome even the physical degradation. Those are the ones to be saved. I'll make you a challenge, Guy. Walk with me through the streets of Soho one evening. I'd suggest tonight if it weren't snowing. What about tomorrow?"

"My mother has some affair. I'd willingly escape it, but I promised her I'd be there. Reluctantly."

"She has some young lady for you to look over?"

Guy swung round violently, beckoning to the waiter.

"Two more brandies. Doubles. Yes, you're right, Daniel. A prissy miss in a crinoline. At the moment, I assure you, I'd rather look over your Soho drabs. But I suppose I can get drunk again. Make it the following day. I'll look forward to it."

"This is hardly meant to be a pleasure."

Guy's eyes were narrowed, hiding their expression.

"I believe you think all this suffering poor stuff is a revelation to me. Have I gone about with my eyes shut?"

"Your eyes see what your mind allows them to. Like those of fashionable ladies dabbling in good works. Otherwise how could they bear it? Make your class *look* at things."

Guy's mouth quirked suddenly, without humour.

"You're an old sobersides, Daniel. Why don't we pick up a

likely looking girl and take her to the Ritz? Feed her, and pick her brains. If she has any."

"My God, I'll prove this is no amusing evening out," exclaimed Doctor Bushey, suddenly losing his temper. "If you are a specimen of the kind of man who sits in Parliament—blind, introverted, selfish, spoilt—then heaven help this country!"

Guy's mouth tightened. But he said with deliberate good humour, "You'll have me taking you seriously, Daniel. I'll find I'm using the poor as more than a stick with which to beat my dishonourable opponent."

"I'll show you. I'll prove it to you!"

"I believe you will."

But the last brandy had slightly fuddled Doctor Bushey, and his flash of anger had tired him. He didn't notice that Guy spoke seriously at last.

3

LALLY CLUTCHED BELLA IN A suffocating grip. They both lay rigid, listening.

"What was it?" Lally whispered, at last.

"Some—" Bella hesitated, "—poor woman in the street. Robbed, I expect."

"No, it was in this house."

Bella had thought so herself. She was still trying not to alarm Lally who was inclined to hysterics.

"It was the same person we heard moaning this evening," Lally said with certainty. She sat up in the dark. "Who can it be? What can be the matter with her? Wouldn't Aunt Aggie have said if there were someone else here?"

The dark pressing on Bella's eyes was intolerable. She groped for matches and lit the candle. Even such a small and wavering light restored her common sense.

"I expect it was Tottie. She probably has nightmares that she's still in that dreadful shed. Perhaps with rats."

"I can hear someone walking about," Lally exclaimed, clutching Bella afresh. "Coming up the stairs," she whispered.

The footsteps, ponderous and slow, were quite distinct. The ancient stairboards creaked. A door clicked shut, softly.

Then abruptly, freezingly, the scream came again.

Without conscious thought Bella was out of bed and standing rooted to the floor.

Lally had begun to whimper, her face ash white.

"What are you going to do, Bella? Don't leave me!"

Bella picked up her shawl and flung it round her shoulders.

"I'm going to find out what's going on."

"Bella, don't! Don't! It might be Noah."

Bella looked at their feeble barricade, the chair propped beneath the doorknob.

"Noah! What would he be likely to do?" she said with a fine pretence at scorn. At the same moment the door handle turned very gently.

Lally's knuckles were in her mouth. Bella, gripping the end of the bed, was able to say in quite a loud voice.

"Who is it?"

"My dears! What's making the door stick?"

It was Aunt Aggie's voice, warm, throaty, reassuring. Bella sprang to the door to remove the chair.

"We heard someone scream. Lally—we were both nervous!"

"So you barricaded the door. In my house! My *foolish* little dears!" Aunt Aggie, in nightcap and voluminous red flannel dressing-gown, holding a candle aloft, looked the picture of cosiness and normality. "I said to Noah, those dear girls upstairs will be alarmed. I must slip up and see if they have been disturbed. I can't stay—" a deep shuddering moan from beneath her stopped Aunt Aggie for a moment. Then she went on quickly, "It's most unfortunate, my poor niece is having her baby quite six weeks too soon. She's a delicate creature. I was afraid this would happen."

"You mean she's been here all the time?" Bella exclaimed involuntarily.

"All this evening? Certainly. And for a week before that. She came to London to await her husband's return from abroad. He's a sailor. His ship's due in any day, any moment. But I fear—" Aunt Aggie chuckled cosily, "his child is going to arrive first. Now settle yourselves, my loves. I didn't tell you Mary was here for fear you'd be disturbed."

"We're doctor's daughters," Bella said, rather stiffly.

"Why, so you are. But I expect your dear Papa sheltered you, for all that." Another cry came from downstairs. "Oh dear, I must go. Mary doesn't show much fortitude. She's very young, poor dear."

"Can we help?" Bella persisted.

"By no means. I wouldn't have your young eyes distressed. Goodness me, I've brought a score of babies into the world. Noah's in the kitchen boiling water. That's all the help I need. Now pull the blankets over your ears and go back to sleep."

The door closed and Aunt Aggie had gone. Bella got back into bed, but didn't blow out the candle. The frail light was a small shield against nightmares.

"Do you know," she said at last, "I think that baby is Noah's."

"You mean Mary is his wife?"

"Well—" Bella thought nothing of the kind. "I think that's why she's here. Because the baby is Noah's."

"Oh," said Lally, shocked but satisfied. "That's why Aunt Aggie wouldn't talk about her."

It was the first light of dawn before the baby's thin, feeble wail sounded.

Bella edged herself out of Lally's clutch that had scarcely slackened all night, and got out of bed to draw back the curtains. It was still snowing.

When she saw the inexorably falling flakes, making the narrow street spotless and silent, her heart sank. This meant that she and Lally would have to remain prisoners in the house for another day.

But prisoners by snow, not by any persuasion on the part of Aunt Aggie or Noah, she told herself firmly. She would pay Aunt Aggie the shilling for their night's lodging and beg her hospitality until the snow stopped. It was the only thing to do. No one could go abroad looking for work with skirts dragging in twelve inches of snow.

Anyway, her night's fears seemed foolish now. A baby had been safely born, which was a wonderful, not an alarming event. Bella only hoped that Lally would wake in a similarly calm state of mind. In this, too, her mind was soon at rest, for Lally opened her eyes and instantly exclaimed, in excited anticipation,

"I wonder what the baby is. I long to see it. Let's get dressed and go downstairs."

A newly-lit fire was burning cheerfully in the little parlour. Before it stood a wooden cradle.

Lally was beside it in a flash, and bending over its occupant.

"Oh, Bella! It's awfully tiny. Come and look. It's no bigger than a doll. It has black hair like—" She bit off her words as Noah's laugh came from the doorway.

"Were you going to say like mine, Miss Eulalie? But you'd be wrong in that. Mary's only my cousin. And I suppose that poor worm of a thing is my cousin, too. Lost me my night's sleep, it did."

But Noah didn't look as if he had lost any sleep. His huge shoulders filled the doorway, his cheeks were as healthily red as ever, his little coal-black eyes intensely alert. It was impossible to imagine him having any sympathy for the young mother upstairs, whether the child was his or not.

"Is it a boy or a girl?" was all Bella could find to say.

"A boy. If you can call it anything at all. It came too soon. Ma says it likely won't live."

Lally gave a cry of distress, and knelt beside the cradle to fondle the baby's incredibly miniature hand. The fingers curled feebly round her forefinger. She gave a softer exclamation, of pity and enchantment. It was as if the little scrap of a thing were appealing to her, asking her to help it to live.

Aunt Aggie had come in carrying steaming plates of porridge.

"Well, look at her, the daft creature," she said tolerantly. "Is your sister soft about babies, Miss Isabella?"

Lally looked up, pleading.

"Aunt Aggie, it won't die, will it? Noah says it will."

"The Lord knows, my dear. It's got a bad start, poor scrap. It won't take any food yet. I fancy it's too weak. I've seen that kind before. They just take a brief look at our sorrowful world and then off they fly to brighter climes. Now don't take on, Miss Eulalie. If the Lord had meant that little being to stay with us He wouldn't have sent it too soon. Come and sup your porridge while it's hot."

"How is its mother?" Bella asked.

"Fine. She's eaten a hearty breakfast and now she's sound asleep."

The porridge plates were liberally filled and there was a jug of milk from which Aunt Aggie urged everyone to help themselves lavishly. Tottie, still dressed in the same deplorable dress that was little better than a piece of sacking, came in to take away the empty plates, clattering them clumsily in her swollen fingers. Her face was not so much white as blue, either from cold or starvation or both. Presently she came back with bread and dripping and thick fried slices of gammon.

"Eat up," said Aunt Aggie comfortably. For all her disturbed night she looked remarkably fresh, her cheeks pink, her eyes round and benign. "Noah, don't forget that you must call on Mrs. Jennings before you go to work. That's the lady I mentioned as might be of assistance in finding positions for you young ladies," she added to Bella and Lally. "Get her to send a message, Noah, if she has any prospects. It's no day for women to be abroad. I haven't seen so much snow in London for years. You two dears mustn't attempt to go out. You'd be mired in a few steps. I'm sorry it will be such a dull day for you," she fluttered her plump hands, "but Noah and I can't be held to blame for the snow. I think I may be right in suggesting you could find worse places to be than this fireside."

Her expression was so kind, her plump figure so attractive in its neat dark dress fastened at the neck with a jet brooch, her cap so crisply starched and snowy, and this all following a sleepless night, that Bella could only nod in helpless admiration. Her apprehensions had been completely vague and unfounded. Even Noah, by daylight, was simply a large uncouth young man with his head hung greedily over his plate.

"Can we see your niece later, Aunt Aggie?" Bella found herself automatically adopting the more intimate form of address. She had caught it from Lally.

"Well, now, that I don't know. She's shy of strangers. She's a country girl. But we'll see. We'll consult. I want her to sleep as long as possible. So as to get strong if her husband should arrive. In the meantime, if you want to be of use, I can find you plenty of needlework. If Mrs. Jennings should call it would be sensible for her to see how nicely you sew."

Noah suddenly made a stifled sound, between a grunt and a cough. He lifted his head and cleared his throat vigorously, as if a crumb had lodged inconveniently. His small eyes were shining, not with distress, but with malicious laughter.

"You're a one, Ma. Getting your mending done for free," he added.

Bella wanted to explore. Lally was content to sit by the baby's cradle, her needle half the time idle in her hand. But Bella kept listening for Aunt Aggie's whereabouts. She had the most lively curiosity about the baby's mother, and a compulsive desire to see her. Once, when she had been sure

28

Aunt Aggie was upstairs, she went into the kitchen, a narrow dark chilly room with damp walls and a stone floor, and a tiny window looking on to a square of snowy backyard. She wanted to see Tottie, too.

She asked Tottie for a glass of water, and while the girl was getting it, said conversationally, "It's nice being here, isn't it, Tottie?"

The little unkempt head nodded warily.

"I noticed you have such bad chilblains, you poor thing. You ought to have something to put on them. My father had a very good prescription. I'll tell it to your mistress and she'll get it for you, I'm sure."

The child stared, shrunk against the wall. Bella had a queerly certain feeling that she could speak if she wanted to.

"But anyway they'll soon get better now you're in a warm house. It's better than that horrid shed, isn't it? Do you really have no mother or father, or brothers and sisters?"

Tottie shook her head violently. Bella moved nearer.

"Tottie, have you seen the lady upstairs? The sick one?"

But before Tottie could make any kind of response the ceiling above them creaked, there were steps on the stairs.

Tottie made a flapping movement with her hands. Her face was full of unreasoning terror. She seemed to be frantic for Bella to go.

Bella's swift instinct of fear had simply been caught from this child who was like a little wild animal, captured and mesmerized. She made herself say lightly, "It's only Mrs. Proudfoot, Tottie. She wouldn't hurt you. Is it Noah you're afraid of?"

But the child had fled through a doorway that led down a steep narrow flight of stairs, obviously to a cellar. Perhaps that was where she slept, down in the dark and the damp. She must have been in hiding from a hostile world for so long that she instinctively preferred the dark.

Surely, if anyone could tame her, it would be Aunt Aggie.

Resolutely reassuring herself, Bella returned to the parlour fire and Lally, with her anxious vigil over the baby.

"Bella, it never cries."

"I expect it's too weak."

"I think that's because it's hungry. It sucked my finger quite strongly."

Bella looked down at the tiny pinched face. It didn't look like the face of a newborn baby, healthily red and crumpled.

It was a curious bluish-white and looked old, a miniature old old man.

But even so weak a child could be coaxed to life. Papa had used to perform miracles with delicate babies. He had insisted on constant feedings, a very little at a time.

All the same, after Tottie scuttering away into her cellar, Bella felt defeated and wasn't sure she wanted to fight for another even more pathetic scrap of humanity. She had a sudden desperate longing for their cottage in Buckinghamshire, Papa coming in smelling a little of rum but hearty and cheerful, the table laid for supper, the fire burning, Lally at the pianoforte singing in her sweet reedy voice, the present, secure and comfortable, lasting unquestioningly forever.

Nevertheless, when Aunt Aggie came in, she would have made the suggestion if Lally hadn't bravely spoken up first.

"Aunt Aggie, I think the baby's hungry. Shouldn't it go to its mother?"

Aunt Aggie bustled over with the greatest interest.

"Do you think it will drink now, the little mite? Well, there's no harm in finding out. I'll take it upstairs."

She was away for a long time. When she came back with her bundle she was doleful.

"I doubt it took much. It hasn't the strength to suck. However, we must trust in the Almighty." She laid the baby back in the cradle. "There, the little lamb. So quiet and good. Not a cry against this wicked world."

Later in the day, just before the early dusk began to fall, there was a great knocking at the street door. Aunt Aggie, for all her bulk, could move lightly and very quickly. She was out of the parlour at once, closing the door behind her. Bella could move quickly, too. Without formulating her reason she had sprung to the door and opened it a crack.

"Bella!" Lally exclaimed, horrified.

"S-sh! I want to hear."

But she couldn't hear much, only disjointed scraps of conversation. Something in a man's voice about fog and ice on the river, and Aunt Aggie oddly emphasizing one word, *awkward, awkward*. Then she said quite clearly, "Tomorrow morning at the latest, fog or not," and in reply to something the man said as he stepped away from the door out of earshot, "A great prize, you can be sure."

She gave her low throaty chuckle as she closed the door.

Bella had scarcely time to regain her seat before Aunt Aggie came back into the room.

"Now isn't that exciting! The ship is in."

"The ship?"

"Mary's husband's, of course. But it can't dock yet because of the fog."

"Then the baby will be going," Lally exclaimed.

Aunt Aggie patted her head benevolently.

"Silly child. You didn't think it could stay here, did you? Any more than you and your sister can. Poor Aunt Aggie is the one who should be sad. She is just a milestone all you young people pass. However, that's life, and we must accept it. Now do you know what Tottie and I are going to do. We're going to toast crumpets for tea. Presently Noah will be home. We'll all have a cosy evening round the fireside."

There hadn't been a sound from upstairs all day. Lately, the dreadful suspicion had been growing on Bella that the baby's mother was dead. She wasn't leaving happily with her newly-returned husband in the morning, she was going to be carried out, smuggled away before it was light. That was what the furtive conversation with the man at the door had been about. That was the thing that was so awkward. Aunt Aggie hadn't wanted to distress them by telling them the news.

Could it be true? Was it only her strained and fevered imagination? It was so uncanny that there was no sound at all from upstairs. Even when Aunt Aggie went up, there were no voices. And she still insisted that her patient wasn't well enough to be visited. Was that why the baby didn't drink—because its mother lay dead?

The same unreasoning impulse that had driven Bella to listen at the door now made her run softly up the stairs while she knew that Aunt Aggie was busy in the kitchen.

There were two open doors on the first landing. They led to small bedrooms, one obviously Aunt Aggie's and the other Noah's. The door to the third room was closed.

Bella knocked gently then, afraid to linger, turned the knob.

The door was locked.

"You!" she called softly. "Mary! Are you awake?"

No one answered. There was a curious musty smell on the landing. It seemed to come from the locked room. Bella called again, more urgently,

"Are you all right in there? I'm your friend. Please speak to me."

She pressed her ear against the door, and fancied she could hear deep breathing as of someone drowned fathoms in sleep. Yes, she was sure it was breathing. Abruptly she was filled with a wonderful sense of relief. Mary was sleeping, as Aunt Aggie had said. Once again, Aunt Aggie's actions had been perfectly innocent. Really, she was awful to have let her imagination run away with her like this. It was only because the day had seemed so long and dark, and the house so claustrophobic. Dead bodies, indeed! There was only a young girl sleeping after the ordeal of having her first baby.

Relief made her quite gay that evening. When Noah came home to say that Mrs. Jennings would be sending for Bella and Lally some time the following evening, she welcomed the news with gratitude and optimism.

"Does she know of some suitable positions? That would be wonderful."

Aunt Aggie tapped her gently with her knitting needle.

"Such impatience! She wants to be gone from us, Noah. No, my dear, Mrs. Jennings doesn't recommend young ladies to positions without having first seen them and ascertained their capabilities and character. She is the soul of integrity. She merely wishes to make yours and your sister's acquaintance. It may be she will know of something you can go to immediately. It's quite probable since it isn't every day one meets such nice refined young ladies as you two. Mrs. Jennings' complaint is the great vulgarity and bad manners of so many modern young women. Some of them without even a curtsey, if you can imagine it."

Aunt Aggie tch-tched with disapproval. Then her needles began clicking busily again and she said cosily,

"But Miss Isabella and Miss Eulalie haven't a thing to worry about, have they, Noah? They'll be taken care of."

Noah suddenly let out his choking hiccuping laughter.

"You're right, Ma. As usual."

4

LALLY COULDN'T SLEEP THAT night. She turned and twisted, and resented Bella sleeping so soundly. Didn't Bella give a thought to the little baby that may not live till morning? Lally couldn't get it out of her mind. Each time she closed her eyes she saw the minute bluish-white face and the wren's claw hands. Why didn't it move more and open its eyes? Why didn't it cry? It had seemed to be starving this morning, but after it had been with its mother it had scarcely stirred again.

It wasn't natural. It should have been awake again and screaming for food. But it just slept on and on, scarcely breathing.

Now she kept listening to see if it were crying. If it were it would be a feeble whimper that perhaps no one would hear.

Bella had worried about the young mother, so mysteriously quiet all day and with her bedroom door locked. But Lally had thought that a grown-up person could speak for herself, and make demands. The baby was helpless.

The worry turned round and round in her mind until at last she did fall into a sleep that was full of fantasies. There was the sound of someone sobbing, the crack of horses being whipped up, and suddenly, quite near, Noah's snorting laugh. That last sound was so real that it brought Lally sharply awake, only to realize that the house was silent and she had been dreaming.

Although could she, very faintly, hear the baby crying? She sat up listening. Then, very cautiously so as not to wake Bella, she got out of bed and crept to the door. She listened intently through a crack. No sound came up the dark stairs. This didn't reassure Lally, but rather alarmed her more. For now she was beginning to imagine the baby dead or dying. In spite of her nervousness of Noah—for supposing that laugh hadn't been in a dream at all—she knew that she had to see the baby.

Surely she could creep down the stairs without disturbing anyone. She put a shawl over her nightgown, and groped for the candlestick. She mustn't strike a match until she was outside the bedroom for if Bella woke she would forbid her going.

On the landing there was still silence. With shaking fingers, afraid she would drop candlestick and all, Lally struck a match and lit the candle. The trembling light reassured her. She began to make the journey downstairs, the violent beating of her heart seeming to make as much noise as the alarming creaking of the stairs. It surprised her that she accomplished the journey without disturbing anyone.

There was still a ghostly glow from the fire in the parlour and the warmth lingered. Holding the candle carefully, Lally darted forward and peered anxiously into the cradle.

It was empty.

The clothes were thrown back, the barest imprint of a tiny head remained in the pillow.

Lally gave a cry of loss and desolation. The baby might be with its mother. It might have been taken into Aunt Aggie's bed for warmth. She told herself this, but her sense of loss remained overpowering. Her eyes filled with tears. She had come downstairs on bare feet, and she was shivering with cold. There was nothing for it but to make the cautious journey upstairs again. She turned disconsolately to do so.

In the passage a sound caught her ears, a tap-tap-tapping that seemed to come from the cellar.

Bella had told her the stairs down to the cellar, where she thought Tottie slept, went from the kitchen. Scarcely knowing why she did so, Lally tiptoed out there, the stone floor striking ice cold on her bare feet.

The noise that sounded like nails being hammered gently into wood was louder now. The door leading downstairs to the cellar was slighty ajar, and a faint glimmer of light showed.

As Lally stood there filled with an unnameable fear there was a final sharp bang, and the noise of a hammer being thrown aside. Then there were footsteps coming fumblingly up the stone steps.

Lally looked round wildly for some place to hide. There wasn't time to do more than blow out the candle and conceal herself behind the door, praying that whoever was coming wouldn't shut it and expose her, trembling, in her nightgown.

Something bumped against the door frame. There was a brief muttered imprecation in Noah's voice. The large shape of Noah, with a candle in one hand, what looked like a shovel in the other, and with a narrow box tucked under his arm appeared. He crossed the kitchen without looking behind him, and opened the door to the backyard. His candle blew out at once. He swore again, and leaving the door open to the icy wind, disappeared.

In a flash Lally was at the window, peering out. The moon

34

shone through torn rags of snow-cloud and lighted eerily the white ground and against it Noah's black form.

He had put the box on the ground and begun to shovel the snow away from a small area near the wall. Lally watched in fascinated horror as he dug steadily, the narrow hole becoming a black gaping wound against the white snow. He didn't waste too much time over the digging. As soon as the hole was deep enough to accommodate the box he picked it up and put it in with a contemptuous toss, and began scraping soil over it.

At that moment Lally could contain herself no longer. She gave a low whooping cry and fled for the stairs. She blundered up them in the dark, falling twice, bruising her knees and her knuckles, caring nothing for the noise she made.

"Bella!" she was gasping. "Bella! Wake up, for God's sake! Bella, we must get the police. Noah's murdered the baby. And now"—her voice choked in unutterable horror, "he's burying it!"

She was at the bedside shaking Bella violently awake.

"It's true! You can go down and see. The moon's shining. It makes the earth against the white snow look as if—as if it's bleeding! And there's Noah—he made the coffin in the cellar. I heard him. Oh, Bella, the poor little baby!"

Bella had somehow got a candle lit and was trying to calm Lally's babbling.

"Hush, love, for goodness sake! You'll have everyone awake. You've only had a nightmare."

"It's true!" Lally beat Bella with clenched fists. "It's true. It's happening now. The cradle's empty. The little b-baby— Noah's murdered it, I tell you!" she shrieked.

There was a click of a door opening and shuffling steps.

"What's the matter up there?" came Aunt Aggie's voice, strangely thick, as if she were half asleep.

"There, I told you!" Bella whispered. She raised her voice. "It's all right, Aunt Aggie. Lally's had a nightmare."

Lally ran to the top of the stairs, screaming, "It's not a nightmare! Noah's burying the baby. I saw him."

Aunt Aggie came up the stairs, slowly, each step creaking beneath her weight. She was in a voluminous flannel nightgown, with her nightcap strings tied beneath her chin. She completely filled the narrow stairway, forcing Lally back with her slow formidable approach.

But her voice was, as usual, kind and mild.

"What's this, my dear? What's this? Noah burying a baby. What nonsense! I declare, it's almost comical. My innocent Noah!"

"The cradle's empty!" Lally whispered, her strength suddenly gone.

"Of course it is. Because the baby's gone, with its mother. Not an hour since."

"In the middle of the night!" Bella exclaimed in disbelief.

"A sailor hungry for his wife and child has no heed of time, my dears. The ship had docked, a fly must be sent immediately. So it came, and the driver was in a rare bad humour, I can tell you. And baby and mother have gone, whisked into living arms." Aunt Aggie yawned deeply. "And now, my dears, can I have some uninterrupted sleep? These nocturnal upheavals," her words were strangely slurred again, "are exhausting."

"Then what," Lally insisted faintly, "was Noah burying?"

Bella took her arm. "It was a nightmare, love. It really was."

"No." Lally shook her head stubbornly. "If you come downstairs you'll see him, dressed, with snow on his boots. Listen! There he is now."

Sure enough there were cautious footsteps on the stone floor of the kitchen. Bella's heart gave a great leap.

"He *is* there, Aunt Aggie."

Aunt Aggie breathed heavily as if she were already half asleep. Her eyes looked peculiar, very large but completely colourless, the pupils shrunk to pinheads. She shrugged suddenly, and said, "Then go downstairs, both of you. Dig up the backyard. Find your dead baby. What cruel nonsense, indeed! How you repay my kindness! Noah, Noah!"

"What's the matter, Ma?" Noah's deep voice, very alert, came up the stairs.

"These young ladies think you've been committing a horrid crime."

"Me? That's a joke. What sort of crime?"

"Why, burying the baby in the yard, if you can believe it!"

"Ha ha! Ha ha ha! That's a rare one. I suppose they heard those tomcats yowling. Thought it was my victim. Ha ha ha!"

Lally seized Bella's hand in her ice-cold one.

"Bella, come! You've got to come. You'll see the hole in the snow. It *is* true!"

Shivering with distaste, Bella nodded. She would go, to quieten Lally. Otherwise there would be hysterics all night.

Besides . . . things happened in this house. That girl with her newly-born baby being spirited away in the night as if no one must see her go . . .

She seized her shawl.

"Come then. Excuse us, Aunt Aggie. But my sister must be humoured when she's in this state. She has a nervous temperament."

Aunt Aggie nodded sympathetically.

"I can see that, my dear. I'll come down with you, and mix her a soothing draught. She's in a state, that's clear."

"Look, Bella, look!" Lally said, at the kitchen window. "It's there—at least—"

The moonlight shone on nothing but snow. There was no dark gash in the earth. True, the snow was trampled but that, Noah explained, at their backs, was because he had gone out to throw something at the noisy cats.

"It's covered up," Lally whispered.

"Neighbourhood's full of pernickety cats," Noah said. "I'd trap 'em, shoot 'em."

"Drink this," said Aunt Aggie, holding a cup to Lally's lips. "Poor little love! You're shivering. You must go back to your warm bed. And sleep."

Lally drank without knowing what she was doing.

"And sleep sound," said Aunt Aggie, her round colourless eyes shining.

"All day, if she likes," said Noah, towering above them, the undercurrent of secret mirth in his voice.

"And some for you, too, my dear," Aunt Aggie said, holding the cup towards Bella.

Bella was about to take it, then suddenly shook her head.

"Come!" Aunt Aggie coaxed. "It'll do you good. Soothe your poor nerves."

Bella was suddenly wondering why Noah laughed at everything, even marauding tomcats. There would be nothing funny about them. Neither would there be anything funny about burying a baby, dead by natural causes or otherwise. Yet he laughed . . .

"No," she said, shaking her head impatiently. "I must stay awake to look after my sister."

The briefest flash of anger seemed to pass over Aunt Aggie's face. Then she said kindly, "But of course you must. She looks ill, poor dear. Take her up to bed. Make her rest. Otherwise Mrs. Jennings isn't going to be very favourably impressed tomorrow. She admires a sound nervous system. Doesn't she, Noah?"

Noah chuckled, softly and intolerably.

When Lally was still asleep at midday and no amount of shaking would rouse her, Bella was thoroughly alarmed.

"What did you give her to drink?" she demanded of Aunt Aggie.

"Just a few drops of laudanum, my dear. Nothing to harm her. I feared a brain fever, the way she was behaving last night. This long sleep will avert disaster and do her all the good in the world."

Papa had often prescribed laudanum for his patients. At least it was reassuring to know that Lally had swallowed nothing more dangerous. And perhaps it was wise that she was having such a long rest. She had been in a state bordering on dementia last night. Bella was too perturbed to go into the question as to whether Lally had been suffering from a fevered imagination or whether she had truly seen the horrible episode she had described. The only thing that mattered now was for Lally to wake up and for them to get out of this house. If Mrs. Jennings didn't send for them they must go of their own accord, snow or not. They might be doing Aunt Aggie an injustice, she might genuinely be the soul of kindness, but too many things had happened under her roof for Bella to be able to endure the thought of another night here.

And however simple Aunt Aggie might be, there was no doubt Noah was far from simple. Bella prayed she would never need to set eyes on him again.

The door of the third bedroom on the first floor stood wide open today. The cradle had disappeared from the hearth in the parlour and this room stood open as if to flaunt its empty bed.

Bella stepped inside, as she was sure she had been intended to. It was a mean little room with scarcely any light coming through its small window that faced the backyard. There were no ribbon bows on the curtains to impress lodgers newly arrived, no washstand with prettily decorated floral jug and basin. There was only the narrow iron bed, a bit of rag matting on the floor and a hard chair. The young woman who had been in here had not been made very welcome. Was it because she couldn't pay a shilling a night for her room, or because she was a poor relation and hadn't needed to be impressed? And have her nervous fears allayed . . .

Or was it simply that with the birth of her baby about to take place it was more practical to have a minimum of furniture and fripperies?

Now she had gone and all that was left of her was that faint curious smell Bella had noticed yesterday. She recognized it now, for Lally's breath carried the same odour. Laudanum. That explained why the girl had been so quiet. Perhaps it also explained why the baby hadn't cried. Papa had said some lazy and unscrupulous mothers didn't hesitate to give laudanum to a fretful baby.

But if it were given to so frail a child, surely the consequences would be fatal. Perhaps they had been . . .

Bella left the horrid little room and ran upstairs for the twentieth time to see if Lally had yet stirred. When she found her lying just as inert and sunk in sleep, her pale hair spread like an illusive sunshine over the pillow, Bella gave a whimper of despair. What was to happen to them? It had stopped snowing at last, but soon it would be too dark and too late to venture out. If Mrs. Jennings sent for them they would not be able to go.

Mrs. Jennings had been like a lifeline in her mind, but now Bella was beginning to wonder about that lady. It was terrible to have to be suspicious of people's kind deeds, but why should this woman be so eager to help two complete strangers? What did she get out of it? Not many people did things for nothing. Even Aunt Aggie was getting her shilling a day.

But she and Lally were in a desperate position. They had to trust someone.

To calm herself, Bella set about packing their bags. She made as much commotion as possible, hoping to wake Lally. It was fourteen hours since she had fallen asleep. Bella was growing more anxious every minute.

At last she went downstairs to find Aunt Aggie who was knitting peacefully before the glowing fire. The picture of comfort she presented made Bella's wild fears subside.

"Aunt Aggie, my sister still can't be woken."

"Let her sleep, my dear. Be thankful she can. This is doing her all the good in the world."

"But isn't Mrs. Jennings arriving at any moment?"

"Not Mrs. Jennings herself. A conveyance will be sent for you."

"Supposing Lally is still asleep?"

Aunt Aggie looked at Bella blandly over the top of her spectacles.

"Then she must be carried, mustn't she? Noah will see to that. Noah's very strong."

She smiled suddenly, disclosing her broken teeth.

"Don't look so alarmed, my dear. Mrs. Jennings is a very influential woman. She's expecting you and mustn't be disappointed."

"C-carried!" Bella whispered. She ran forward to seize Aunt Aggie's arm. "Who is Mrs. Jennings? What does she want with an unconscious girl? *Tell* me!"

"Tch tch tch! I thought it was only your sister who indulged in hysterics. Mrs. Jennings has positions for you. Haven't I told you a dozen times? Doubting Aunt Aggie, indeed! There's ingratitude for you. Ah dear, it's a hard ungrateful world."

Bella drew back staring, seeing suddenly not the cosy kind old woman who had helped two strangers so astonishingly, but a mealy-mouthed hypocritical creature with unknown depths of cunning. The moment of illumination was shattering. She twisted her damp hands, praying that this was imagination, unreliable intuition.

But thinking of Lally helpless upstairs, and listening to Aunt Aggie's unperturbed plan to carry her *unconscious* to a strange house, Bella knew that she had to face this new terrifying position, and revile herself for her innocence and blindness.

Tottie's state of terror should have told her. Noah's unholy amusement should have been revealing. The disappearance of the young mother and baby should have been not innocent but sinister. But it had taken this last desperate state of affairs, herself a prisoner here because she couldn't carry Lally bodily away, to make it plain what was happening.

How could she have been so gullible? She forgot her fear in the hot anger that swept over her.

"Mrs. Proudfoot, would you be good enough to tell me exactly what you were planning to do with Lally and me, what secret scheme you had in mind?"

"Eh? Eh, my dear?"

"Don't tell me your friend is finding positions for us, because I no longer believe you. Or perhaps I do. Only I daren't imagine what the positions are. Oh, what a fool I've been! Listening to your blandishments. But not any more. I'll pay you what we owe you and the moment Lally stirs, we're leaving this house."

"But, my dear young creature—"

"How can you sit there so calmly," Bella stormed, "while my sister may be dying from that drug you gave her? Yesterday you watched the poor little baby dying—heaven knows what you did to its mother—"

"My dear, what *fantasies!* Your sister told me about your romantic imagination. Dreaming of a rich world. I fear that isn't your destiny. But how pretty you look when you're angry. I believe you'll do very well—in your new life. You are almost my best— Where are you going?"

"To the kitchen to tell Tottie to make plenty of black coffee. And then out to find a doctor. And don't dare to stop me."

"I won't, my dear." Aunt Aggie chuckled with slow relish. "But I rather think Noah will."

"Noah!"

"He came home early today. He's been busy in the back. Shovelling snow. Snow is pretty when it first falls, but later, when cats and other animals scatter it about—" her owl's eyes were on Bella without a flicker, "then it's a nuisance. Noah is tidy-minded."

Sheer horror sucked away Bella's fine flood of anger. So what Lally had seen was true. Noah was not tidying snow. He was smoothing away all traces of a grave . . .

"And Tottie doesn't understand orders from anyone but me," said Aunt Aggie "She's dim-witted. Besides," she went on, after a moment, "I have the key to the front door here in my pocket, and if you think to go by the back way, Noah's there."

But Noah wasn't in the backyard. His voice came from the doorway, making Bella start violently.

"What's up, Ma?" he asked, standing there swinging his large hands loosely.

"Miss Isabella is getting impatient to begin her new life." Noah grinned. He opened and closed his hands slowly.

"Then she'll have to be a bit patient, won't she? The fly don't come till after dark. Didn't you tell her?"

"I must have a doctor for my sister!" Bella insisted.

"Ma knows more than any doctor. We don't need no doctor in this house." Noah had taken something out of his pocket. He now dangled it ostentatiously. It was a key. The key to the back door no doubt, since his mother had the front door one in her pocket. His bright little eyes were full of malice.

"I'll scream for help," said Bella, between tight lips.

Noah flung back his untidy black head and roared with laughter.

"Try it in this street, love. It's natural noise in these parts."

"Yes, my dear," said Aunt Aggie, knitting placidly. "No one is going to go to the help of a Soho drab."

Bella caught her breath sharply. Suddenly she flew to the door, pushing past Noah contemptuously, and ran upstairs. In the bedroom she banged the door shut, and stood against it, panting. As soon as she could listen above the sound of her harshly indrawn breaths she realized that no one had followed her. But downstairs Noah was still laughing. And on the bed Lally stirred at last.

Bella was at her side in a flash.

"Oh, Lally! Wake up! We've got to get away from here."

Lally's heavy eyelids lifted showing her eyes cloudy and unfocused. Then they fell again and she breathed in deep sleep-drugged breaths.

Bella shook her violently.

"Lally, wake up! We're in great danger."

Lally mumbled, then slept again, and Bella, dropping her limp body, wondered what was the use anyway. For the doors were locked, and Noah guarded them.

But was she to sit here helplessly until that fly came furtively in the dark to carry them away—to what? So much for being thought a Soho drab. She would scream. Noah and Aunt Aggie would hear how she could scream.

She flung up the narrow window and leaned out into the foggy yellow murk. The moment a passer-by appeared—Holy Mother, let it be someone with ears that listened—she would open her lungs.

Two ragged children huddled in a doorway opposite, their rags drawn lovingly over their bare feet. A very small boy trudged past in the snow and slush, pushing a barrow laden with a miscellany of junk. A little later a woman appeared, hurrying. Bella caught only a glimpse of her white drawn face beneath her bonnet. The street was empty for a minute, then two men appeared, and Bella's heart lifted. But they were drunk, stumbling and singing. A third companion was trying to catch them up. but he fell sprawling in the slush.

And there were footsteps on the stairs . . .

The doorknob rattled.

"What you got against the door, love?" It was Noah's voice, coaxing. "Move it, will you, or I got to use my strength."

Two more men had appeared in the gloom. There was no time to wait and see if they were drunk or sober, friends or evil-doers. Bella leaned out of the window and screamed at the top of her lungs.

"Help! Help, I beg you! I need a doctor! My sister's ill! We're in great danger!"

The men had stopped and looked up. One was short and square, one very tall. They wore top hats, Bella now observed. Thank God, they were gentry. And they had stopped to listen.

"Please help—" There was a great clatter as Noah burst into the room. In two strides he was at the window and had flung Bella away. "Little bitch!" he muttered. Then he had thrust his own head out and was saying in a blandishing voice that would have done credit to his mother.

"Take no notice, sirs. It's my wife. She's a bit weak in the head, like."

On the floor where she had fallen Bella put her head in her hands and sobbed.

Noah closed the window and turned slowly. He stood over her, enormous, menacing. His voice was very soft.

"Think you'd get away with that, did yer—"

And then there was a great thumping on the street door.

"Open up!" came a clear, arrogant, autocratic voice. "Open up. My friend is a doctor. And I intend fetching the police."

The voice brooked no refusal. It was the most heavenly sound Bella had ever heard.

5

IT TOOK ALL BELLA'S STRENGTH to hold Lally upright in the coach. She concentrated on that, and nothing else. She had no idea where the gentleman who had introduced himself as Mr. Raven was taking them, but she trusted him. She had to. Anything was better than the house from which they had escaped.

The last hour had been the worst nightmare of all, and Bella was only glad that Lally had been too drowsy and stupid to take in what had happened, the stalwart police constable guarding Aunt Aggie and Noah in the parlour while a sergeant and another constable searched the house, and, on Bella's directions, since Lally was not able to give them, dug in the backyard.

The flimsy packing case was unearthed, and the lid lifted to disclose the tiny frozen body. Bella thought she would have fainted then, but that the young man in the caped greatcoat kept so firm a grip on her arm that the pain kept her conscious. His friend, the elderly doctor, examined the baby, and lifted a grim face.

"I think there could be more investigations done here, sergeant. This is a newborn infant. Its death could have been natural but its burial isn't. This yard may hold other grisly secrets. What can you hold that fine pair on?"

The sergeant had an impressive flow of legal conversation.

"Detaining young females unlawfully with intent of immoral purposes. Concealing a death and illegally disposing of the body. Smuggling away the infant's mother, whose whereabouts have still to be traced. Don't you worry, sir, I'll have a charge sheet a yard long."

"Just keep them under lock and key," said the doctor. "My friend and I will see to the young ladies."

"If you can be letting me have their address, sir. Their evidence will have to be taken."

The younger man spoke authoritatively.

"They'll be my responsibility, Daniel." He handed a card to the sergeant. "You'll find my address there."

The old doctor lifted his matted brows.

"Is this wise, Guy? Wouldn't they do better with me. Betsey—"

"No, they'll come to me. You wanted me to have a crusade. I believe this is where I begin." He glanced at the mummified infant and his face had a hard look of anger and outrage. "You were right, Daniel. There are things to be uncovered in this city. Let's get out of this damned place. What about the other girl? Will she be all right?"

"She's recovering from a heavy dose of laudanum. Try and get some hot milk into her. She should do very well by morning. I'll call and take a look at her."

The last thing was Aunt Aggie's language as she was taken away. She burst into a string of vile oaths directed at Bella and Lally. Her face beneath the respectable black bonnet with

44

its velvet ribbons was a mask of fury, her large pale eyes so full of cold, malignant hate that Bella shivered. Noah was bad enough. Held between two burly police he was sullen and furious. But Aunt Aggie had let the evil show through her pink and white innocence. She was like the stinking sewers that ran beneath the city's comfortable buildings and ornamental parks and gardens. Bella prayed that neither she nor Lally would ever need to set eyes on her again.

But ten minutes later, in the jolting cab, Bella suddenly sat upright.

"Tottie!" she exclaimed.

The young man sitting opposite, his gloved hands folded over the nob of his cane, listened attentively.

"Tottie? Another waif?"

"We are not waifs, Mr. Raven," Bella said haughtily.

The young man's calm eyes went over the two girls, observing their neat but plain clothing, their obvious air of distress and dishevelment.

"Of course not, Miss McBride," he said politely. "But Tottie?"

"She was Aunt—I mean, Mrs. Proudfoot's servant girl. Noah found her living in some derelict building a few days ago and brought her home. At least he said it was a few days ago, but now I'm not sure. She might have been there much longer."

"This is interesting. Certainly she must be found. She'll be a valuable witness."

"She can't talk. She's dumb."

"Dumb? She was born dumb?"

"I don't know. I had the thought it might be from terror. She was very afraid of—that old woman—and Noah." Bella's eyes darkened. "They let her be dressed in rags and she had dreadful chilblains. She was probably hiding in the cellar."

"The police will find her," said Mr. Raven. "They'll be searching the house thoroughly. Then Daniel—my friend, Doctor Bushey, will take care of her. Rest assured."

He smiled, and Bella thought what cold eyes he had, blue and aloof, occupied with their own thoughts. He had rescued Lally and her from a fate she didn't dare to think of, and she was intensely grateful to him. But now it seemed to her that their plight had suited some private purpose of his own. She began to wonder uneasily where he was taking them, and

45

what he intended to do with them. She wished it had been the old doctor who had taken them, with Tottie. He was bluff and kindly. She would have trusted him completely. But Mr. Raven was a swell. His clothes were exquisite, from his silk cravat to his well-polished boots. Doctor Bushey had looked at them with a gentle and fatherly eye. This haughty young man merely considered them waifs.

And perhaps, after all, Bella reflected honestly, that was unpalatable only because it was so near the truth.

The cab drew up at last outside a tall, grey, imposing house, one of a row of such houses flanking one side of the road, while on the opposite side were the trees of a broad park.

"This it, guv'nor?"

"That's right, cabby." The young man had sprung out lightly, and was looking up at Bella. "Can your sister be roused, or must she be carried?"

From that angle he looked younger, and anxious, almost boyish. Bella was suddenly ashamed of her misgivings. She shook Lally energetically.

"Come, Lally. Wake yourself up. Do you want to be lifted like a baby?"

Lally moaned and shivered, and with a great effort sat upright.

"Where are we?" She clutched Bella, memory touching her drowsy brain. "It's not—Noah?"

"It's Mr. Raven. He wants to help you out. Come along, love. You can manage very well."

Somehow Lally contrived to climb down. Mr. Raven paid the cab-driver, and with a last curious glance at Lally, the man whipped up his horse and drove off. Mr. Raven unceremoniously put his arm round Lally's waist and half carried her up the steps to the shining mahogany front door. He rang the bell vigorously, and when the door swung open, didn't seem at all perturbed that the stooping white-whiskered old man in butler's dress should see him standing there with a swooning young lady on one arm and Bella beside him laden with the bulging carpet bag which contained all hers and Lally's possessions.

"Take the young lady's bag, Doughty. Tell Mrs. Doughty to prepare—let me see—I think the blue room." He had motioned Bella in and helped Lally over the last step. Lally was now standing upright, her eyes round with amazement. She thought she was dreaming, poor creature, and who

46

wouldn't, to find herself in this luxurious hall, with rich rugs on the floor, a shining stair-rail leading up into the gloom, and huge bowls of flowers in midwinter scenting the air.

With calm aplomb Mr. Raven took the girls' shawls and handed them to the astonished Doughty.

"Hurry, man. Can't you see my guests are exhausted? As soon as Mrs. Doughty has the fire alight, tell her to come to us in the library."

"Yes, sir. At once, sir."

Lally gave a sudden nervous giggle, then clapped her hand to her mouth. Bella nudged her sharply to follow Mr. Raven across the hall into a large book-lined room. A fire burned invitingly, throwing its flickering light on to the leather-covered armchairs and sofa. Mr. Raven motioned the girls to sit down, and again Lally had to be nudged into obeying, she was so dazed and open-mouthed.

But Bella had kept her wits. She sat primly on the edge of the sofa, and inquired stiffly what Mr. Raven intended to do with them.

"Why, get you justice, if I can." He looked at Bella, and for the first time his mouth quirked in amusement. "What plan did you think I had?"

He was amused that Bella should be afraid he had evil designs on them, Bella thought in the greatest indignation. He might have realized she was not as naïve as that. She might be simply dressed, and Lally might at present look a bit daft, but he needn't think they were ignorant servant girls.

"I don't know what you mean by justice, sir," she answered coolly. "All my sister and I have come to London for is to find respectable occupation. I would hardly have called that justice."

"What I meant, Miss— I'm afraid I don't even know your name."

"I am Isabella McBride and this is my sister Eulalie."

Mr. Raven bowed with a courtly air that momentarily fascinated Bella. She had a passionate admiration for good manners.

"Will you go on and explain about the question of justice, sir?"

"Certainly. I want to make the plight of young women like yourself and your sister public. I still have to hear how you fell into the clutches of that monstrous old

47

woman, but the important thing to prove to the world is that people like that woman and situations like this exist. I tell you, I'm shocked and horrified. If it hadn't been for the happy intervention of Doctor Bushey and myself, where might you be now? I'd make a guess and say on your way to the docks to be forcibly put aboard a ship bound for some Middle Eastern port."

"W-what for?" That was Lally, sitting upright, her eyes sticking out.

"Why, to be thrown into some low brothel," replied Mr. Raven. "For the use of foreign sailors and worse."

Bella started, meaning to reprimand him for speaking so brutally to sensitive Lally, but then she realized he hadn't been thinking about delicate ears, he was so genuinely incensed about the existence of such crime and depravity.

"I will take this matter into the House," he declared. "There will have to be a complete investigation into this kind of thing. One walk through a slum area and I stumble on it. Is such a thing happening every day, every night? There'll have to be more police, new laws, greater penalties."

His words had galvanized Lally into life.

"Will Aunt Aggie go to prison?"

"Aunt Aggie? You call that old witch aunt? Certainly she'll go to prison. I hope for life."

"And—Noah?"

"Him, too."

Lally sighed deeply and murmured into Bella's ear, "Now we can feel safe."

The young man stopped his erratic pacing up and down. For one moment the hard anger left his face, and he was looking down at Lally's pale face with its drooping eyelids and tumbling fair hair with a detached interest. He had noticed her at last, as people always did, though most people much sooner. She was so pretty.

"Yes, you can feel safe, Miss McBride. But we shall need yours and your sister's help to put them in prison. You will both have to give evidence in court."

"We will have to be witnesses?" Bella exclaimed.

"Yes. Tomorrow you'll give statements to the police. That's the beginning. Later, when the two are tried—"

"Oh, no!" Lally cried out. She buried her face in Bella's shoulder. "I couldn't bear to see them again. I should die."

"S-sh, Lally!" said Bella absently, her mind on the more

practical issue. "So you intend keeping us here, Mr. Raven, until the case is tried, and, as you say, justice obtained."

"Is that so great a hardship? Mrs. Doughty, my housekeeper, is very respectable, and quite kind."

Bella flushed. "I didn't mean that. I mean, are you asking us to represent all unfortunate young women? What is that going to do to our future?"

She saw that he had never thought of them as individuals. He had suddenly noticed that Lally was pretty, but they were still two anonymous young women to be used for a cause. Respectable servant girls, no more. And wasn't that what they were, anyway? Why had she to be so high and mighty because Papa had brought them up as ladies, and she had filled her head with romantic novels, and they had been almost within sight of Covent Garden Opera House?

She was aware of the quickly-veiled surprise in Mr. Raven's eyes when she had mentioned their future, and suddenly she saw the truth as he saw it. They would, with luck, be governesses, or perhaps assistants to a milliner or a dressmaker, so would it matter if their names had appeared briefly in the newspaper as the innocent victims of a wicked old woman and her son? If their plight could help other unfortunates, then the ordeal ahead must be faced.

Diamonds, operas, grand houses . . . Bella gave a little philosophic shrug, facing reality at last. Visiting London had made her grow up very quickly.

"I assure you, Miss McBride, neither your reputation nor your future will be harmed. I will guarantee you positions when this is over. In the meantime—ah, here is Mrs. Doughty. Mrs. Doughty, these two young ladies are Miss Isabella and Miss Eulalie McBride. They are to be my guests for a short time. I trust their room is ready?"

Mrs. Doughty was as short in stature as her husband, but much broader. She had a fleshy red nose and the high colour of someone who might conceivably, Bella reflected shrewdly, help herself to a little port after the dinner guests had departed. But, as Mr. Raven had said, she looked kind, if at this minute completely flabbergasted.

"Yes, sir. It's ready. The fire's alight. The beds are scarcely aired. If I'd known guests was expected—if I'd had a warning—" Her little pouched eyes rested incredulously on the two girls again.

"None of us had a warning, Mrs. Doughty. Events take charge of us. But I'm sure you'll manage. I think the young ladies would prefer a tray in their room tonight. So I will say good night."

He gave his small courtly bow again, and Bella felt a little twist of excitement in her stomach. But again it was Lally at whom he looked. No doubt he was reflecting how she would look when her hair was tidied. Perhaps he might find the little servant girl amusing . . .

The room was the most beautiful Bella had ever seen. She found herself tiptoeing across the soft carpet towards the dressing table with its gilt-framed mirror and its elaborate array of toilet necessities. There was a huge bed, covered with a snowy-white tasselled bedspread, and with mahogany steps, to make climbing into its dazzling softness the easier. There was a washstand, with jugs of steaming hot water and fleecy towels, and on the opposite side of the room, a writing desk equipped with candlesticks, a silver holder containing quill pens, and silver inkwells, pin cushions, and a blotter in an elegant red leather frame. The curtains of rich blue brocade were drawn across the windows, the walls were a paler blue damask. In the grate the fire, which was just beginning to take hold, sparkled on the shining brass fender and fire-irons. Two low chairs, in quilted white velvet, were drawn up invitingly to the blaze.

It was a room that almost brought back Bella's romantic dreams. But not quite. She and Lally were here only temporarily, while a rich young man indulged himself in his passing whim for a crusade. As he had pointed out, for the sake of other unfortunates like themselves, they must support him.

Mrs. Doughty had opened the carpet bag and spread out their simple flannel nightgowns. No doubt she was used to handling fine lawn and linen, and this would be another reason for the perplexity in her face. But, as a well-trained servant, none of this came into her voice.

"Would you be liking your supper now, miss?" She addressed herself to Bella, for Lally was plainly now beyond speech. "A nice bowl of soup would do you both good."

"Thank you, Mrs. Doughty. That is kind of you."

The woman obviously liked the way Bella spoke, for she said briskly, "I'll bring it up myself. That stupid Annie does nothing but gawp and gape."

The moment she was out of the room Lally clutched at Bella.

"Bella, we must say our prayers!"

50

"Whatever for, you goose?"

"What are we doing in a place like this?" Lally looked wildly round the room. "That fine gentleman wants us for his own purposes."

The excitement turned again in Bella's stomach, a barb of mingled pleasure and apprehension. She knew exactly why Mr. Raven wanted them because he had explained his impersonal and lofty reason to her and she had believed him. She was still hearing his voice, deep, quiet, completely confident. Above all, a man should have confidence and be in command of others. That was a quality to be admired. Sentimentality was unnecessary.

She took Lally by the shoulders and swung her round to the mirror.

"There! Look at yourself! Would a fine gentleman be interested in a fright like that? Your hair coming down, your face smudged. Why, you look no better than a street girl."

Lally pushed at her hair shamefacedly.

"I didn't know. I'm so sleepy still. Why did you let me go out looking like this?" She added, with sudden defiance, "Perhaps he likes street girls."

"Perhaps he does. So does Noah. Would you rather be back with Noah?"

Instantly Bella was sorry for her sharpness, for the quick terror was in Lally's face again.

"Don't say his name!"

"Then be thankful to Mr. Raven for what he has saved us from." More gently she said, "Don't cry again, Lally. We're safe now. And look at this lovely bed. I'll help you undress, and you can have your supper in bed."

Lally shivered and sighed.

"You're so calm, Bella. How can you be so calm? Didn't you care at all about the little baby?"

"I care about Aunt Aggie and Noah being punished for it. Off with your boots! There! Your feet are frozen. Do you know, I think Mrs. Doughty would bring a warming pan if we asked her."

At that moment there was a knock at the door, and Mrs. Doughty was back with a laden tray. She set it on a table by the fire, and whisked the covers off steaming bowls of soup, and hot toast.

"Now, come and eat up, young ladies. You both look fair starved."

While she had been away she had obviously decided on

the manner she would take to these perplexing guests. It was a nice blend of respect and equality, by no means concealing a very lively curiosity. But there was no doubt she had a warm heart. She wouldn't turn a dog from the door in this snowy weather, much less a pair of nicely-spoken young ladies fallen on bad times. If the master decided for some mysterious reason of his own to give them the best room, then obeyed he must be.

"Thank you, Mrs. Doughty." The fragrant smell of the soup had made Bella's spirits rise instantly.

"Is there anything else you might be wanting, while I'm here? Coming so sudden-like, you might have overlooked some requirements."

"All the belongings we have in the world are with us," Bella answered, with dignity. "We shall manage very well. Only my sister is very chilled. She hasn't been well. Could she have a warming pan?"

"But of course, miss. I could see at once your sister was poorly. Has she caught a chill? Perhaps she's been sleeping in a damp bed."

Bella smiled slightly at Mrs. Doughty's delicate way of obtaining information.

"No, the bed wasn't damp. It was a very good bed."

"But the baby was buried in the snow!" Lally cried suddenly and wildly.

Mrs. Doughty's mouth fell open. Her broad-tipped nose glowed scarlet.

"Bless me! She's wandering, poor dear!"

"No, she isn't," said Bella. "We had a terrible experience. Mr. Raven rescued us. You'll hear all about it, I expect. There's to be a court trial. Aunt Agg—. . . the people concerned are to be punished. Mr. Raven is anxious to see things like this can't happen again to unprotected females. He mentioned something about a law in Parliament."

"Why, yes, he's hoping to be elected to Parliament. Ah, so that's what it is. Doughty will understand better than me. He says it's a wonderful blessing Mr. Guy—Mr. Raven, that is, we keep calling him Mr. Guy, knowing him from a small child, you understand—it's a blessing Mr. Raven has decided to do something for his country. It takes him out of his dreadful grief."

"Grief?"

"He lost his sweet young wife two years since. Her and the baby." Lally gave a gasp. "A baby!" Bella motioned to her to be quiet. She realized that her curiosity about their host was as strong as Mrs. Doughty's about Lally and herself.

"How sad! Did he love her very much?"

"It was a marriage made in heaven. And in heaven it ended, poor souls. She was like an angel, so fair and sweet. When she died, he went wild. We all thought he'd ruin himself, gambling, drinking, taking no respect for anything, laughing. You should have heard him laughing with his friends, late at night. I used to say to Doughty, 'Listen to that. Laughing like a devil and crying inside.' But Doughty knew it would work itself out, all that wildness, and so it has."

"He's recovered from his grief?" Bella was remembering the cool emotionless eyes, and wondering suddenly what they had been like while his young wife was living.

"Never. But he's come to terms with it, like. Oh, he can still be wild, I'm telling you. But he's going to be a member of Parliament so he's got to be respectable and serious. And he will be. Whatever Mr. Guy does, he puts a great fire into it. Indeed, you might say, what he wants he intends to get. Nothing will stand in his way. Only excepting the Almighty who took Miss Caroline and the child away."

Mrs. Doughty sniffed, and touched her eyes with her apron.

"But there, I'm talking too much. I'm only telling you nice young ladies—and you do look nice, I said as much to Doughty—that now Mr. Raven's helped you from whatever this dreadful experience of yours was, it's your plain duty to help him to make a law in Parliament, if he wants to. It'll be for the good of all, I can assure you. And you can rest safe here."

6

LALLY HAD A NIGHTMARE ABOUT Noah in the night, and Bella had to light the candle and soothe her. She awoke perfectly dazed, and quite unable to grasp her surroundings. At last she seemed to recognize the luxurious room, with the embers of the fire still glowing, but instead of being reassured lay quietly sobbing, "What is to happen to us, Bella? What is to happen to us?"

Finally Bella said sharply, "For goodness' sake, Lally, stop

53

being so dreary or I'll think a ship to Marseilles the best place for you. Can't you have a little optimism?"

Lally was quiet then, but her large eyes were curiously empty, and Bella couldn't rouse her again. She decided that Lally was suffering still from the after-effects of the laudanum and she must try not to be impatient with her until she was quite recovered. By that time Bella expected her to be feeling the same growing excitement and pleasure that she herself felt. Couldn't Lally enjoy their stay in a luxurious house while it lasted, for it would be brief enough?

In the morning Bella was at the window, with the curtains pulled back, and a fascinating new world spread before her, when there was a tap at the door, and a very small maid-servant struggling with a large coal bucket appeared.

"Do your fire, miss," she said, shooting an inquisitive glance at Bella, and at Lally, still submerged in the big bed.

"Thank you," said Bella. "What's that out there?"

"What, miss? Oh, you mean Hyde Park, and that's Rotten Row."

Bella gazed, entranced. She knew all about Rotten Row where the fashionable people rode and drove in their carriages and even sauntered by on summer evenings. This was very different from Seven Dials, and the mean dirty streets where screams were unanswered, and children walked barefoot in the snow. This was really the London of her dreams.

Where would they be in the spring, when the ladies emerged from their winter hibernation and sported their new bonnets and parasols? Far from the fashionable world of Rotten Row and Hyde Park, Bella thought. But at least there it was now, beneath its glistening coverlet of snow, and one brave gentleman rider was cantering by, the snow flying off his horse's hooves. The trees spread their leafless branches in a faint lilac-coloured mist. A hackney coach clattered by on the road beneath, and already the newsboys were shouting in their cracked rasping voices. "Lord Palmerston says more troops for Crimea. Big losses in Crimea." An organ grinder had begun a turgid melody, errand boys were hurrying by. Even in this quiet part far from the incredible jostle and confusion of Piccadilly and the Strand, the city was awake.

The fire had begun to glow. The undersized maid, who must be Annie whom Mrs. Doughty had mentioned, got briskly to her feet and said she would bring hot water immediately. She opened a cupboard and brought from it a

54

hip bath painted white and decorated with pink flowers, which she placed in front of the fire. Then she disappeared on her way for the pails of hot water.

Bella shook Lally awake.

"Do look, Lally! We're to bath before we dress. Oh, I do enjoy luxury."

Lally sat up, blinking and rubbing her eyes. But she seemed, thank goodness, to be in possession of her senses again.

"Don't start enjoying it too much because it won't last. It'll be us lighting the fires and carrying the hot water in our next place, most likely."

Bella undid her plaits and shook her black hair in a curtain over her shoulders. She picked up a brush and sat in front of the mirror saying softly, "I wonder whose face last looked out of that glass. A rich spoiled one, I expect. But it's mine today."

She studied critically her white skin with the almond blossom tinge on the cheekbones, the slanted slender black brows, the heavily lashed topaz eyes. Her face was pleasant enough but, she decided honestly, not nearly as pretty as Lally's. Her nose was too short and had a dusting of freckles. And she had that long neck. Papa had used to say she looked like a flamingo. She took after his family, while Lally was all her mother, fair and pink and white, with her little prim mouth and innocent eyes.

All the same, Bella thought she didn't do the beautiful mirror a disservice. She looked pretty enough, with the thick shawl of her black hair.

"Bella, don't dream again! It gets you nowhere."

It was Lally's turn to be practical, and Bella reluctantly had to agree. She had forsworn dreaming since yesterday.

During the morning the nice elderly doctor, Doctor Bushey, called. The girls were asked to come down to the library to see him.

He smiled at Bella's urgent question, "Did you find Tottie? Is she all right?"

"Tottie's very well, although I didn't know her name until this minute. Betsey's pampering her in my kitchen, feeding her and warming her. But I can't get a word out of the child."

"She's dumb," said Bella. "She's been dumb ever since Noah found her."

"Not before?"

55

"How would I know? But I thought—Noah's a very alarming person."

"That's very intelligent of you, my dear. How did you guess there's such a thing as hysterical paralysis, sometimes of the limbs, sometimes of the vocal cords?"

"Our father was a doctor."

"Ah! So!" Doctor Bushey exchanged a glance with Mr. Raven, who was standing silently before the fire. "Well, then, I'm inclined to share your diagnosis of Tottie's condition, but I'm not prepared to say how long it will last, or indeed whether she'll ever regain her power of speech. And she doesn't appear to be able to read or write, so we'll get no help from her. Beyond exhibiting her rags or her condition of semi-starvation, of course. But the Proudfoots can swear they found her only last week, or the week before. There's nothing to prove she's been living like a rat in a hole in their house for longer than that. Though I suspect it. The poor child will take months to stop being terrified of a human being, let alone begin to talk. But I'm not here to discuss Tottie. How's the younger Miss McBride today?"

He was looking at Lally, who flushed and said, "Oh, no, Doctor, I'm the elder. Though most people don't think so. I'm not as—as advanced as Bella."

Mr. Raven was looking from one to the other, the expression of aloof interest in his face again. They were exhibits, that was all. Bella found herself flushing, too, though not with shyness but indignation.

"Well, older or younger, you seem to have thrown off the effects of the drug. Not sleepy today? Now, now, don't flinch, child. I only want to feel your pulse."

Lally submitted, her eyes wide and nervous.

"Splendid," Doctor Bushey murmured. "But I recommend rest and quiet. There's been a shock to the system. Miss Bella?"

Bella held her arms to her side, then reluctantly extended one of them.

"There's nothing the matter with me."

"No. I see that. A much stronger constitution altogether. Well, they'll do very well, Guy."

The girls were dismissed. They were not required again until a policeman who said his name was Inspector Gulley called to take a very long and complete statement of the events of the past three days, from the moment of meeting Aunt Aggie on the coach until Mr. Raven's and Doctor

Bushey's arrival. He particularly wanted to know about the young woman who had had the baby, and seemed disappointed to hear that neither Bella nor Lally had set eyes on her. Bella recounted the conversation overheard at the door between Aunt Aggie and the man who had come by fly, and Lally told a confused story about hearing someone sobbing, and horses being whipped up in the night. "But I thought I dreamed it," she added.

"There's no actual proof," the Inspector said aggrievedly to Mr. Raven. "If, as we suspect, the ship concerned was the *Star of Asia,* she's well up the Channel by now, and she'll have discharged passengers at her first port before we can get word through to have her searched. Anyway, from the state of this young woman's health, drugged, and recovering from a premature birth, she'll probably be dead and dumped overboard—sorry, miss."

"There's no doubting the proof of the dead infant," Mr. Raven said crisply.

"No, sir, we'll get them on that. But if we can prove this other thing they'd be in for a life stretch."

Beside Bella on the sofa, Lally shuddered convulsively.

Bella said, "Is that all you require us for, because my sister's distressed?"

"Is that all, Inspector? Then certainly go upstairs. Ring for some tea." Mr. Raven's voice was kind, but still impersonal. He was speaking again to the Inspector before they had left the room.

Later there was a tremendous commotion outside, horses stamping, the yapping of dogs, and a high clear voice giving peremptory orders.

"Hannah, bring Loulou. You know the fuss she makes if I'm out of her sight."

Bella, who had been growing bored with their luxurious imprisonment, and who had more than her share of curiosity, had thrown up the window and was leaning out to watch a lady, elegantly dressed in a lilac-coloured crinoline, with a fur-trimmed cloak over her shoulders, sweep up the steps and ring the bell. The impatient clangour must have been audible through the entire house, for even Lally started up from her fire-drugged lethargy.

"Who is it, Bella?"

"I don't know. A lady. Her maid's carrying her dog. One of those hysterical French poodles. She seems very much at

57

home. She's awfully fashionable. I'm going to find out who she is."

"Bella!" Lally exclaimed, shocked again at her sister's new-found shameless propensity for listening at doors.

But Bella had no time now for the niceties of etiquette. Hers and Lally's lives had suddenly become too extraordinary. One not only needed good ears but good eyes as well.

She went softly down the stairs and paused where they curved to give a view of the hall.

The visitor, with her black-clad maid holding the struggling poodle, stood in full view. Mr. Raven was out of sight but his voice perfectly distinct.

"Mamma, what brings you out in this weather?"

"Gossip spreads," said the lady tartly. "Whatever is this new indiscretion of yours?"

"Indiscretion, Mamma?"

The lady tapped a tiny extremely well-shod foot. Bella could see only half her face beneath the brim of a lacy nonsense of a bonnet, but the whole of it she judged to be exquisite. Exquisite and pampered and artfully young, as a face always sheltered from ugliness would be.

"Guy, don't hedge. You know very well what I'm talking about. This abduction of servant girls!"

"Abduction? The word's your own, I trust, Mamma."

"The word's the one being used, I regret to say."

Mr. Raven laughed softly, and with apparent enjoyment.

"Don't tell me the story's out already. Or should I say the most popular version of it? And what version have you heard?"

"Why, that you're sheltering these two creatures whom you picked up in some unmentionable slum—though for what reason I'd rather not know."

"Then you needn't know, Mamma," Mr. Raven said indulgently. "You shan't distress yourself. A little thing like cleaning up the slums—giving the submerged tenth of the population of whom you've never heard a chance to live decent lives—need hardly concern you. Take Loulou home and give her the food a starving child would sell its soul for. Leave me to my own brand of crime."

"Guy! I won't be laughed at!" Mrs. Raven's voice was sharp and angry.

"Neither will I, Mamma."

"Good heavens, I'm far from laughing at you. I've come to beg you not to ruin yourself."

"Ruin myself?"

"My darling boy, haven't you any sense? Oh, I know well enough your motives are probably quite honest. I can't see you finding a servant girl irresistible." (Bella caught her breath in quick anger. What a hateful stupid *impossible* woman!) "You've much too fastidious an eye. But what are your enemies going to make of this?"

"You mean Sir Henry Shields?"

"And others. You're like your father. You don't care two figs about making enemies and then you underestimate them. Politics can be dirty, hadn't you realized?"

"I've realized."

"This is playing into Sir Henry's hands."

"On the contrary. After I've finished with white slaving I shall begin on the children in mills. Sir Henry's among others."

Mrs. Raven had thrown up her gloved hands in a gesture of horror.

"White slaving!"

"What did you think, Mamma? That I was entertaining prostitutes for my private amusement?"

Mrs. Raven sucked in her breath audibly.

"Guy! I don't believe a word of your philanthropy. I give you up. White slaving, pro—" She couldn't bring herself to repeat the unforgivable word. Her lifted face was full of outrage. "I believe you're enjoying this disastrous situation."

Mr. Raven's voice was meticulously polite.

"Would you like to meet the young ladies, Mamma? I assure you, they are human beings."

"Never! This is madness. Get them out of the house. Send them to some sort of home, can't you?"

"No, I'm afraid I can't. Actually, I'd thought you might help in finding situations for them after this is over."

Mrs. Raven seemed to have difficulty in finding her voice. "You're preposterous! You've lost your senses! Can't you listen to me? What will happen isn't just my imagination. I shan't dare to look at a newspaper for weeks. They'll tear you to bits. You know what those low-class journalists can do. Your reputation—"

Mr. Raven laughed again.

"Reputation? That comes long long way after an empty belly or a raped—"

But there his mother gave a faint cry and turned swiftly to the door.

"Hannah! I apologize for you having to listen to this. Come. Loulou—my smelling salts—Guy, if your father, if Caroline—"

"This," Mr. Raven's voice cut in icily, "has nothing whatever to do with the dead. It has to do with the living. Of whom I sometimes doubt you are one."

For all her appearance of fragility, Mrs. Raven obviously was no person to swoon for anything but effect. The faintness went out of her voice. She was stung back to aggrieved life.

"How I could have such an imbecile son! What about Mademoiselle Hortense, pray? She took a fancy to you, and I rather thought you did to her."

"Mademoiselle Hortense is enchanting. But she isn't in danger from greedy and evil people. She isn't penniless and in want. She's on the right side of society. Forgive me, Mamma, but suddenly I find that impossibly tedious."

"If you must have a new fad, why do you choose one like this? The poor! So unwashed, so ignorant! You'll soon tire of this, as you do of everything else. But you'll have lost your reputation in the meantime."

"You don't begin to understand, Mamma. I'm not just pursuing a new fad. I'm deadly serious. I've found something worthwhile to do at last. I even regard it as worth losing my reputation for."

There was a brief silence, then his mother exclaimed,

"Then play with fire, you fool! Burn yourself up! But don't expect me to reverently scatter your ashes."

From nowhere Doughty appeared to open the door. With a great swishing of skirts, the lady swept out. The meek Hannah in her sober black followed. After a moment Mr. Raven sauntered across the hall. From her vantage point, still perfectly fascinated by what she had heard, Bella looked down at the sleek honey-dark head. Her cheeks burned with the unfair insulting remarks that horrible elegant alarming woman, his mother, had made about her and Lally. She wanted to rush down the stairs and beg Mr. Raven not to ruin himself for their sake. If it were likely he would be ruined. Yet she had a contrary desire, so overwhelming it made her blood grow hot to think of it, to see that well-bred face lose its slightly chilling composure and grow ardent in their defence. She could pray to see that . . . She knew she was never going to beg him to give up his quixotic crusade.

"Who is it, Bella?" Lally cried. "Could I hear someone quarrelling?"

"Mr. Raven's mother," said Bella briefly.

"Oh! Doesn't she like him?"

"I should think she adores him. It's us she doesn't like."

Lally looked perplexed.

"But she's never seen us. Oh, it's because we're here and shouldn't be. Is she very terrifying?"

"She doesn't terrify me."

That evening Mrs. Doughty came up to tell them that the master wanted to see them in the drawing-room. She scarcely gave them time to tidy their hair.

"Come along, young misses. The master doesn't like to be kept waiting. He has a rare temper at times."

Lally was all eyes for the beautiful room with its gold silk hangings, its chandelier with its central glowing rose of flame where the gas jets came through, its pictures and portraits. Bella looked straight at the man standing before the fire, and saw nothing else.

Had he been thinking over the wisdom of his mother's words? Was he going to send them away?

He asked them to sit down, and offered them Madeira wine. Lally took her glass because she was afraid to refuse, Bella because she had an odd idea it might give her more confidence in her prayer being answered.

He trusted that Mrs. Doughty was looking after them well, and that they were comfortable and happy. When they assented, he went on,

"I merely wanted to tell you that I'll be away for ten days or so. I have to go down to my constituency and make speeches. I'm a candidate in a by-election to be held shortly. I can't neglect the people whom I hope will vote for me."

Lally sipped her wine and murmured something inaudible. Bella said plainly, "So what are we to do, Mr. Raven?"

"Why, stay here, of course. I want you here until after the trial, which will be held in two weeks' time. You understand that, don't you? You're under subpoena as witnesses, and it would be an offence against the law if you disappeared."

"We have no intention of disappearing, Mr. Raven." (Where would they disappear to, Bella thought ironically.)

"No, I'm sure I can trust you. You're quite free to go

61

out, of course. Only I'd suggest you don't go without Mrs. Doughty or Annie."

"W-why?" Lally gasped.

Mr. Raven looked into her huge alarmed periwinkle eyes, and again, ever so little, his face softened. She reminds him of his dead wife, Bella thought suddenly and fiercely. The fair sweet Caroline . . .

"Because it's customary for young ladies to be accompanied by chaperones. Not because the streets are full of Noah Proudfoots. Not in these parts, at least. You'll be quite safe." He was formal again, moving away to pick up the wine decanter and refill his glass. "I hope you won't find it too tedious here. You may use the house as you wish."

"The library?" Bella asked eagerly.

He did look at her this time, but not as he looked at Lally, merely with faintly lifted brows and polite interest.

"I'm afraid I have very few novels, Miss McBride. My mother is the person for those. If she should call you must ask her to lend you the latest."

"Is it likely she will call?" Bella asked.

"Most unlikely. We quarrelled today. But Mamma is a person of whims. However, that's beside the point. I merely wanted to tell you that as from tomorrow until my return you are in charge of my house."

He smiled and gave his courteous bow, dismissing them. Upstairs Lally found her tongue, and chattered without stopping.

"Isn't he kind, Bella? Isn't he a gentleman? And so good-looking, but if only he would smile more. He looks sad. Yesterday I thought he was merely scornful and superior, but now after hearing about his dead wife I know it's sadness that makes him so cold. I wonder if he will marry again. Surely he will. He must be very rich, and he has that big house in the country Mrs. Doughty told us about. Bella! Bella, aren't you listening? Aren't you interested?"

"He imagined I'd only want to read novels," Bella said resentfully. "He puts people in a category."

"In a—what are you talking about? If you ask me, you read too much."

"He'll have to learn better," Bella said.

The restlessness grew on Bella. The house was a haven, but who wanted to hide forever, smothered in richness. The next day she persuaded Mrs. Doughty to allow Annie, the sharp and alert maid, to put on her bonnet and shawl and

62

accompany Lally and herself on a walk in the park. The snow had at last disappeared, and she was sure she could see the gold candle flames of crocuses beneath the trees. Then there were more riders out in the Row, too, and carriages bowled past drawn by shining and mettlesome horses. Bella longed for her first look at fashionable London.

But the outing came to nothing. The three girls had barely descended the steps of Mr. Raven's house before a man pounced on them. Lally screamed, but the man, who had a lean, hungry, avid face, said at once in quite a cultivated voice,

"Don't be alarmed, miss. I only want to ask you a question. How long is Mr. Raven intending to shelter you? What is his object? Oh, come now—" Bella was dragging at Lally, hissing, "Don't say a word, Lally. It's a newspaperman. We mustn't talk to him."

The man was pursuing them up the steps. "Come, please, miss! Just a few innocent questions. What's your occupation? Does the gentleman offer you better prospects than you had before?"

Furious at the man's growing insolence, Bella hustled Lally and Annie indoors, and said with deceptive calm,

"What is your newspaper?"

"The *London Clarion*, miss. I only want a short story about you. But I promise you headlines." His bright, avid eyes glinted unpleasantly. "You're news, miss."

"If one word about us is printed in your paper," said Bella, and now her face was blazing, "I can promise you a very great deal of trouble."

She swept in and banged the door. Old Doughty who came hurrying across the hall showed a reluctant admiration.

"You sent him packing, miss. Good riddance to him."

"I lost my temper," said Bella. Already she was uneasily suspicious that this wasn't the way to treat the press. That little rat of a man would know she couldn't make trouble for him. How could she? But he could print a malicious story if he pleased, in revenge.

She brushed away angry tears.

"We can't even have a peaceful walk. We can't see the Row. I never knew London was such a wicked city."

When the newsboys started shouting the next morning she asked Doughty to go out and buy a copy of the *London Clarion*. Surely the man wouldn't have dared to make up a story about them. They couldn't be headline news as he had suggested. Not her and Lally, two unimportant country girls.

The man had kept his promise. There were headlines.

Mystery in Knightsbridge. Who are Mr. Guy Raven's beautiful protégés?

They were dressed for a walk in fashionable Hyde Park, these unfashionable young ladies in their unpretentious bonnets and shawls. But they were unduly modest—or had they had instructions from their host—and refused to talk to our reporter. We can, however, confirm the rumour that they are extremely comely, the one fair and the other dark. But perhaps it was hardly to be expected that the aspiring candidate for Hertfordshire would give sanctuary to any of the fair sex less well-endowed with good looks. Would he get so heated about the wrongs of a squint-eyed Polly or Mary Ann? Let us leave him his foibles while he remains a private citizen, but do we want this sort of thing intruding into the serious affairs of Parliament?

Bella gasped over the article. "But it's wicked! It's evil! Why, it's suggesting—"

"What?" asked Lally nervously.

"Why, that we may be more than—" (Oh, why was Lally so *innocent!*) "—than just guests."

"I don't understand, Bella."

"It's what Mrs. Raven meant when she said this would ruin him. I thought she was just a jealous old woman, but now—"

She hadn't finished speaking before Mrs. Doughty knocked on the door.

"Oh, miss—" even the phlegmatic Mrs. Doughty looked flustered, her nose a hot and angry scarlet, "—the master's mother is downstairs demanding to see you both."

"Mrs. Raven!"

"Aye. And she's a character to be dealt with, for all her delicate looks. Shall I say you're poorly?"

"Oh, yes, please!" Lally began, but Bella interrupted her with an imperious, "You'll do nothing of the kind, Mrs. Doughty. Go and tell her we'll be down immediately. Lally, tidy your hair! Put on a clean fichu." Bella was at the mirror, smoothing her own hair, noticing the flush in her

64

cheeks and the blazing brilliance of her eyes. Good! She could outstare Mrs. Raven. She was ready for battle.

The lady sat very upright in the drawing-room. She had a roseleaf complexion, a haughty little parrot's beak nose, and sparkling dark eyes that gave her face an appearance of great vivacity. She was very delicately made with a waist as small as Lally's, and long fine hands that were arranged composedly in her lap. She was dressed with a richness that Bella instantly suspected was deliberate. She intended to over-awe the two servant girls.

Lally, of course, was overawed. She curtseyed too deeply and was then overpowered with shyness. It was left to Bella to say politely, "You wished to see us, Mrs. Raven? I am Isabella McBride, and this is my sister Eulalie."

"I am not interested in your names," said Mrs. Raven. She looked at the girls sharply and inquisitively. If she were surprised by their neatness and good looks she concealed the fact. She sat erect like a displeased queen.

"I only want to tell you that you must leave here at once. Whatever schemes may be in your heads, I don't think either of you would want to ruin my son."

"Schemes!" Lally gasped, surprised into speech. "We have no schemes. Have we, Bella?"

"I think you're upset by the newspaper this morning, Mrs. Raven," Bella said calmly. "We are, too. We're terribly sorry such a thing happened. The man simply waylaid us. We told him nothing. I suppose he was frustrated, so this is how he has taken his revenge."

"A revenge against my son."

Bella's chin went up. "It isn't exactly flattering to my sister and myself, either."

"Then you must see it doesn't happen again, mustn't you? By packing your bags—if you have any—and leaving here at once." Her insolent tone made it difficult for Bella to keep her temper. She made herself speak reasonably,

"We can't do that, Mrs. Raven. We've promised Mr. Raven to stay until he returns from the country and the trial takes place. He has committed himself to making public this kind of crime. It's a horrible crime, Mrs. Raven. Perhaps you didn't know?" She waited a moment for Mrs. Raven to answer, but that lady merely tapped her fan restlessly, the jewels on her fingers flashing. Bella went on, "So it becomes the duty of my sister and myself to stand by him, no matter what it does to our own reputation."

"*Your* reputation!" Mrs. Raven gave a high tinkling laugh. "But, my dear young woman—" She caught the look in Bella's eye, and cleverly changed her tactics. "I think you must both be grateful to my son for what he has saved you from. A fate literally worse than death, I believe. Yes, I see your sister agrees with me. So couldn't you perhaps show your gratitude by nipping this deplorable scandal in the bud? You have only to leave here at once. I personally will find you situations in some other part of the country. I promise you shall have unsullied reputations. All I beg of you is not to ruin my foolish, impulsive boy's future. You know he's standing for Parliament, of course, and you realize that any more of this kind of publicity will be fatal to his chances. I can see you're intelligent young women. You must be sympathetic, too. Poor Guy suffered a tragedy in his marriage and it's been the greatest relief to us all that at last he's emerged from his sorrow and begun to show what he can do. He has a brilliant brain. It's our duty not to deprive his country of that."

Lally was looking intensely distressed.

"Bella, we must—"

Bella interrupted her with an impatient, "Hush, Lally! Mrs. Raven, I don't think you understand the position at all. We *are* part of all that you say about your son's future. He's making our unfortunate experience part of his electioneering campaign. So we have to be here as proof to his story. We can't disappear. It would be most ungrateful to him. I think he would furious."

"Of course he'd be furious!" Mrs. Raven snapped. "Because he has no sense. And neither have you. Or have you—" her eyes narrowed "—a great deal of sense as to where your own fortune may lie?"

Bella bit her lip, determined to control her temper.

"We made a promise, Mrs. Raven. We don't break promises."

"Oh, tush, girl! Don't take that high-flown attitude with me. I see through you. You're nothing but an adventuress. The whole thing is a plot. You're hand in glove with that old woman in Seven Dials."

Lally was scarlet and on the verge of tears.

"Oh, no, Mrs. Raven! How can you say that! Bella, tell her it isn't true! Tell her we'll leave and not make trouble."

"What about the baby, Lally?"

"The b-baby?" Lally's eyes fell before Bella's fierce regard. "What do you mean?"

"Are you going to say that it doesn't matter that it died? Have you forgotten it already? Don't you care that other innocent babies die that way? Are you *really* going to let Aunt Aggie go free? What are you made of, you, my own sister!"

Lally was crying in earnest.

"Bella, you know I'd do anything for the baby. But this l-lady—"

"She never saw the baby," Bella said, her quiet voice belying the high points of colour in her cheeks. "It's difficult to feel for someone you've never seen. She's naturally only concerned for the good of her son. But he's a grown man and how he manages his life is his own affair. We can only do what we promised."

Mrs. Raven was snapping her fan open and shut. Her mouth was sucked into her cheeks, making her look suddenly old, but far from feeble. On the contrary, her abruptly bony face had a frightening intensity, as if hate burned beneath it. She was not used to being thwarted. She was certainly unfamiliar with such a humiliating situation as a young woman of much inferior standing defying her. She would never forget it. Beneath her own anger, Bella was soberly aware that she had made an enemy not to be underestimated.

But did it matter? When this affair was over she was unlikely ever to cross Mrs. Raven's path again. And how *dare* the old woman treat her and Lally like subhumans to be whisked out of the path of her precious son?

"I think you don't entirely understand the situation, Mrs. Raven."

"Oh, I understand it very well," Mrs. Raven said tightly.

"No, I think you don't. I think you expected to find my sister and me illiterate and common. You thought we could be patronized and intimidated. You don't like us to have a sense of honour—"

"*Bella!*" whispered Lally, scandalized.

Mrs. Raven was on her feet. She was quite small, smaller even than Lally. She stood so erect, she looked eight feet tall.

"On the contrary, Miss McBride," her voice was ice, "you're exactly what I expected you to be!"

Then she swept out. For all that Lally was still there, snuffling and drying her eyes, the room seemed extraordinarily empty. And Bella had an uncomfortable suspicion that she had had the worst of that interview.

"Bella, how could you be so rude?"

"She was ruder."

"No, she wasn't. She was only worried for her son."

"She was rude in the things she was thinking about us. I could read them if you couldn't. I'm never going to let people patronize me! Never!"

"Now she hates us."

"That's better than despising us. At least she knows we're human beings. She didn't before she came. She thought we were faceless and anonymous the way she thinks of anybody not in her own class. I can't endure snobbery. Somehow I don't think Mr. Raven can, either."

"Bella, I think you're getting above yourself," Lally said soberly.

The flame was still in Bella's cheeks.

"I'm *being* myself, that's all. I'm not going to truckle to anybody. Why, you'd have let her make us run away. You'd not even have fought for the dead baby."

Lally's fist was in her mouth. But she said stubbornly, "Suppose all this scandal does ruin Mr. Raven."

"It won't. Oh, I grant you it's true it might damage his career for a while. But don't you see, it will make his character. It wasn't after he met us, but before, that he was ruining his life. Didn't Mrs. Doughty tell us? All that idling and gambling. Now he has a cause to fight for. Haven't you noticed how he's changed already?"

"No."

"He has. He's lost that world-weary look."

"Oh, Bella, you're imagining things," Lally said uneasily. "You never saw him until two days ago."

Bella had a pang of surprise as she realized the truth of this. She had such an extraordinarily clear image of Mr. Raven when he was surrounded with fashionable young people, and bored to death. She knew exactly how he had looked, with the carved lines of weariness in his cheeks. Now he was not weary. He was cool, calculating, alert, and not to be intimidated by slanderous attacks in the press, or anywhere else.

The now familiar excitement was twisting inside Bella again. She began to smile dreamily, running her fingers caressingly over the beautifully carved mantelpiece. "Anyway," she murmured, "I confess I like being here. Ring the bell, Lally. We'll have the fire lighted in this room today."

"Bella!"

"Oh, don't be such a mouse! Didn't Mr. Raven say we were to use any room we pleased?" The smile was curving her mouth again. "I enjoy luxury. I intend making the most of it."

7

"SO YOU HAD A VISIT FROM MY mother?"

Mr. Raven had arrived home long after dark. He was still in his greatcoat, and walking restlessly about the hall. Lally had retired early. She was working herself into a fever about the trial tomorrow, and Bella had been down to the kitchen to ask if she could prepare the soothing drink that Papa had always administered when Lally was in one of her states. She was carrying it upstairs now, and that was how she had encountered Mr. Raven.

"Yes. We did."

"You found her not particularly well-disposed towards you?"

"She thinks we are doing you harm."

His mouth quirked in what could have been the beginning of a smile.

"I gather you were more than a match for her."

The humiliation of that scene, with Mrs. Raven looking down her little beaky nose with that arrogant contempt, was still too vivid.

"I was rude to her. But not as rude as she was to me." She held his gaze defiantly. "I think you should have remedied your mother's misapprehensions about Lally and me, Mr. Raven."

"Do you think she would have listened?"

Bella wanted to burst out with all her brooded-over grievances, that Mrs. Raven was arrogant, disdainful, narrow-minded, selfish, intolerably snobbish. Instead she heard herself saying, quite meekly,

"Are we doing you harm?"

He did smile then, with a kind of retrospective pleasure.

"Indeed you are. I had some stormy meetings. They were very exhilarating. Sir Henry is rubbing his hands in glee."

"Sir Henry?"

"My opponent. He boasts of influential friends in the press. I suspect he buys them. Unscrupulous reporters. Or simply editors who don't like my brand of politics. It's all in the game."

"We couldn't help it about that reporter," Bella said. "He waylaid us. We didn't tell him a thing. What he wrote was all made up. We haven't dared to go out since."

"Don't worry. There'll be much worse, especially after the trial tomorrow. What's that you have in that glass?"

"It's for Lally. She's dreading having to see Mrs. Proudfoot and Noah again. It doesn't do any good to tell her they'll be safely in the dock. She's just scared to death."

"I'm sorry to hear that." There was genuine concern in his face, the first that Bella had seen. It was because he was thinking of pretty Lally with her highly sensitive feelings. Bella unreasonably thought she would rather have him remain aloof and detached. "But she won't need to be in the witness-box long. She only needs to describe seeing the baby buried. She does understand that, doesn't she?"

"She has to re-live a nightmare," said Bella.

"Yes, yes, I know. I'm sorry. It can't be helped." He was growing impatient. "It began when you talked to a stranger in a coach. Now you have to see it through."

"Yes, Mr. Raven." Bella began to move towards the stairs. His voice called her back.

"But you, Miss Isabella. You don't share your sister's nightmare?"

He was forcing her to look inside herself again. She had an uneasy feeling that it wasn't feminine to anticipate so much satisfaction from seeing Aunt Aggie and Noah prisoners in the dock. Nor feminine to have secretly enjoyed defying Mr. Raven's mother. Nor should she be so fiercely ready to fight all the slander a hostile press may make about him as her and Lally's protector.

She should be like Lally, inconspicuous and tearful and in need of petting and sympathy.

She met Mr. Raven's inquisitive glance.

"I have a much stronger constitution than my sister," she said levelly.

The gloomy courtroom was crowded. Bella hadn't seen the newspapers that morning but Doctor Bushey, who had called to accompany them to Bow Street, admitted that there had

70

been a great deal of publicity given both to the forthcoming trial and to Mr. Raven's so-called philanthropy.

"One or two of the papers are kind," Doctor Bushey admitted, when pressed by Bella. "They say it's important that we should have some members of Parliament who are interested in the cause of humanity. It's refreshing when a rich young man is deeply concerned for the poor."

"But the others?" Bella persisted.

"The others are the sensational press."

"What do they say? What do they call Lally and me?"

"They are very complimentary about your appearance, Miss McBride."

The old doctor, in his gruff kindly way, was so like Papa, that Bella felt completely at home with him. Mr. Raven may have been sympathetic—who knew?—but there was no doubt he was using them for his political ends. Doctor Bushey was genuinely a friend.

"You're not telling me everything, Doctor Bushey. Do they say that Mr. Raven is only pretending to care about justice, that—" Bella flushed and went resolutely on, "—he is really keeping us for immoral purposes?"

"Well—if you insist, lassie—they do suggest you might be a certain aspiring young politician's lights of love. But don't take the slander to heart. I assure you Guy isn't. He's enjoying the tussle. It's doing him all the good in the world—if that interests you." The doctor gave Bella a shrewd penetrating look, which she evaded.

"It won't do him any good if he loses the election."

"If he loses, he'll fight again. But he won't lose. Today's trial will bring out the truth. Anyone only has to look at the innocence in your two faces. Don't worry yourself, my dear. All will be well."

But Doctor Bushey's reassuring words were forgotten when Bella stood in the witness-box and looked directly at the prisoners. Noah's small coal-black eyes, smouldering with fury, his great shoulders and lounging body, and beside him the dumpy form of his mother, a humble respectable deeply distressed old woman who kept her eyes meekly downcast, and her black-gloved hands quietly clasped in front of her, brought back all the terror she and Lally had suffered.

Whatever it cost, hers and Lally's reputation and even Guy Raven's political figure, this evil pair must be prevented from ever again exercising their designs on other innocent young women.

71

Neither the police nor Mr. Raven need have been afraid that she would forget her lines or be afraid to speak them. She saw no one in the stuffy crowded room but the two in the dock. She gazed unflinchingly at them and told her story. Once she noticed Noah bare his teeth and lick his lips. But Aunt Aggie never lifted her eyes. She was a wronged old woman, her only weakness her too kind heart.

Bella told how Lally had run upstairs in the early hours of the morning scarcely able to speak about the terrible thing she had seen, the tiny narrow box in the snow, the great stooping form of Noah. She said that as a doctor's daughter she had been able to identify the odour of laudanum, both on Aunt Aggie's and her sister's breath, and almost certainly from the locked room of the young mother whom she had never seen. She finished by relating how it was intended that her sister should be carried unconscious—here her voice rose with remembered incredulity—to interview a strange woman about a possible position, and how, when she had become suspicious and frightened, she had been told it would be useless to scream for help.

"I understand," the magistrate murmured, "that this is an area where screams of distress are less heeded than, let us say, birdsongs. Go on, Miss McBride."

But Bella had finished her story. The anger and indignation that had carried her along had burnt out, leaving her exhausted.

"That's all, sir. That's when Doctor Bushey and the other gentleman, Mr. Raven, happened to be passing. They did hear my cries for help, and so—" she couldn't bear to speak their names, she pointed at the pair in the dock with her accusing finger, "they were wrong when they said no one would listen."

It was then that Aunt Aggie very slowly lifted her eyes and looked at Bella. Her lips moved. Bella could hear her whispered, "Tch tch!" Her round pale eyes were sad and forgiving. She looked so neat, so round and soft and cosy, her cheeks a clear baby-pink, her expression gently disillusioned with the ingratitude of the human race, that Bella was suddenly convinced she would never be found guilty. The press, already eager to tear Mr. Raven to bits, would find pink-cheeked Aunt Aggie a dear kind misunderstood and wrongfully accused old lady.

The policeman beside Bella was indicating that she was to step down. She ignored him and leaned forward, crying passionately to the magistrate, "You must believe me, sir. Don't let her deceive you with her look of innocence. She is a wicked old woman."

"This court is interested only in evidence, Miss McBride," the magistrate reproved, in his detached voice. "Step down, please. Call the next witness."

The next witness was Lally. Bella saw at once that she was in a fine state of terror, her cheeks blanched, her eyes dilated. She looked everywhere but at the dock. She hadn't the courage to face her nightmare again.

Her evidence had to be coaxed out of her and was almost inaudible. She stumblingly whispered about the empty cradle, the hole in the snow. Her very incoherence was, Bella realized, far more convincing than Bella's own angry story. Everyone in the room was listening with fascinated attention to poor Lally's terror.

The magistrate was gentle with her. He listened attentively, coaxing her when need be, and shortly told her kindly that she could stand down.

Mr. Raven was the next witness. In spite of having to soothe the half-fainting Lally, Bella was immediately conscious of the rustle through the court, and suddenly she realized the number of men present with notebooks and stubby pencils. One of them was looking intently at her and Lally, and obviously sketching their likeness. Bella quickly turned her head away, only to look directly into other insolent eyes. The benches at the back of the gloomy little room were crowded with people who had come to see, not a pair of evil-doers, but herself and Lally, and the man, now standing composedly in the witness-box, who had protected them.

She felt hot and angry and curiously naked. She was thankful that Lally had given way to her distress and was weeping quietly into her handkerchief. At least she needn't be aware that they had enemies other than the two in the dock. It was Bella's first experience of being a public exhibit, of knowing that the onlookers were consumed with curiosity, hostility, perhaps even a certain lewd admiration. Noah and Aunt Aggie might be found guilty and sent to prison, but she and Lally were being labelled as loose young women without even a trial.

Mr. Raven was having to answer what seemed impertinent questions. Standing in the witness-box he seemed very tall, very cold, very definite.

"You say it was pure chance that took you and your companion down this particular street?"

"It was. We had been to visit a Ragged School in that area. We were already in a state of great concern and indignation about those unfortunate children."

The magistrate leaned forward.

"Keep to the point, if you please."

"Then let me say we were in the state of mind to be very conscious of distress. I merely wish to emphasize there was genuine distress in Miss McBride's calls for help. It was immeasurably shocking to stumble on such persecution in an English city."

The magistrate was becoming irascible.

"The witness stand is not a political platform, Mr. Raven. We want your evidence only."

"Doctor Bushey and I broke into the house," Mr. Raven went on. "We found these two unfortunate young women literally prisoners. I offered them the shelter of my home. I admit I wanted this particular depravity existing in our seemingly enlightened civilization to have as much publicity as possible."

The pencils wrote furiously. Mr. Raven stepped down and Doctor Bushey took the box. After his evidence the prosecuting counsel asked that the prisoner Mrs. Proudfoot be put in the witness-box.

It was growing dark and the gas had been lit. The flaring jets accompanied counsel's monotonous impersonal voice.

Was it the prisoner's habit to take as lodgers only young women obviously in trouble? Was that why she made the room disarming, with pretty furnishings, so that a suspicious young woman would be pleasantly surprised? Wasn't it strange that her friend Mrs. Jennings, who apparently was so useful in finding positions for these completely strange young women, couldn't be traced? Perhaps Mrs. Jennings didn't exist, perhaps she was, in reality, a completely different article, a ship anchored in the Thames, due to sail for distant ports?

And if the woman whose baby the prisoner had delivered —and subsequently buried—was actually her niece, as she maintained, wasn't it strange that she too couldn't be traced? Wouldn't she have been a little grateful to her "aunt" for successfully delivering her, even if, sadly, the baby hadn't survived for many hours? And wasn't it odd that a new-born baby's stomach showed traces of opium which could have come from a drug known as laudanum? Moreover when it was obvious the baby wasn't going to live wouldn't it have been natural to call a doctor, certainly to get in touch with the proper authorities about its burial?

And wasn't it a still further coincidence that a ship called the *Star of Asia* that had sailed at dawn, scarcely three hours after the baby's burial, had had on board a mysterious passenger who had had to be carried to her cabin? Perhaps the prisoner wasn't aware that the *Star of Asia* had had to put into Gravesend to shelter from high winds, and there had been searched. It might interest the prisoner to know that no young woman was found on board, but there were certain articles of women's clothing discovered hidden in a locker. Wasn't the prisoner distressed that her "niece" had obviously been put off the ship hastily? It may well be that she had not survived her son by more than a few hours, so that one lay buried in the snow and one beneath the bounding wave?

The quiet monotonous voice pounded on and on until at last Aunt Aggie's glib answers and denials became fumbling and incoherent. Finally she was silent, her mouth open helplessly showing her rotting teeth, her eyes quite empty.

Bella was tiredly exultant. She heard the magistrate saying that the prisoners would be kept in custody while awaiting trial in the central criminal court before a judge and jury. There was something about a charge of infanticide, and then suddenly it was all over. Aunt Aggie and Noah were being led away between two burly policemen. Aunt Aggie had composed herself again, her head was meekly bent, her whole posture suggesting injured innocence. But Noah threw back his wild black head, searching the courtroom until his eyes rested on Mr. Raven. Then his expression became frighteningly malevolent.

"Curse you!" he said audibly. "Curse you!"

Lally trembled and her hot hand clutched Bella's. Even Bella, confident as she was that Aunt Aggie and Noah would be safely under lock and key, felt a shiver of premonition.

The room was shuffling itself empty. Everyone could go home.

Home?

8

SONGBIRDS IN SOHO? THAT was the headline in the London Clarion the next morning. With flaming cheeks Bella read the article.

"As the Magistrate aptly remarked in Bow Street courtroom yesterday, screams are more common than birdsongs in some areas of our fascinating city. But the Raven's ears were attuned to both the goldfinch and the blackbird. Obviously he found it impossible to decide which had the greater charm. The simple solution was to carry them both to his love nest. And who, whose eyes rested on the fair forms of the Misses McBride, could blame him? It is entirely right that such charming examples of our English beauty should not be criminally smuggled out of the country. We sincerely wish Mr. Guy Raven the greatest happiness in his private life. But let him now have the good sense to give up all thoughts of a public life. Or, if he fails to heed our advice, let the people of Hertfordshire think carefully before electing such a man to Parliament."

"We are notorious!" Bella exclaimed. She thrust the paper at Lally. "Read that."

Lally frowned over the small print.

"What does it mean? Are they trying to say we only pretended to need help?" Lally's eyes grew stormy. "They should have seen that poor baby for themselves. Aunt Aggie said she gave him laudanum to stop him crying, but he never cried. He never cried, Bella!"

"The baby's dead. Forget him. We have to think of ourselves now. What is to happen to us if we have no character?"

"You didn't seem to care about that when you talked to Mrs. Raven," Lally said, with unexpected sharpness.

"That was because she was patronizing us. I've told you I hate to be patronized. I don't think I could let even Queen Victoria do that to me. And I didn't think I could endure it in the courtroom yesterday when all those men stared and drew pictures of us. If only there was some way to show them how we look down on them and despise them."

"I only want to be safe," Lally murmured, her eyes dark. "Noah looked as if he would like to kill us. I keep having nightmares that we meet him again, in a dark street."

"Don't be silly, Lally. He'll be locked up for years. But we have to go on living in the world. It's all very well to have new laws made for the protection of women and children, but they're too late to help us. Who *is* going to employ us now? I can think of no one but some lecherous old man who likes to pinch servants in dark passages, and has a wife who is too timid to protest about it. Don't look so scandalized. There are plenty of those."

"Mr. Raven will look after us," Lally said uncertainly.

"I think Mr. Raven will be quite occupied in saving his own reputation."

Lally didn't seem to understand any of this. She was so unworldly and concerned only with the fundamentals. A baby had been murdered, and probably also its mother. What did reputations matter? But Mrs. Doughty was more practical. She arrived upstairs, breathless, to announce that the master wanted to see them in the library, and that he was in a fair taking.

"He's got all the morning papers, and dear to goodness, they're slandering him something cruel. There's a sketching of you two in one of them. It's wicked. It makes you look bold and sly. Doughty says politics is a dirty business, and that's true."

Mr. Raven was pacing up and down the library, frowning, his mouth hard, his eyes a wintry blue. He didn't greet the girls but said immediately.

"This is developing into a real fight, isn't it? I seem to have underestimated my opponent. Mind you, I've played right into his hands, getting involved in a scandal."

"It's only the newspapers that have made it a scandal," Bella said hotly.

"That's true. I hadn't realized I was so unpopular. I knew I wasn't approved as a Parliamentary candidate, of course. Too young, too irresponsible, too lax in my morals. Now they're having a fine time proving they've been right all the time. Look at that."

He tossed the paper depicting Bella and Lally sitting on a bench in the courtroom on to the table.

"Oh, I don't look like that," Lally said indignantly. "So bold. And my nose doesn't turn up like that."

"No, it doesn't, does it," said Mr. Raven thoughtfully. "The artist wasn't very observant, or he'd have noticed you have a much prettier nose."

Lally flushed, looking pleased. This, thought Bella, was a fine time for Mr. Raven to indulge in polite flattery, even though in such a withdrawn and curiously calculating manner. She was just beginning to realize, uneasily, how little she knew him, and how lightly she had been taking this scrape into which she and Lally had got. She should never have agreed to stay in this house. She had been even more unworldly than Lally. To help Mr. Raven in his fine principles, indeed! The world had no time for fine principles. It preferred to crucify.

"What are we to do?" she asked bluntly.

"Do?" The question seemed to astonish him. "Why, fight, of course. Do you think this muck frightens me?"

"We are only women."

"Well?" A trick of the light made his eyes look silver. There would never be any warmth in them, Bella thought, angrily, hopelessly.

"A man can live down a tarnished reputation. A woman can't. Surely you must know that."

"Is your reputation of more value than your life? I don't think that was in your mind when you screamed for help."

"In this society there's almost no difference. With a ruined reputation a woman doesn't have a life. Oh, I know you saved Lally and me from a dreadful future. I'm very grateful. But how was I to know this would happen, this muck, as you call it?" She indicated the spread newspapers. "I can see only one thing for Lally and me now. We'll have to emigrate."

Mr. Raven stared at Bella's flushed and angry face. Then suddenly he began to laugh.

"Don't be a coward, Miss Isabella."

"A *coward*!" Bella's eyes sparked. "Don't dare to call me that! I'm not being a coward. I'm being realistic. It's time someone was."

Lally was clutching Bella's arm.

"Leave England? Oh, Bella!"

"On the contrary, Miss Isabella," Mr. Raven said. "I'm being realistic, too. You're so taken up with your indignation that you haven't bothered to inquire why I wanted to see you. I was going to explain to you both that there's only one way to silence these malicious rumours."

"Can that be done?" Bella asked in surprise.

"Certainly it can be done. Very simply. By my marrying one of you."

Momentarily Bella was beyond speech. She simply stared at Mr. Raven unbelievingly. He couldn't be proposing marriage in that cool emotionless way, with nothing but calculation in his eyes. This was the greatest indignity of all.

And yet the lightning had shot through her stomach, making her feel faint.

"You don't have to emigrate, Miss Eulalie," he was going on. As he looked at Lally, his gaze had again softened, as it always did for Lally. Always! "It would be ironic if I subjected you to almost the fate from which I thought I had saved you. At least, that's how the newspapers would interpret it. So I want you to be my wife."

"Me!" Lally gasped. She had gone paper-white. "Oh, Mr. Raven, thank you, I couldn't!"

"Couldn't? Come, Miss Eulalie. You don't flatter me. I won't make pretty speeches. I won't even pretend that I love you. How can I? I scarcely know you. Besides I must tell you now—I lost my wife and I will never love again. This would be a marriage from expediency only. But you would be mistress of this house, and of Ravenscroft. We'll drive down to Ravenscroft when the weather improves. I promise you you'll find that a very beautiful house. My grandfather built it."

Lally was gazing at him with a hypnotized look, her soft mouth open, her wild childlike eyes full of a dazed terror.

"Confess," Mr. Raven went on, "that it has passed through your mind more than once since you have been here that you would like to be mistress of a house like this."

"No, no!" Lally managed to say. "That's Bella. I've had no such thoughts."

The cool blue eyes raked Bella.

"The realist again?"

She was furious that the blood rose in her face, furious with Lally for being so naïve, for looking so innocent and gentle and untroublesome, indeed, for promising to be the kind of wife whom a man could conveniently ignore. She was most furious of all with this man for putting them in so ignominious a position. Yet already her honesty was telling her that he had meant well from the start, and was now choosing the best method he knew to save their reputations.

She could still, by a tremendous effort, keep her voice cool.

"Who doesn't enjoy luxury?"

"Exactly. And it would, of course, be yours also after your sister and I are married."

"A *ménage à trois?*" said Bella sharply, and he put back his head and laughed delightedly.

"That's scarcely language for someone assumed by the press to be a Soho drab. I believe we can still set London by the ears. In a very different way, of course, from what we have achieved already. My mother could dress you both. Yes." Finger on lip, he surveyed them thoughtfully. Why, he even notices now that we have bosoms and waists, Bella thought in angry sarcasm. And reflected on the extreme unlikelihood of that haughty little parrot woman, Mrs. Raven, condescending to advise them on wardrobes.

"We aren't *playthings!*" she declared, and incredulously heard her voice tremble.

The laughter had gone out of Mr. Raven's face, too. He looked suddenly tired, the lines unnaturally deep in so young a face.

"I never thought you were, Miss Isabella. I assure you this isn't a joke that has gone too far. It's a deadly serious thing I set out to do, and I simply don't intend to be thwarted by a lot of vicious scandalmakers. I've explained that marriage means little to me now. But it will afford permanent protection for your sister and yourself. For myself, it may whitewash me sufficiently to scrape by with my electorate. If it does, then I can begin on the really important business of social reform. It's a barbarous thing that young women like yourselves, without family or dowry, should have no real place in our society. And even less place now that you've unfortunately been caught up in the publicity treadmill. Well, I'm offering amends. And damn it—" he said with sudden impatience, "I see no reason at all for going down on my knees to do it."

Bella gave Lally a little push.

"Go on, then."

Lally looked at her piteously.

"Go on?"

"Say you'll marry him, of course."

"But, Bella—forever?"

"Marriage is forever."

Lally twisted her fingers in the greatest distress. Her eyes were swimming in tears.

"I thought—I meant to l-love—the man I marry."

"Love?" said Bella in a high voice, as if the word were one

80

she had never understood. "Don't be a dolt!" she said, and picking up her skirts swept out of the room.

She couldn't bring herself to speak to Lally again, even after she had heard Mr. Raven calling in a loud impatient voice to Doughty to get him a cab, and later heard him leaving the house. Lally, she knew, would be looking for her to pour out her terror and excitement, and triumph. For of course she must feel triumph. Who wouldn't? Mr. Raven was one of the most eligible men in London. Lally only had to play her cards right and she could win for herself an important place in society. It would take time, of course. People had long memories. But with her gentleness and innocence and angelic prettiness, Lally must eventually win even Mr. Raven's mother. That was, if she used her commonsense and didn't go on babbling forlornly about love. Who could expect love in this world? Only a baby or a simpleton.

As for herself, with the respectable chaperonage of her sister and new brother-in-law, and the background of rich houses, there may eventually even be someone to marry her. A music master, perhaps, or an elderly widower.

Bella paced up and down the little morning-room. She felt on fire. She couldn't sit still, she didn't want to engage in an interminable conversation with Lally, she abhorred the thought of a little soothing needlework which would only serve to remind her of all the long useless days to come, dabbling with painting, pressing wild flowers, netting purses, being neither wife nor mother nor servant. Being nothing . . .

Yet this marriage was undoubtedly the way to save all their faces. Wasn't it? Or was there any other way?

An impulse seized Bella. She flew upstairs to get her bonnet and shawl. Lally was standing at the window of their bedroom, a handkerchief to her eyes.

"Oh, Bella, there you are!" she exclaimed in relief. "Bella, I truly can't face—Bella! Where are you going? *Bella!*" Her piteous voice followed Bella down the stairs.

But Bella was in the hall asking Doughty for the address of Doctor Bushey, and would he please get her a cab.

Doughty disapproved. "There's pesky newspapermen lurking outside, miss. I don't think the master would like you to expose yourself."

"Please do as I say," Bella said haughtily.

The old man, recognizing the voice of authority, hastened to obey. But he was right about the men outside, and Bella had to hold her shawl about her face, and shake off impertinent hands.

"What about your life story, miss? We'll pay you good money."

"Can we hear your plans for the future, miss? Don't be shy, dear. Let's have a look at your lovely face."

"Then if you won't talk about yourself, how about telling us of your patron's plans?"

Scarlet with rage, Bella reached the waiting cab and clambered in. In a calmer mood she would have enjoyed the drive across the park past Tyburn Hill to the Edgware Road and then to Wigmore Street with its rows of neat respectable houses. As it was, she was scarcely aware of the lavender-coloured morning, with the mud splashing up in fine style from the wheels of passing carriages and coaches, the bustling throngs, the incredible welter of noise and vitality. By a great effort of will she composed herself, and sat still in the cab that smelled of wet straw and old tobacco smoke. But she could see nothing except Mr. Raven's stony eyes and the implacable set of his head. Perhaps Lally did well to be afraid . . .

Doctor Bushey was at home, and expressed himself astonished and delighted to have a visitor. The neatly-dressed maid who showed Bella in to the small cosy parlour smiled and bobbed when Doctor Bushey told her to fetch Tottie.

"Miss Isabella would like to see Tottie."

"That wasn't why I came."

Doctor Bushey's eyes didn't lack warmth or humanity or understanding. Indeed, they had a little too much of the last quality. Bella was very well aware he had noticed at once her flushed cheeks and distrait air. But he preferred to wait until Tottie arrived.

Her hair had been brushed and pinned back, her face was clean and her cap and apron spotless. But she still had the look of a caught animal, her eyes flying from Bella to Doctor Bushey in instant apprehension. She stood cringingly just inside the door, as if ready to fly if anyone moved.

"Don't be afraid, Tottie," Doctor Bushey said quietly. "Miss McBride is your friend. You remember her, don't you?"

Tottie nodded jerkily, but her gaze went beyond Bella, as if she expected to see Aunt Aggie or Noah spring up from behind the furniture.

"You must learn to say 'How do you do' to your friends, Tottie. But all in good time, eh?"

"Her chilblains are better, I think," Bella said.

"Yes, Betsey's been treating those. Hasn't she, Tottie? All right, you can go now. But slowly, child. No one's chasing you."

Tottie's impulse to dart out of the room was overcome. Bella found her eyes tightening with sudden tears as she watched the suddenly deliberate and pathetically dignified departure of the little figure.

"She's learning," she said in amazement.

"Yes, she's learning. She hasn't spoken yet, but I'm quite sure she will, in time. We don't even know how long she was with that terrible pair, but I'd make a guess at about two years."

"Two years! A mere child, and living like that!"

"Yes, my dear. Living like that."

"Doctor Bushey, are there many Tottie's in London?" Bella asked in the greatest distress.

"I hope not. Although I fear so. But that's better, my dear."

"What's better?"

"You're looking less agitated. You've found someone with a bigger problem than your own."

"You brought Tottie in deliberately!"

"Of course. Of course. A little emotional therapy is good for everyone. Now tell me, what has my headstrong young friend, Guy Raven, been up to?"

"The newspapers, Doctor Bushey!"

"Yes, yes, I saw them. They've found a good story and they'll thrash it to death. They need boiling in oil, the lot of them. But don't tell me Guy is intimidated by this cheap sensationalism."

"No, he isn't," Bella admitted. "He has found a solution."

"So?" Doctor Bushey nodded interestedly.

"He proposes to marry my sister!"

Doctor Bushey leaned back, surveying Bella with his bright shrewd eyes. The knowledgeableness in them brought the colour to her cheeks again. She hadn't meant her voice to be so full of indignation, but it had been, and now this kindly old man who might have been her father was reading entirely the wrong meaning into it.

"Guy never does things by halves," he murmured.

"You don't seem at all surprised."

"I'm not. Except perhaps," the thick brows flickered, "by his choice."

"I think Lally reminds him a little of his first wife. Isn't it true a man always admires the same kind of woman? Though he was perfectly honest and explained he would never fall in love again. Anyway," Bella's voice grew resentful, "he has scarcely looked at us. It's all a matter of convenience only."

"And what are you asking me, my dear? Whether your sister should accept this offer of marriage?"

"Is there any other way out?" Bella said desperately. "Supposing it doesn't remedy the situation but does Mr. Raven even more harm? Frankly, Doctor Bushey, my sister hasn't the temperament to meet such a situation. She's timid and inclined to hysteria. Things must go gently and smoothly for her. For instance just having to encounter Mr. Raven's mother again would put her in a state of collapse. So if there is still persecution after the marriage, then wouldn't tarnished reputations be better for us all, after all."

"Tell me, what have you advised your sister to do?"

"Advised—"

"You haven't remained entirely silent, I take it."

Bella's eyes fell before the sharp humour in his eyes.

"If you must know, I told her to fly into his arms! The silly dolt!" She met Doctor Bushey's gaze defiantly. "Thinking tears are the answer to everything."

"And Guy thinks an advertised respectability the answer to everything. I warned him of this at the beginning."

"You knew this would happen!"

"Not perhaps this precise predicament. But some sort of one."

"Then should he do it? Should Lally do it?" Bella leaned forward earnestly. "I love my sister and want her to be happy. Is there any chance of happiness for her now?"

"Or Guy? He is *my* particular care."

"But he says he will never love again, anyway."

"Oh, come, Miss Isabella! Is someone who could act so spontaneously and generously towards two unknown young women incapable of love?"

Unconsciously, Bella pressed her hands to her heart. Why must she go on wondering whether those cold impersonal eyes could grow alight?

"He was pursuing his own ends," she muttered. "He wanted a cause. A picturesque cause, I think."

"Tottie was not so picturesque. Nor are a thousand others. Nor did you think you and your sister were at the time. My dear, be fair. Guy deserves his chance, his career. It can be a notable one."

Bella rose.

"Then he is to marry Lally."

Doctor Bushey held out his hand. His eyes twinkled kindly, conspiratorially.

"He is to marry one of you."

9

MRS. DOUGHTY CAME HURRYING downstairs when Bella arrived back.

"Thank goodness you're there, miss. Your sister's nearly out of her mind. I don't know as you shouldn't call the doctor."

"She can't be as bad as that!" Bella exclaimed in alarm.

"She is, too. Crying and sobbing. Saying she's been abandoned. You didn't ought to have gone off like that, miss."

"I had an errand," Bella said stiffly. Kind as she was, Mrs. Doughty was becoming too familiar. From now on they were no longer equals, as Mrs. Doughty imagined, but mistress and servant. This was a bridge Lally would have to learn to cross. She must understand that there was to be no more weeping on Mrs. Doughty's shoulder.

Lally, however, was in no state to understand anything. Bella found that Mrs. Doughty hadn't exaggerated her condition. She was prostrate, her eyes swollen, her little nose (which Mr. Raven had glibly admired) pink, her breath fluttering exhaustedly. When Bella, her bonnet still on, bent over her, her eyes widened in a moment of purely instinctive terror before she recognized who it was.

Then she whispered faintly, "Why did you leave me?"

"Good gracious, I've only been gone an hour. You were perfectly safe."

"Safe!"

"Oh, Lally, of course you were safe. Aunt Aggie and Noah are miles away and locked up."

"But now there's Mr. Raven."

Lally's voice was so low as to be almost inaudible. She

searched Bella's face with her wide strained eyes. Her fingers, feverish and alarmingly claw-like (she seemed to have lost weight overnight) were tightly wound round Bella's wrist. It was too late to be impatient with her or to attempt to scold her out of her panic. Her state of mind, Bella realized, was serious.

"When he touched me—after you had gone out of the room—" she was speaking in a low murmur, as if to herself, "—he only laid his hand on mine—but it was as if he were suddenly Noah. Or someone—as bad as Noah. I couldn't stand it. I snatched my hand away. And he—"

"Yes?" said Bella. "What did he do?"

"He smiled, I think. He said I was not to be worried, he would not be a demanding husband, but for the sake of propriety, I must sit at the head of his table, and receive guests, and—and share his room. Bella, I can't! I can't, I can't, I can't!"

Lally's voice had risen in the hiccuping cries of hysteria. Bella slapped her face and ordered her to control herself. Then, when she was silent, very white and scarcely breathing, Bella said gently,

"Lally! Sweetheart! Don't you realize how lucky you are? Why, it's like a fairy story. At one moment you were practically a waif, and now you're to be mistress of two fine houses. Think of the clothes and jewels you can have. I warrant Mr. Raven is generous. And he won't be unkind. He's a gentleman."

"It's another trap," said Lally restlessly. "We thought how kind Aunt Aggie was, too. We liked the pretty room. But see what happened. No one is to be trusted."

There was a knock at the door. Mrs. Doughty stood there with a laden tray.

"I've made some hot chocolate, miss. It's very soothing. I wouldn't let Annie bring it up. All agog she is."

"Why?" Bella asked, wondering if it were possible for Annie to be more agog than Mrs. Doughty, whose eyes were positively starting out of her head.

"All them milliners' and dressmakers' boxes arriving. The area bell's scarcely stopped ringing for the last ten minutes. What those rascally newspapermen are making of this, I'd not like to say. What is it, miss? Are you and your sister to be dressed up and flaunt the town?"

"Are the boxes addressed to us?" Bella asked faintly.

"Certainly they is." Mrs. Doughty's speech was a little

86

garbled, as if she might have had recourse to the port decanter to fortify herself against further excitements. "The Misses McBride, 16 Knightsbridge. That's no mistake."

"Then you'd better ask Annie to bring them up."

"You mean you was expecting them?" Mrs. Doughty gaped. "Surely you wasn't out shopping this morning, miss!"

"No, I wasn't." Bella had recovered her composure, and even Mrs. Doughty's goggling eyes could not see how her heart was beating. "I think they were sent to help my sister recover from her nervousness."

"Nervousness?"

"That will be all, Mrs. Doughty. Have the boxes sent up."

Lally could take no more than a sip of the chocolate. She gazed in a stupor as Bella took the lids off the exciting boxes, and displayed the ravishing contents. Bonnets, one pink and one blue, with French silk ribbons and roses as soft to the touch as real ones, two gowns, one the palest blue satin with a low-cut bodice and a gently stiffened skirt belling out from a tiny waist, the other pink, also in rich satin. The material gave Bella a sensation of sheer sensual delight. She had never seen such lovely gowns. There were evening slippers, too, and long white satin gloves, and two cashmere shawls.

Like a summer garden, the room had sprung into bloom.

Bella held the pink dress against herself and looked at her reflection in the mirror. But although it was beautiful and expensive it was too insipid a colour for her. So was the blue. Wouldn't Mr. Raven have realized that with her black hair and vivid cheeks she needed jewel colours, ruby reds and sapphires. But of course he wouldn't realize that. He had never looked at her.

"The things are for you, Lally," she said pettishly. "Can't you sit up and take an interest in them?"

Lally's eyes wandered dully over the strewn finery.

"There are two of each. One bonnet and gown must be for you. The pink, I expect."

"I detest that baby pink!"

"Then have the blue. You could have them both," Lally said longingly, "if you would have Mr. Raven, too."

Bella was suddenly very still, a tremendous excitement mushrooming inside her.

Then her mind fastened feverishly on smaller things. She noticed a letter in the bottom of one of the boxes and snatched it up. It was addressed to "Miss McBride" which, strictly speaking, meant Lally, but Lally was in no mood to make sense of the thick black writing. Bella tore open the envelope and unfolded the thick notepaper.

"My dear Eulalie,
It may lift yours and your sister's spirits to have a pretty gown and other gee-gaws. I hope that you will both do me the honour of dining with me this evening.
                                        Your affianced husband,
                                        Guy Raven."

"We are to have dinner with Mr. Raven tonight," she said.

"Oh, I can't, Bella. I can't, truly." Lally's lip was trembling again. "I only wish I need never face him again."

Bella lost her patience.

"Don't you want to put on that lovely gown? Don't you want to thank Mr. Raven for it? Don't you want him to see how pretty you can look?"

"I should be sick if I tried to eat. I know I should. And why does he send us these expensive things? Is it another trick?"

"Lally, nothing's a trick any more. You're to marry him. He wants you to look the way his bride should, that's all."

"That's why he rescued us!" Lally exclaimed. "I see it now. He only wanted to get one of us at his—at his mercy. The way Noah would have, too. Or any man. And then there would be another baby—to be buried in the night."

Lally was frighteningly colourless, her eyes enormous and sunken, her little hands beating at her breast.

"Lally, Lally, little love! Be quiet." Bella was genuinely alarmed. Lally seemed to be going out of her wits. The dreadful experience to which they had been subjected in Aunt Aggie's house had burnt itself too deeply into her mind. Her marriage now to a man who terrified her could complete her breakdown. Bella had sufficient medical knowledge to realize that.

And she saw that what had flashed into her mind, no, what had been there all the time, the impossible outrageous alternative, was now to be a necessity.

At once, now the decision was made, she became calm and assured.

"Lally, you shan't go down to dinner tonight. You shall rest quietly here by the fire. You shan't do anything you don't want to."

Lally's eyes took on a wild gleam of hope.

"Really, Bella? Not even marry—"

"Not even marry Mr. Raven." Bella's voice was quiet, definite, protecting. "If he still insists on having one of us, it will have to be me."

"Oh, Bella, you're so brave! I do so admire you. Mr. Raven must see you would make a much better wife than me." Lally clutched at her in a passion of gratitude. Then she said less certainly, "I don't have to tell him, do I?"

"I shall tell him myself. Tonight."

He was standing in his usual posture with his back to the fire. He looked very handsome in his black dinner-jacket and gleaming white cravat. There seemed to be a certain anticipation in his eyes as he looked up at the sound of Bella's entrance. He was no doubt curious to see how his bride to be and perhaps her sister, also, looked when dressed as elegant young ladies.

But his expression immediately changed to a polite question as he saw Bella, alone, and in her best gown of grey tarlatan which was a little dowdy and old-fashioned, since it had been made by Miss Anstruther in the village quite eighteen months ago. Miss Anstruther had never been able to achieve a clever cut, and had an obsession about what she called a ladylike neckline. Nor was grey Bella's colour, but Papa had bought the cloth when he had bought Lally's blue, and certainly, if nothing else, the grey gown was dove-like in its modesty.

It made her look like a governess.

"Didn't the dressmakers' boxes arrive?" Mr. Raven immediately inquired.

"Yes, they did. Lally and I found the contents—very extravagant. But—" Now she was faced with it, how was she to make this incredible suggestion?

"They perhaps didn't fit? I had to make a guess as to size. But where is your sister? She's coming down, I hope?"

"She asks to be excused. She has a very bad headache. She—Mr. Raven, you know us both equally little. Why did you decide it was Lally you would marry?"

She hoped she looked more composed than she felt. Her heart was pounding so violently that the lace trimming on her bodice trembled visibly. She had meant to be cool and tactful, and now she had blurted out the question like a schoolgirl.

She didn't know how she had expected him to react. Certainly she wasn't prepared for his deliberate survey of her. His gaze went assessingly from her coiled dark hair to her feet. It lingered on her throat, her bosom and her waist, and finally rested on her slippers peeping from the hem of her gown.

"Not because her charms exceed yours, Miss Isabella. Simply because she is the elder of you." He laughed. "I had to have some distinction to make."

How *could* one marry a man like that, cold, insolent, assessing one's advantages as he might an animal he wished to purchase? Lally was right to be afraid.

Then why wasn't she herself afraid? Why did she feel only this terrific sense of challenge and destiny?

Bella lifted her head proudly on her long neck.

"I thought perhaps my sister reminded you a little of your dead wife?"

He moved sharply, turning to the fire.

"That's an impossible assumption. My wife has no duplicates."

"Then, Mr. Raven—if you have no special preference for Lally, will you marry me instead?"

He swung round, staring at her.

"My sister has a much more delicate nervous system than I have. She's suffered dreadfully from shock, she has nightmares all the time about Noah and the dead baby. Now the thought of marrying someone virtually a stranger terrifies her."

"Terrifies? Not a nice word, Miss Isabella."

"It's only that you're a stranger. I'm afraid another ordeal so soon would make her brain give way. She begged me to——"

"Offer yourself instead? And doesn't the thought of such an ordeal terrify you, too?"

She hated his growing amusement.

"I've said I'm much stronger," she said tartly.

"Yes. Yes, I can see that. You'd be capable of making a sacrifice."

"A sacrifice?"

"That of a loveless marriage."

"It isn't a sacrifice but a solution. You explained that yourself."

"I did." He laughed again, suddenly looking as if he were enjoying himself. "Sit down, my dear. Let's drink to this extraordinary situation. I lose one bride and gain another in the space of twelve hours. Incredible. Damned amusing, really."

"Then—you will do this?"

"Why not? It makes no odds to me which one of you I have." His eyes met hers blandly. "The goldfinch or the blackbird, as the newspapers so cleverly put it."

10

THE NEWSPAPERS LOVED THAT catch phrase about the goldfinch and the blackbird.

They were able to use it to full effect the next day when most of them carried a discreet announcement of an impending marriage.

> *"All London is agog to know the identity of Miss Isabella McBride. Is she the fair beauty or the dark, the golden-feathered finch or the black songster? It is rumored that bets are being laid in all the elite gambling houses. Indeed, it is the kind of wager that Mr. Guy Raven would have enjoyed himself in the recent past, before he became so oddly reformed a person. We feel his new personality is greatly to fashionable London's loss, and not at all to the country's gain. Sincere congratulations to clever Miss Isabella, but can a belated marriage certificate white-wash a man's reputation?"*

That was the scandalous *London Clarion*. The more respectable papers confined themselves to a bare announcement, or a few lines that contained only a mild jibe.

On the whole Guy was not too dissatisfied. There was every chance now that he could weather the storm. Except as far as his mother was concerned.

She sent him a note by hand.

"Since I will never set foot in your house again while those scheming and unscrupulous creatures are there, I will expect you here at eleven."

She was waiting for him in her elegant drawing-room that looked over Chelsea embankment and the turgid yellow waters of the Thames. She was dressed entirely in black. Guy recognized the gown as the one she had had made when in mourning for Caroline. He didn't suppose she had put it on deliberately to remind him of Caroline, but because she felt this occasion required black.

She sat rigidly on a straight-backed chair, her poodles yapping and quarrelling about her feet. Hannah, the elderly maid, hovered in the background, but was immediately dismissed. Things had gone too far even for Hannah's trustworthy and sympathetic ears.

"Well, Guy! At first you were a fool, now I can only think you're a raving lunatic."

Guy kissed her on her exquisite pale pink cheek. His mother was now sixty-five. He was her only child whom she had borne at the age of thirty-five after several tortured years of thinking herself barren. She loved him with a demanding possessiveness. Even for the gentle well-bred Caroline she had not been an easy mother-in-law. Guy could only hope that, at the most, she would reluctantly acknowledge his new wife.

"I want to bring Isabella to meet you, Mamma."

"Isabella! Stuff and nonsense! That won't be her real name. It will be plain Bessie or Bridget. Can't you see the girl for the scheming hussy she is? She was only waiting for someone like you and that gullible old fool, Bushey, to come along and fall into her net. Heavens, boy, at your age to be taken in by the oldest trick in the world."

"And when you've met her, Mamma," Guy went on imperturbably, "perhaps you'll be good enough to advise her on a suitable wardrobe. Something simple to be married in, since we plan a very quiet wedding, but after that you can let yourself go. See that she's dressed the way my wife should be. Will you do that for me, Mamma?"

The sound that escaped Mrs. Raven's lips could only be described as a hiss. Her beautiful, heavy-lidded eyes blazed with outrage. She thumped her ivory-headed cane on the floor several times, and a poodle yelped.

"So the slut expects to shelter under my wing! That she should *dare!*"

"Be careful of your language, Mamma." Guy's voice was mild, but his mouth had tightened.

"I'll use exactly what language the subject deserves. The girl obviously is a slut. Both of them are. By the way, which one is this Bella, or whatever her name is?"

"Are you interested, then?"

"I met them," his mother said tightly.

"She's the dark-haired one. The younger."

"I expected it! The saucy one. At least the other might have been manageable. But you would have an eye for cheap vivacity. Don't begin to think you'll be the master with that one. Isabella, indeed! She's already been abominably rude to me, and yet now you expect me to forget her gutter manners and introduce her to society."

"Perhaps you were rude to her first."

"I merely told her the truth. In any case, I was brought up not to answer back to one's elders."

"The girls have been under considerable strain, Mamma."

"I should think so! I should think so!" the old lady crowed. "Catching a rich husband. Quite an ordeal. Oh, Guy! I'd never have thought a son of mine could be so stupid. Let your career go, if it must. What does that matter compared to a lifetime of misery? Do you realize, for one thing, you'll never see me in your house again? Neither in London nor at Ravenscroft."

"Don't be absurd! Ravenscroft is as much yours as mine. You know you love it."

"And I shall sacrifice it. Guy! My boy!"

He met the appeal in her lifted eyes, and his own hardened.

"I'm sorry, Mamma. You call me a lunatic. I'm afraid I must call you a narrow-minded, intolerant, cowardly old woman."

"You'd dare!" Her moment of softness had gone. Her beaky nose was held high, her expression that of a malevolent old parrot. "Cowardly! You think I haven't the courage to introduce that woman to society. Why, I'd introduce a worm if I felt so inclined. But not a schemer. No, not if I have to endure loneliness until my dying day."

"You should have been on the stage, Mamma."

"And you should be back in an infant school!" she screamed.

The memory of that little funereal figure like an angry wasp infuriated him, perhaps because he saw so much of himself in her. He, too, enjoyed the histrionic gesture, and the flouting of public opinion. He even had an odd satisfaction in making this improbable and wildly unsuitable marriage. He would find imposing his will on society highly stimulating. His bride would be accepted and he would make his mark as a politician. The future promised to be lively, at least, a welcome change from the dark, lonely nightmare of the last two years.

Only one small thing nagged at him. He had had to give way in his choice of his bride. It was a detail, it mattered little which of the two girls he married, it amused him more than anything that the elder should have been afraid of him. He had liked her soft prettiness. The other, Isabella, Bella, whatever he was to call her, had a tendency to dramatize things. Sauciness, his mother called it. Perhaps it was better that his wife (how he hated and resented using this word of another woman!) had spirit. Lifting herself from a nondescript background to that of wife of a rising politician would require all the skill and courage she possessed.

Would it ever work?

Well, if it didn't, she could stay down at Ravenscroft with her sister and enjoy a rural life.

In the meantime, she must be properly outfitted. She had looks and would make a presentable figure.

Yet when he tried to remember how she looked he found he could only remember that her eyes were a curious dark yellow. He remembered that because they had blazed at him, like an angry cat's.

He knew, at least, that she would not be a coward.

For the rest, as long as she behaved with discretion and cut a reasonably good figure in public, she would get by. He didn't think she would have too much trouble with the servants. If she did, they would have to go.

But he suspected she would manage them excellently, since she had already, and very definitely, got her way with him. The thought did rankle, damn it. But apart from the money and the clothes, the houses and the servants, she would find she hadn't made much of a bargain.

Probably the material things would content her very well.

But she must be dressed properly. Since Mamma wouldn't undertake this chore, he must send for Cousin Henrietta.

Lally perked up amazingly when she found that she was no longer required to go through the ordeal of marriage to a stranger. She became quite high-spirited and giggled obligingly at Mrs. Doughty's sallies. Bella said Mrs. Doughty was not to be encouraged, considering their changed status in the house, but it was difficult to restrain Mrs. Doughty's exuberance. She found all weddings delightful, and this one particularly so.

"It'll make the master a human being again," she declared. "I never did like those la-di-dah young ladies who've been trying to catch him. You'll learn to understand him, miss, and make him happy. And you've class, for all the newspapers say. I've said to Doughty all along, them young ladies has class."

Bella was touched, in spite of her decision to permit no familiarity from servants.

"I hope everyone will be as kind as you, Mrs. Doughty."

"Pish to them as isn't. Warm hearts in your own home is all that's needed."

Mrs. Doughty obviously cherished the romantic notion that all marriages were made for love. If she had suspected the enforced bargain, she had as quickly put it out of her mind. She expected Bella to be blushing and starry-eyed, and it was a shame to disappoint her.

But it was Lally who did the laughing . . .

Then Cousin Henrietta arrived.

She was a dumpy plain dowdy little woman who stood in the hall surrounded by a multitude of bags and boxes and peered at Bella and Lally through a lorgnette.

"Which one is the bride, Guy? They both look remarkably young."

Guy led Bella forward and presented her.

"Ha! Well, my dear, let me congratulate you on your courage."

"Courage, Cousin Henrietta?" Guy queried good-humouredly.

"From the little you've told me, and the great deal I've gleaned from the newspapers, the situation would alarm any woman. But," the old lady peered again, "she has a good chin, I see. Well, when do we begin shopping?"

"As soon as possible. The ceremony—" (He didn't, Bella noticed, say wedding), "is to be next Wednesday. It was good of you to come, Cousin Henrietta."

"I did it to annoy Edith, if you must know." The old lady gave a loud cackling laugh. "Is she still sulking?"

"You know Mamma."

"She must be as mad as a March hare. Deliberately losing her son, losing a charming daughter, losing her grandchildren. Don't blush, young lady." Cousin Henrietta poked suddenly at Bella with her stick. "You're a fine healthy-looking female. And it's time there was a filled cradle at Ravenscroft. Now, where's my room? I must take a nap before we lay our plan of campaign. I'm not as young as I was, and the roads were atrocious. By the way, Guy, any limits to expenditure?"

"None within reason."

"Good. Splendid. The sister, too?"

"Eulalie, too, naturally."

The old lady gave her hearty cackling laugh.

"It isn't naturally, at all, and you must admit it. Ha! I confess I enjoy this situation. It's titillating. Ha, ha, ha! Trust a Raven. Did you ever hear that story about your grandfather and the Maharajah's third wife? No, well, neither did I officially. But it was a rattling good one. Have my bags sent up. I've brought my own pillows."

"She's *mad*!" said Lally.

"Anyone can see that," said Bella furiously. "Does Mr. Raven really think I'll wear what a crazy old woman chooses for me. We were perfectly well able to do our shopping ourselves. I told him so. But, no, he said we must be suitably chaperoned and advised. His mother would at least have had good taste, if she had deigned to have anything to do with us. But this old frump—"

"I hope you're not referring to the Countess of Lyminster, my love," came Guy's voice.

He had followed them to the drawing-room and stood in the doorway looking at them unsmilingly. Already like a reproving husband, Bella thought, as she exclaimed, in confusion.

"Not Cousin Henrietta? Not that—"

"Frump? I'm afraid so. I apologize for not making it clear to you earlier. I thought I had."

"You never did!" Bella said indignantly. "How could you be so thoughtless! Making us look foolish. You know very well she looks exactly like a gardener's wife."

"Bella!" Lally protested.

"A gardener's wife doesn't travel with twelve pieces of luggage. You must learn to be more observant, my love. Well, can I leave you in Cousin Henrietta's capable hands? I assure you they are capable."

He wasn't angry at her outburst. Bella wished he had been. He was only faintly amused. Nothing she said or did seemed to rouse him to any emotion. It was like talking to someone through a closed door. She wanted to beat at him with her fists, and believed she would, after they were married, if he continued to behave like this. She tried one more small protest.

"If she dresses us in her own taste—"

"Trust her, Isabella my dear. You may be surprised."

"Now, if you have to curtsey to the Queen—"

"The Queen!"

"I sincerely trust you will be invited to one of Her Majesty's drawing-rooms. We might arrange later for one or two lessons in the royal curtsey. To continue. If you entertain Lord Palmerston to dinner—"

"The Prime Minister!"

"He was a friend of Guy's father. Didn't you know? Hasn't that young man told you anything?"

"He didn't even tell us you were a countess!"

The infectious high cackle broke out. The old lady's sallow, weathered face was seamed in a thousand wrinkles.

"Did he think it would alarm you?"

"He should have known better," Bella muttered.

"Yes." Cousin Henrietta's voice was suddenly absent, as she studied Bella. "Yes, I can see that. But don't give him too many surprises too quickly. You must ride him with an easy rein at first. He's been abominably spoiled by that doting mother of his. He's arrogant like all the Ravens, selfish by nature, unobservant. Remarkably unobservant. Yes." The old lady tapped one gnarled finger against her teeth. "We must do what we can to open his eyes. But where was I? Ah, yes. If the Prime Minister comes to dinner, you will place your guests so—"

"I won't wear pink," Bella said defiantly.

Cousin Henrietta poked at a roll of taffeta with her stick.

"That," she said to the salesman. "I have a camellia that colour at Lyminster. It makes me think of a rosy dawn in the East. Romantic. Full of promise. Of course you'll wear pink, my dear. The right shade of pink."

She went on buying and buying. Silk, taffeta, velvet, fine wool. Buttons, braids, exquisite hand-made lace, yards and yards of ribbon. Elegant little buttoned boots, satin slippers, silk stockings, gloves, and lengths of lawn and linen for petticoats and nightgowns. Bonnets, a fur-trimmed cloak for daytime, and a glorious chinese-red satin for evenings.

In the middle of it all, Bella suddenly burst into tears.

"Now what? Now what?" Cousin Henrietta said impatiently.

"I keep thinking of Tottie."

"Tottie! Who has that absurd name?"

"She hadn't a dress. It was only a bit of sack somehow

stitched together. It seems so wicked to want all these lovely things."

Cousin Henrietta waved to the discreetly goggling shop assistants.

"Some sal volatile, and hurry. Have you never seen a bride in tears? You!" Her expressive stick was pointing at a very young salesman. "Fetch that brocade. I think for a grand toilette—Lord Palmerston admires well-dressed women, I believe—we must find you a maid who is clever at hair dressing. Your task, my dear, is to please your husband. Let him look after the unfortunate Totties."

She was right, of course. If Bella could do her part in making Guy a successful wife it would help him enormously in his career, and ultimately Tottie and her kind would find the world a kinder place.

She crushed down her feelings of guilt that she should feel such avid delight in the luxurious clothes. Now she would be able to face the world with the greatest confidence. Now, she told herself in secret breathless joy, her husband must notice her.

He was not quite her husband yet. After an exhausting week spent almost entirely with dressmakers and milliners, her wedding day had come. She was dressed in grey with a little bonnet trimmed with modest pink roses. She hated the mousiness of the clothes, and wore them only because of Guy's insistence on extreme simplicity. Indeed, Lally looked gayer than the bride in her favourite blue. Cousin Henrietta looked a fright, and Doctor Bushey, the only other person present, did nothing to mark the special occasion except wear a rather drooping rosebud in his buttonhole.

It was a curiously furtive wedding, Bella thought resentfully, not, she sensed, because the pavement outside was crowded with inquisitive sightseers and newspaper men, but because nothing must be done to make it seem like a festive occasion. It must in no way resemble the happy and glorious occasion of Guy's wedding to his first wife three years previously. Caroline's ghost must be discouraged from attending such a modest ceremony.

Anyway, where was her good sense? They were not in love with each other. She was thankful to escape the hypocrisy of obvious festivity. She didn't tremble, though only by the exertion of tremendous will-power, when Guy slipped the ring on her finger. She noticed that his hands were square and strong. She began to think confusedly of them on her body that night, and was scarcely aware that the meager ceremony was over, and she, Bella McBride, was the wife of the most talked-of young man in London. She was suddenly wishing there had been some way of letting Cousin Sarah know. It would have made the marriage seem more real.

There was gaiety in the house that night, as it happened. Mrs. Doughty, on her own initiative, had prepared a celebration dinner. Bella had thankfully shed her grey mouse wedding gown and put on one of the new ones, the apricot silk. It bared her shoulders and set off her lovely long neck.

Her husband had not so far spared one glance for his bride, she could have been a blackamoor for all he had noticed her at the church. But he should look at her tonight.

Lally, also, took a timid pleasure in dressing in a pretty gown and twisting up her fair hair. Cousin Henrietta had not yet found them a maid who came up to her highly critical standards, but she promised to do so before leaving for the country.

Doctor Bushey had come back to dinner and when Bella went downstairs she found two strange men whom Guy introduced as political colleagues. Bella was not unaware of the startled look of admiration that came into their faces. Her heart began to bound. If she were to be actually admired by her husband's friends, things would not be too difficult after all.

But she found the dinner had not been arranged for her pleasure. The men had too many absorbing political topics to discuss, and she was too nervous and inept to get control of the conversation. Cousin Henrietta, who might have helped, chose to be silent, and Lally, unexpectedly faced with strangers, was tongue-tied.

There was champagne, certainly. Bella found it a much over-rated drink. It merely made her miserable. She had wanted to sparkle tonight. She would have sparkled if Guy (she was making herself call him Guy in her thoughts as if, by doing so, he would become less of a stranger) had so much as given her one approving glance. But for all his determination that she should be correctly dressed to sit at the head of his table, he now seemed to find her part of the furniture.

She drank her champagne rather quickly and hoped Doughty would notice and refill her glass—which he did. The second glass did make her sudden onset of misery less acute.

She decided the table was much too long, Guy much too far away. When they dined alone she would insist on sitting at his side. The candle-light caught gleams in his thick dark gold hair. He was animated as she had never seen him before, but about some wretched school in the East End.

"Every boy an Oliver Twist, I swear it. You read Mr. Dickens, I take it? He doesn't exaggerate."

Cousin Henrietta was tapping Bella's arm. Bella recovered herself hazily. Was dinner over? She had almost forgotten to eat. She realized she was to rise and leave the gentlemen to their port.

Followed by a relieved Lally, she led the way to the drawing-room. Cousin Henrietta at once excused herself, saying she had had a long day and would go up immediately.

"If you ask me, you'd be wise to do the same. They'll be in there for hours."

"Hours! But—"

"Port and politics. Even a new bride provides little competition to that irresistible combination."

"You mean this new bride," Bella said with sudden bitterness. "I don't expect you faced such a situation when you married, Cousin Henrietta."

"No. I grant you the circumstances were completely conventional. A tediously dull affair, a conventional marriage. Comfort yourself with that knowledge."

"But your husband at least *looked* at you!" The champagne had made sad work of Bella's pride.

"I don't believe he really saw me once in thirty years. Not that he didn't have an eye for a pretty young woman. I was constantly dismissing maids. But I had my roses." Cousin Henrietta shrugged philosophically. "That's how it is, my dear. Marriage is a state on earth, not a state in heaven. Far from perfect. How it succeeds is largely up to oneself. Now don't ask me how to behave, child. Use your instinct."

Instinct was all she had to use, for she had the vaguest notion of what to expect when Guy finally came to share the room that had been hastily re-decorated and furnished for their needs.

Lally had even less, Lally was in a flutter of nervous apprehension as if it were she who had to climb into the big bed and wait. She insisted on coming up with Bella and helping her to undress and put on the snowy-white lawn nightgown with its ruffle of lace at the throat and wrists.

"Shall you braid your hair or leave it loose? Shall I brush it for you?"

"No. Yes, just a little." Bella wanted Lally to go and at the same time to stay. She felt a little calmer when her sister was there, the waves of excitement not washing so shudderingly over her.

He hadn't noticed her naked shoulders at dinner and now they were covered. But the nightgown was flimsy, easily discarded.

His body would be like his hands, strong, hard . . .

"Bella, you're trembling."

"I'm cold."

"You don't look cold. You look on fire." Lally nodded sagely. "It's the champagne."

It's the thought of my husband's naked body. I've never seen a man naked . . .

"Yes, it's the champagne. I drank two glasses."

"I didn't. The bubbles went up my nose. Get into bed and I'll brush your hair there. Don't braid it, Bella. It'll look pretty against the pillow. So black and shiny. Bella," Lally's voice came in a breathless rush, "are you afraid?"

"Afraid?"

Lally began to giggle helplessly.

"You sound so haughty, just like Cousin Henrietta. I can tell you, I'd be scared to death. I'm just so glad it isn't me. I don't think I'll ever marry."

"Of course you will."

"I'd keep seeing Noah's hands. Those big crushing hands . . . Oh, Bella!" Lally's voice quivered. "This is the first night we've ever been parted."

"By one flight of stairs," said Bella. "Goose!"

Nevertheless, she clung to Lally tightly before Lally went. She wasn't sure whether it was Lally's tears that wet her cheeks, or her own.

But when she was alone the enormous anticipation swept over her again. She was trembling one moment, her body taut the next. She didn't know how to compose herself. She sat up primly against the plump down pillows, laying her hands flat on the counterpane and staring at her wedding ring.

Mrs. Guy Raven . . . She was that not from love or ambition, but expediency. She had to keep reminding herself of this fact, for obviously her husband needed no reminding. He was in no haste to join his bride. Far-off gusts of laughter sounded from downstairs. The port decanter must be being passed round again. And again . . .

A wind had risen and beat against the window, and presently there was the thin sound of rain flung against the panes like fine gravel. It must be late for the traffic was only spasmodic, a weary cab-horse being whipped up or a carriage rolling past. There was a little French gilt clock ticking on the mantelpiece over the embers of the dying fire. Bella lifted the candle to peer at it and saw the hands pointed to one-thirty.

Such an ardent bridegroom . . .

She got out of bed, and went and turned the clock's face to the wall. Then she was acutely conscious of its officious knowing ticking. She contemplated dashing it to the floor. But it would be like stopping a heartbeat, the only heartbeat in the room beside her own.

Suddenly she realized that Guy was not coming.

She got back into bed and blew out the candle. The rain blew in icy flurries against the window. Her body was icy, too, all its heat put out.

11

THERE WAS A TAP AT THE DOOR and in response to Bella's sleepy "Come in," Mrs. Doughty appeared, carrying a breakfast tray.

She set it down and briskly drew back the curtains.

"The master gave orders you were to have your breakfast in bed. I'll send Annie up at once to tend the fire."

Bella frowned at the thin winter sunlight.

"Has Mr. Raven breakfasted?"

"An hour since, madam." Mrs. Doughty was remembering to be very prim and formal. But her watery eyes held a gleam, and by the look of her purplish flush the gentlemen hadn't drained the port decanter last night. "He said you weren't to be disturbed until now."

Bella suddenly thought of the unoccupied side of the bed, pristine, clearly unslept in. But it wasn't so pristine, after all. She must have tossed and turned a great deal, for the pillows were rumpled and the blankets awry. Mrs. Doughty had noticed nothing amiss. Indeed, her knowing look indicated a very mistaken interpretation of the reason for Bella's weariness. Bella supposed she would make nothing of the bed in the adjoining room also having been slept in. Ladies and gentlemen liked their occasional privacy. They were not like the lower classes who got into a double bed on their wedding night and stayed there, willy-nilly, for the rest of their lives.

All at once Bella was envying them . . .

"Has Mr. Raven gone out yet, Mrs. Doughty?"

"Not yet, madam. He's in the library with his secretary."

"Tell him I'd like to see him before he goes out."

"Certainly, madam."

It was an hour before Guy came. Bella had thought to toy with her breakfast, but the coffee, the hot rolls, the lightly boiled eggs and the thin toast and marmalade were too good. She recovered her spirits by the minute, telling herself that this luxury was no longer a temporary one, to be snatched away as soon as she became a governess or a seamstress. It was hers for the rest' of her life. Even alone in a double bed . . .

She had put on one of her new robes and brushed her hair, although it still hung loose to her waist, when the knock at the door announced Guy.

He came in saying in his formal voice, "Good morning, my love. You wanted to see me?"

Naturally I wanted to see you. Isn't it usual for a wife and husband to say good morning? Even to kiss?

But it was impossible to burst out with her angry and bewildered thoughts. They were exactly as they had been two days ago, two weeks ago. Strangers.

"I wondered if there were anything new in the papers?"

"Only a rumour that there will be questions in the House today."

"About us! Oh, why can't they mind their own business!"

"If I'm to be a public figure, I must accept this." He was speaking painstakingly to her as if she were a child of dim intelligence.

"But our marriage was to have solved the trouble," she said miserably.

"I hope it will have. Forgive me, but I must be off."

He had never seen her with her hair down. He didn't see her now. Bella stamped her foot softly.

"Mr. Raven! Guy—"

He turned politely.

"Yes, my dear?"

"You were very late last night. You perhaps didn't want to—disturb me?"

Now he did look at her. But his eyes hated her. He was wishing for her long black hair to be corn-coloured, her face to be gentle and aristocratic. His thoughts were as clear as if he had shouted them. And she didn't know what to do about his ravaged face, his loneliness.

"Don't let me—keep you," she managed to say, but when he had gone, willingly, she tormented herself that she had not behaved differently, made him touch her, shown him that her body, too, was soft and desirable, that all hair looked the same colour when it was entangled in one's lips and eyes.

She ached for him, and at the same time hated him for the way his cold good manners froze her. Cousin Henrietta had told her to use her instinct. But she found she had none. She had nothing when faced with that resentment. She was as inarticulate as Lally.

Lally, incidentally, had to be faced, and she was as bright-eyed with curiosity as Bella had expected.

"Bella—did you sleep well?"

It was a question her husband should have asked her. She replied coolly,

"Very well, thank you."

"Those men stayed awfully late. I heard them leave in the small hours."

"You should have been asleep yourself."

"I know. I was lonely without you." Lally's naïve eyes searched Bella's face shyly.

"Goodness!" Bella exclaimed. "You're behaving as if I'm suddenly a stranger. I'm still your sister. And today we'll order the carriage and drive down Rotten Row."

"The carriage!"

"Why not?" said Bella with asperity. "It's mine."

Guy was not home until just before dinner. Bella had been listening for him for hours. He went straight to his room. She realized, startled, that she had the right to follow him if she wished. But she deemed it wiser to wait until he came down.

When he did so, she saw that he looked tired and unapproachable. She had determined to make pleasant chatter this evening, to show him that she knew a wife's duty. But Cousin Henrietta was there, and had no similar qualms about displaying too much curiosity.

"Well, my boy, how was it in the House?"

"Impossible! They give a man no chance to prove his good intentions."

"They don't believe such a thing exists," Cousin Henrietta said dryly. "Certainly not that old money-grubber, Henry Shields. I suppose this came from his party friends."

"I imagine so. Oh, there was a great air of politeness about it all. The question was merely asked as to the suitability of an electoral candidate who has been the subject of a scandal in the newspapers. The honourable member assumed an air of innocence and asked what the House made of the fact that although the candidate—no names mentioned, mark you—had so far put a veneer of respectability on the affair by marrying one of the young women with whom he was reputed to be associated, he still kept the two women in his house, and what did everyone make of that?"

"But Lally being here is innocent!" Bella cried out. "They ought to see."

Lally had gone pale and looked extremely distressed.

"It means I should go away? Oh, Bella—"

"You'll not go away! At least, not without me."

"There's no question of anything of the kind," said Guy irritably. "The public only seems to be annoyed that I can't marry you both." Perfunctorily he added, "I'm sorry to burden you with my affairs. I hope you all spent a pleasant day."

"I shall go home tomorrow," said Cousin Henrietta. "I've had enough of London. Mucky place. I want my garden."

Bella made a sound of protest. She had grown very fond of the plain, downright, warm-hearted little countess, and she was far from ready to sail the seas of fashionable London life without the old lady's sage advice.

"I haven't deserted you, my dear. I'll be back when that cradle has an occupant. Eh? Eh, children?"

But Guy was in no mood to laugh, and Bella could only try not to let Cousin Henrietta see the hurt of her words. Already her marriage seemed to be in ruins. For the words spoken in Parliament today seemed to have made it a wasted gesture. Her husband clearly thought the same thing. He seemed to have no intention of occupying the conjugal bed.

Before Cousin Henrietta departed she finally declared herself satisfied with one of the many lady's maids she had interviewed. Louise, an angular young woman with sharp quick ways, was installed. Bella disliked her on sight, but had to admit she could create a most elegant coiffure. She also knew the powders and lotions that could completely conceal freckles and enhance one's natural colour. She was clever. She contrived immediately to put at least five years on Bella's age. There was no outward trace left of the unsophisticated country girl.

She took a pride in her work, but Bella had an uneasy conviction that curiosity and nothing more had brought her here. She wanted to see for herself the most notorious woman in London. Her respectful manner hid contempt.

And however much simple port-fuddled Mrs. Doughty might be deceived by the rumpled bed, Bella was certain Louise was not. She knew how to deal with contempt from an uppish maid, but not pity.

All the same, Cousin Henrietta's wisdom was proved by Guy announcing that Bella and Lally were to be prepared to go to the opera the next evening. He had taken a box, and they were to make a grand toilette.

Lally said it was like a dream come true.

"Do you remember, Bella, the very night we came to London, you said one day we would go to the Covent Garden Opera House. Could you have thought it would happen so soon? How good and generous Mr. Raven is!"

"He wants to show us off to the world," Bella said.

"Then he must be proud of us," Lally said, pleased.

Sometimes Bella wondered how they could be sisters, Lally was so simple, where she herself always turned everything inside out, looking for the hidden motive.

"He's not proud of us in that way," she said crossly. "He only wants to defy the gossips. He intends to have us accepted. You'll have to be prepared to be stared at all the way up the grand staircase."

Lally immediately looked nervous.

"Oh, dear! I know I shall trip on my gown. Bella, do you think I must go? Won't people say again how odd it is Mr. Raven always has us both, as if—as if—" Lally couldn't bring herself to put the dreadful suggestion into words.

"Mr. Raven says we are both to go. So please don't argue. Wear your blue satin. I'll send Louise to you as soon as she has finished with me. She'll help you with your hair. And Lally, if you trip, or giggle, or do anything awkward, I'll never speak to you again."

She knew how important the occasion was from Guy's set face. It was the first time he had come to her room while she was dressing. As it happened Louise had just finished her hair, doing it very modishly on the top of her head so that she looked taller and older and with a dignity she didn't feel. She was wearing the Chinese red gown, because the colour gave her courage. No one could shrink out of sight in a colour like that, and she had no intention of shrinking.

She told Louise to go up to Lally and as the woman went couldn't resist spinning round in front of her husband, and saying breathlessly, "Will I do?"

He examined her toilette in every detail. At first she flushed with pleasure at his interest, then she began to pout as she realized she was being studied like a beribboned filly being prepared for a championship. He hadn't noticed her desire to please, not a fashionable audience at the opera, but just him, her husband. He was stupid and unimaginative and cruel.

"Haven't you a gown in quieter taste?"

"No!" she flared. "I'll wear this one."

His eyes flickered in surprise. "Keep calm, my dear. I only mean you to be looked at, not stared at."

"Is it only harlots who wear red?" Bella asked daringly. "Perhaps it's because they enjoy a little admiration."

He took a flat narrow box from his breast pocket.

"You'll enjoy plenty of admiration when you wear these."

He opened the box and the diamonds glittered like a sun dazzle. Bella gasped. She said, crazily, the first words that came into her head.

"They are your wife's!"

"Yes. Put them on." Since she stood gaping he gave her a push towards the mirror. "Or do you enjoy your role of harlot too much?"

"I meant— I didn't mean—"

Because she made no attempt to touch the glittering necklace, he picked it up and fastened it round her neck. The light touch of his fingers on her skin sent such a wave of giddiness over her that she dared not look at her face in the mirror. She kept her head down, waiting for the fire to go out of her cheeks.

"You can't be a harlot and my wife also." His composed voice came from a long way off. "The diamonds were my grandmother's, and then my mother's. Now—" he scarcely hesitated at all, "they're yours."

Suddenly she longed for Lally's ability to weep or to swoon. Then her mind could become a merciful blank and she needn't think at all of that other neck round which this necklace had once been clasped. There would have been no casual air about that ceremony. If the touch of her husband's fingers had enflamed her, Caroline could have turned and flung herself into his arms. She wouldn't have needed to sit rigid, struggling to hide her emotions. But now the stones were heavy, cold, like death.

"Well, hold up your head and look at them." Guy was being very kind and humouring the bedazzled little girl from the country.

Slowly Bella lifted her head. She had recovered her composure. The effort had left her pale and strained, but this her husband wouldn't notice any more than he had noticed her distress.

"I'm sorry if I talked foolishly. I expect it's because I still find it difficult to believe I'm your wife."

He turned away.

"What did you expect?"

Could he be so lacking in imagination that he didn't know about the long lonely hours, the ticking of the clock, the listening, the sleeplessness? She wanted to burst out that she knew very little about marriage, but she did know it shouldn't mean an empty pillow by her side. And the lonely rain on the window, and the listening . . .

Lally could have managed this situation better. It would have been what she had hoped for. And Lally would have adored these horrible diamonds. But she, impulsive hopeful fool that she was, had literally thrown herself into the arms of a stranger, confident that she could make them welcoming.

Isabella McBride, she told herself ashamedly, was a vain creature who had overestimated her desirability. Now she had had a salutary lesson.

"You have been very good to my sister and me," she said soberly.

"I told you I would never love again," he said, as if he in his turn found her lack of imagination surprising. "But you wear my wedding ring, so you will also wear the diamonds."

"To show the world?"

"Exactly. That was our bargain, don't you remember?" He put out his arm, smiling. She saw that his eyes held no hos-

108

tility, after all. They held nothing. "Come! Don't let us make
it an impossible one."

If she had pinched herself until she was black and blue,
Bella could not have believed that this was anything but a
dream, herself going to the opera in silk and diamonds.
Lally, on the other hand, seemed to have forgotten her
luxurious state and as the carriage neared the Opera House
she shrank closer to Bella.

"This is near it, isn't it?" she whispered.

"Near what?"

"Aunt Aggie's house. I can smell the same smell."

"This is the Strand," said Guy. "Aunt Aggie, as you will
persist in calling her, lived some distance away. In a mean
dark street. Look out of the window. There are lights and
people everywhere."

"Aunt Aggie should see us now," Bella said.

Lally gave a forlorn giggle. "Yes, she'd be— Listen, I can
hear a baby crying!"

The thin squall sounded for a moment above the medley
of other sounds, and then was lost.

"It's only someone kept their child out late," Bella said
impatiently. "You'd better not be thinking about babies and
Aunt Aggie in the opera."

"No," Lally whispered obediently.

Her sister's temporary lapse into her state of nervous
terror made Bella forget her own qualms about the ordeal
ahead. She thought how handsome Guy looked in his tall
opera hat and cloak as he waited outside the carriage for them
to get down. Then her attention was taken by the succession
of carriages drawing up and discharging their glittering passengers. The great doors of the theatre stood open before
them. Guy said that as it was late they would go straight to
their box.

"Come," he said, and to Lally, "Don't be afraid. No one
will see you in this crush."

So it was not an ordeal after all to reach their box and
settle down. They had scarcely shrugged off their wraps
before the curtain rose, and in the next moment Bella, too,
had forgotten her apprehensions in the magic of the scene
before them.

For the next hour she was transported. She hung forward
in a daze of delight as the scenes unfolded and the heavenly

voices sang. When the curtain fell she had to be prodded back to reality.

"Stop star-gazing," came Guy's voice, tolerantly. "Let us go and get some refreshments."

Bella blinked at the lights that had sprung on in the vast dusky semicircle of the theatre. She was aware of the movement of people, of jewels winking, of heads turned their way. Someone, she noticed, had lifted opera glasses to look in their direction.

Her heart gave a great bound. This was the moment. This was what Guy had planned. They were to walk slowly, nonchalantly, if possible, down the grand staircase while everybody had the leisure to stare at them.

Guy had opened the door of the box and was standing as easily as if accompanying two notorious young women were a thing he frequently did. Bella, still transported by the music and magic of the opera, felt a sudden surge of overpowering excitement. She was conscious of no fear at all, only pride. She nudged Lally and hissed, "Hold your head up! If you shrink, I'll kill you!" then put her hand gracefully on her husband's arm and walked out.

Lally did stumble once on the stairs, but quickly recovered herself. Bella held her head so proudly, she had to virtually float down the carpeted steps. But it wasn't so high that she couldn't see the people moving back so as not bar their passage, staring. Staring frankly, rudely. The women's heads moved stiffly in their direction, someone held up a lorgnette. There was a titter in the crowd. No one nodded or smiled. Then suddenly Bella saw a familiar face, exquisitely pink and white, the little arrogant beak-shaped nose lifted towards them.

Mrs. Raven! Guy's mother!

She was aware of her husband making a welcoming sound. But the lady's elegantly curled grey head turned deliberately away from them. With a vivacious movement of her fan, Mrs. Raven began an animated conversation with her companions. She had cut her son dead.

The strange stillness lasted another moment. Then it was broken by a long sound, curiously like a hiss. By some instantaneous consent, backs turned everywhere. And the long sigh, the indrawn breath, that had resolved itself into that hostile sound turned into a hubbub of noise that deliberately excluded Guy Raven and his protegées.

Just as Lally had been a little earlier, Bella was jolted back to the night of their arrival in London when, plodding after Aunt Aggie through the mean snowy streets, she had indulged in a dream of going to the Covent Garden opera. Then, as now, her dream had been rudely broken by the sound of a hiss. It was a curious little vignette come true.

"What will you take, my love?" That was Guy's voice, attentive, solicitous. "A little lemonade? Some mulled wine?"

Bella's wrap was slipping, and he adjusted it, his hands lingering on her shoulders.

"Eulalie? A little wine? Did you enjoy the first act? I can promise you fireworks in the next."

Lally's hand trembled so violently she could scarcely hold her glass of wine. Bella slid her hand within her sister's arm, and pinched her warningly. Lally instantly looked about to cry, but Bella smiled sweetly and began to talk as composedly and quite as animatedly as she had seen Mrs. Raven do.

"It's so wonderful. I adore every moment of it. Do you know that moment when you see a Christmas tree alight? This seems like a thousand Christmas trees, all at once."

Guy listened to her with his courtly air.

"I'm glad you enjoy it," he said, smiling, "because, as you must be aware," he didn't bother to lower his voice, "we are being cut by everybody, my mother included. We're being made social pariahs. I always find new experiences amusing. I hope you do, too, my love." His fingers again adjusted the heavy satin cloak over Bella's shoulders. He continued to smile, but she was seeing his eyes come alive at last. Repressed fury glittered in them. "Shall we return to our seats? Eulalie? Did I tell you how charming you look? Especially when you smile."

Talking easily, his hands protectingly on their elbows, he guided them up the staircase and back to their box. There was no hurry, no dismay. They might have been strolling alone in a garden. Nothing in Guy's calm face showed that he knew his death-knell had sounded. He had been rejected, not only by the popular press, but by his own world.

Why, why, why? Bella was seething with rage and resentment. Were she and Lally lepers? Couldn't people see that they were ordinary decent young women undeserving of the reputation with which they had been credited? Was Guy hated so much because he had had the generosity to help them, and the courage to become completely involved? Were his friends jealous of him? Had he stirred their social conscience too uncomfortably? Or was this exhibition just that ugly thing, mob hysteria, mob cruelty?

Whatever it was, Bella found herself too deeply disturbed to see or hear anything more that happened on the stage. The magic had gone from the opera. She sat rigidly, her hand still clutching her husband's arm. She couldn't let it go. Beneath her resentment she was conscious of a fierce racing joy. Guy's performance of a loving husband had been irresistible. She was daring to hope that when they got home it wouldn't stop.

It stopped as soon as they were in the carriage. "I forgot to tell you," he said in his now too-familiar aloof voice, "the Proudfoot trial begins at the criminal court next week. As soon as it's over, I will take you to the country."

"For always?" Bella asked sharply.

"For the summer, at least."

Lally sighed with relief. For her London was already a terrifying place, haunted by Noah and Aunt Aggie and the ghost of the dead baby. Now, added to that, was the hostile stare of apparently civilized people. In the country she would be safe, and able to sleep without nightmares.

But Bella saw the move as a sign of defeat. She couldn't endure defeat. She wouldn't allow it, either for herself or her husband. Being linked ostentatiously with him in public had stirred her to a fierce possessiveness. His battles were now hers whether he liked it or not.

"Isn't retiring to the country running away from the problem?" she asked politely.

"My dear Isabella," his voice was as chilly as the night air, "I shall be immediately returning to London. I have no intention of running away."

So she and Lally were an embarrassment to be hidden away. The fine flamboyant gesture tonight had failed so another tactic must be tried. Retirement, oblivion, an awkward mistake kept out of sight until forgotten. For how long? Forever?

Bella fretted angrily, "It wasn't our fault tonight. None of this was our fault. We were in trouble and you were good to us, but you did it with your eyes open. Didn't you?" When Guy, sitting opposite, his face in shadow, didn't answer, she went on dangerously, "If you ask me, your mother's as much to blame as anyone. She turned her back on you tonight and set the fashion for everyone else. I think it was a wicked thing to do to her own son. How could she? She must be a monster."

"Bella!" Lally protested, shocked.

"It's true," Bella stormed. "I shall make a point of telling her so. How can she be so cruel and unnatural?"

"Be quiet!" said Guy ominously.

"Why must I be quiet? You have the courage to speak about injustices done to Lally and me. I intend to speak to your mother about this injustice. If Lally and I have ruined your career it was unintentional. She did this tonight deliberately."

"I asked you to be quiet. Next week we go to Ravenscroft. That's final."

Bella's temper was getting out of control.

"And turn us all into gardeners like Cousin Henrietta? I have no taste for gardening."

"Then you must acquire one, my love. Just as you must acquire a taste for an absent husband." His voice was tightly controlled. He sounded as if he hated her.

It had all been too much for Lally. She was trembling with fatigue and nervous strain, and had to be helped upstairs. She needed support and encouragement, but for once Bella couldn't give it to her. She was unable to calm herself, much less her sister. Louise, who had waited up, a grudging look on her thin face, was sent to undress Lally, and then told to go to bed. Bella preferred to get out of her finery alone.

The tumult of her feelings had left her unbearably stimulated. She let her elegant gown and petticoats fall to the floor and left them there. She dropped the diamond necklace carelessly on to her bed where it lay glittering like tears. Her slippers were kicked off, and the pins tumbled out of her hair. Although the fire had been allowed to die down and the room was chilly, she felt as if the sun were inside her skin. She couldn't contemplate getting into the big bed and lying quietly. Her head was full of fragments of music, scraps of conversation, her own chaotic thoughts. Tonight she had had a husband who had shown a loving care for her in public, and had hated her in private. The hate was far far more exciting than the pretended love. It was a genuine emotion, the first he had shown towards her. She had roused him out of his deliberate cool neutrality. The scene had been unplanned, she had had no idea her temper could carry her so far, but now that it had happened she was fiercely glad.

If they could not love, they could quarrel. It was being alive, at least.

But she was too much alive tonight. It was past midnight and the thought of sleep was impossible. She felt as if she would never sleep again. She forced herself to sit at the mirror and brush her hair, a calming occupation if ever there was one. It failed completely to calm her. She found herself constantly stopping, the brush poised in her hand, to listen.

Her husband hadn't yet come upstairs. She would hear the carefully muted sounds in the adjoining room when he did come. The fire crackled a little and the clock ticked. Bella stared into the mirror, and saw not her cherry bright cheeks and the golden blaze of her eyes but the long sweep of the staircase in the Opera House, the white shoulders and the jewels of the women, the inquisitive stares, and then the turned backs. She hugged her own shoulders, remembering Guy's deliberate caress as he had adjusted her wrap. Were all their caresses and tender glances to be made in public? Forever? No, she wouldn't again tolerate that word!

Bella sprang up and began to walk about in her nightgown, her hair making a dark shawl over her shoulders. The clock ticked mercilessly. Suddenly she picked it up and flung it to the floor. It gave a small ping and was silent.

Now time has stopped, she thought exultantly. If I can create one miracle, I can create another. And I will . . .

Guy lingered downstairs until after one o'clock. He had yet another glass of port and decided that, a little befuddled, the world looked slightly rosier. His mother had been right, dammit. He had married the wrong girl. She was already becoming a shrew. So she wouldn't live at Ravenscroft and interest herself in the garden. Perhaps she would prefer a filthy Middle Eastern port and her body at the service of all comers.

Where would she have been—no, that wasn't fair. He had used her and her sister as much as she had been used. They had been the flame to kindle his great political career. But flames got out of control and had to be put out. The two girls could count themselves lucky to have the shelter of Ravenscroft while he returned to town and repaired the damage done. Perhaps later they could patch up some sort of a life together—if Isabella would turn herself into an obedient and unobtrusive wife. He had never wanted a wife with opinions.

She had scorned the diamonds (wasn't she feminine?) and

would have had a scene in public with his mother. She held her head as high as if she had been a duchess. She dared to tell him what to do.

He should have married the sister, who could weep in private to her heart's content.

But that wasn't the point. The point was to continue the work he had begun. If he failed at the coming election, there would be another. Nothing had been irretrievably lost.

But nothing had been gained, either, except two females for whom he was forever responsible.

He had thought the solution of marriage easy. Well, so it would be when he got the girls to the country.

One more glass . . . The travesty of the evening was beginning to recede a little. It was time he went up.

The fire in his bedroom was only embers, but the light was sufficient to show him the figure sitting in the armchair before it.

She had no wrap on, only her flimsy nightgown. As she rose slowly, stretching and sighing, he could see the outline of her body.

Surprise, and the abrupt beating of a pulse in his throat, made his voice harsh.

"Why aren't you in bed?"

"I was waiting for you." Her voice was slow, husky, as if with sleep. "You were so long."

"Why are you waiting? Is there something worrying you? Can't it wait till morning?"

"No. Being my husband can't wait till morning. Can it? If you can be my husband in public, so you can in private. I don't like half measures."

There had been other women since Caroline, but never in his house, never wearing his wedding ring. He seized this stranger, for she was suddenly completely a stranger, by the arm, roughly.

"Do you know what marriage is?"

"No." Her voice was naïve, innocent. "You must teach me. I want to learn." She gave a sudden low gurgle of laughter. "I threw the clock on the floor. It was ticking away too many hours. I want to be a woman." Her arms were round his neck. "Even if I must first behave like the harlot they say I am."

"You don't love me."

"No. Perhaps I can learn that, too." Her skin was soft, her lips provocatively near his. She was still laughing a little.

115

"I think you're a little drunk, my darling. But you must understand me. I won't be your wife to the world and not here, in your own bedroom."

He had his hand entangled in her hair, jerking her head back. The candlelight shone on her white face and the burning gold of her eyes. Teach her, she said. She looked like a witch. No golden-haired angel, but a witch. He had made a mistake. He had married the wrong girl, the bold one, not the gentle one. He hated her, but now his pulses were throbbing so that he could scarcely breathe. He would teach her what she wanted to know.

Flung across the bed, and only half-undressed himself, his clothing wrenched open, he took her without patience, violently, having no thought for her virginity.

He heard her cry out. Afterwards she lay so still he thought she had fainted.

But it was the sister who would have fainted. Not Isabella who lay so motionless, her eyes glimmering through mere slits. She was reflecting on marriage, he supposed.

He remembered suddenly his long-controlled infinitely loving initiation of Caroline and got up abruptly, turning his back on the silent figure on the bed. He had not meant this to happen, and vowed it never would again.

12

IN THE MORNING BELLA SAT UP in her own bed, a frivolous lacy scrap of a cap on her neatly braided hair, her arms and throat modestly covered by a fleecy bedwrap. She was tapping the top of her egg, her face expressing a healthy anticipation for her breakfast, nothing more.

"Good morning, Guy," she said composedly to her husband. "Have you brought me the papers?"

"They're downstairs. I'll have them sent up, if you wish. I don't recommend them."

Bella opened her eyes wide.

"Are they still slandering us? Didn't they admire Lally and me last night?"

She wasn't going to show a sign of her true feelings. Had she been shocked, badly hurt, resolved now that marriage

116

must be endured, not enjoyed? Guy knew very well that neither of them were thinking of the fresh insults in the newspaper.

"They don't like people who flout conventions. It frightens them, makes them conscious of their own lack of courage. To the devil with them all!"

"Guy, this is very serious for you, isn't it?"

"I've never pretended it was anything else."

"We mustn't give in. We must fight. Do you still insist on Lally and me going to the country?"

"Yes, I do."

Bella sighed. Then she said, "I shall enjoy seeing Ravenscroft, of course. By the way, I've decided not to keep Louise."

"Louise?" He didn't know what she was talking about.

"The maid Cousin Henrietta found for me. I don't like her. I don't see why I should put up with someone I don't like. I intend to engage Tottie instead."

"Tottie?"

Bella burst out laughing.

"I believe you did drink too much last night, my love. You forget everybody. Tottie's the little dumb girl who was at Aunt Aggie's. She's been at Doctor Bushey's, as you very well know. He'll let her come to me, and I'll teach her how to be a good lady's maid. Let me do this, Guy. It will be helping with your own work. We can set an example by employing only these poor desperate people."

He had sensed her strong will and her boldness, but he could scarcely believe that she would so quickly try to run his affairs. As if that deplorable episode last night had given her unlimited confidence.

"If you want to struggle with a speechless maid, do so. That's your province."

"Thank you, my love. I'll see Doctor Bushey today. At least the country is the place for poor Tottie. And Lally, too. I wonder how Lally is this morning. I hope she didn't have a nightmare last night. I feel guilty, deserting her." She shot a look at her husband beneath her long lashes. "By the way, that pretty little clock will have to be mended. I dropped it last night. Such a pity. Are you going?"

"My secretary will be waiting."

"Oh! Of course." She lifted her face for his kiss. She was behaving as if they had been married for years. Her black hair on the pillow was an outrage. And he wouldn't endure her interference. Yet his blood was beating again, violently.

He had this overpowering impulse to hurt her, punish her, because she was pretending to be his wife, to take Caroline's place. He would have to keep her out of his sight as much as possible. Leave her safely down at Ravenscroft. He had thought to get a gentle grateful self-effacing wife out of his unlucky predicament. Not this pert confident usurper . . .

When Guy had gone Bella lay back on the pillows, no longer needing to check her tears. She had made a vow to herself last night, as she lay aching and violated on the bed, that she would never cry in front of her husband. Which would mean a great many lonely tears in the privacy of her room.

Yet her life could be mended in other ways. She could order the servants to do as she wished, she could dismiss Louise because the girl displeased her, she could make herself enjoy being the mistress of a large house, no matter how much the present thought of it scared her. She could buy unlimited clothes, pamper Lally, take care of Tottie. She could hold her head as high as her mother-in-law held hers. Her life was certainly not over, even if romance had left it. Who expected love? She had scornfully asked Lally the identical question.

One thing was very sure, she would never again allow herself to lie here counting the minutes until her husband came to her bed. Nor would she ever beg him to love her. She must hope, by gathering the scraps of her pride about her, to overcome the humiliation of still wanting him. For, even as he stood conversing politely to her, a visitor scarcely within the doorway, she had ached for him to come near, to touch her. She had had to make it plain that she expected at least a formal kiss, and when he had bent over her she had had to prevent herself from flinging her arms round his neck. She would not be a beggar. She would not be humiliated twice.

The trial of Noah and Aunt Aggie before a judge and jury took place three weeks later. It went on for two days. The ordeal was almost too much for Lally. Constantly anxious for her, for she seemed at times to think she was a prisoner in the court just as they had been prisoners in the house in Seven Dials, Bella found it impossible to follow every detail of the trial. There was a great deal of wrangling between the opposing counsel about proof, proof that there had been a woman smuggled on board the *Star of Asia*, proof that there had been other young women similarly smuggled out of the country in the past, proof that the baby, being so small and delicate, had not died from natural causes, most of all proof that Aunt Aggie's intentions regarding her latest "lodgers," the Misses McBride, had been criminal.

In the end it was lack of this vital proof that went in favour of the prisoners. Their sentences were extraordinarily light, each of them getting only one year's imprisonment.

Aunt Aggie, who had maintained her air of injured innocence during the whole of the trial, kept her eyes downcast as she listened to the sentence. She was still the martyr, wrongfully accused by a thankless world. Bella was certain her drooping eyelids hid triumph.

But Noah was not going to take even so light a sentence philosophically. He smouldered with anger. When asked if he had anything to say, he lifted his shaggy black head and stared across the courtroom at Guy and Bella and Lally.

"What about them adulterers?" he shouted. "Make them pay! Prissy-mouthed bawds!" He stared back viciously at Bella and Lally as he was hustled away down the stairs out of sight. His great voice came hurling back, "A year ain't forever. Wait—"

Wait . . . Bella had no time to experience more than a momentary shiver at that threat, for Lally had slid from the bench in a dead faint.

When, an endless ten minutes later, she recovered consciousness she could only whisper frantically, "We must hide! Bella, we must hide!"

She recognized neither Guy nor Doctor Bushey. When Guy said, with unexpected gentleness, "We'll get you to Ravenscroft. You'll feel better there," she clutched Bella's hand and said fearfully, "Who is he? Where is he taking us?"

"It's Mr. Raven, Lally. You know we're safe with him. Surely you remember."

Lally frowned. For a moment she was frighteningly like a dim-witted child. Her lovely blue eyes had an empty look.

"People hissed," she said. She lifted a trembling finger to point at Guy. "Because we were with him. Oh, Bella!" She hid her face. "Can we trust him?"

Bella, very much aware now that a small group of people had gathered round, let a note of aggressive pride come into her voice. "Don't be silly, Lally! He's my husband."

Here was another scandal, she thought, and was suddenly angry with Lally for her stupid childish weakness. How dare she make things more difficult for Guy. Babbling nonsense that all the newspapers would solemnly print.

"Come, Eulalie," said Guy, the gentleness still in his voice. "We're going home now. Tomorrow we'll leave for the country."

"When she's fit to travel," said Doctor Bushey restrainingly. "I doubt that will be for a few days."

As it happened, it was another three weeks before Doctor Bushey pronounced Lally fit to travel. She had had a complete collapse, and it was several days before she recognized her surroundings or people, except Bella, again. After that she began to mend slowly, and seemed to forget a little of her fear about Noah and Aunt Aggie. She allowed herself to be convinced that she would be safe in the country, that people like Noah and Aunt Aggie didn't leave their city haunts, and that anyway they were now safely behind bars.

Her illness was not the only event during those three weeks. The worst was the Prime Minister's action. He had a long private talk with Guy, and advised him to postpone his political career. The scandal about the two women had now reached major proportions and threatened to damage not only Guy but the party. This came well from a man whose own private life would scarcely bear looking into, Guy thought bitterly. But for all that, Lord Palmerston was a personal friend, and his advice could not be ignored. Indeed, it was the only advice that Guy was prepared to accept.

He could stand again at the next election, when all this would have blown over.

"Get the other sister married," Lord Palmerston urged him. "Have children yourself. Become an exemplary family man, and there'll never be another murmur against you. Bless you, my boy, I understand. I'd have done the same in your shoes. Two attractive young women in distress. An irresistible combination. But these impetuous actions have to be paid for. What did your criminal, the Proudfoot fellow, get? A year? Then you have approximately the same, before we set a date for the next election. Perverted justice, eh? But you'll be all the better for being a little older, and I must say," the glint of the roué shone an instant in the older man's eyes, "from the glimpse I've caught of your wife, a year's private life shouldn't be any great hardship."

So the two young women with their impeccable names,

their innocent eyes and their pitiably distressed faces, had ruined him after all. And now he had to live with them.

An exemplary family life? Lord Palmerston, the old dog, had been rather more than a trifle optimistic when he gave that advice. Did he really think Guy Raven the type to vegetate in the country? With a wife for whom he felt nothing but resentment? She had deliberately misunderstood his lofty interpretation of their marriage and had already tricked him into a physical indiscretion for which he loathed himself. He had nothing whatever about which to talk to her. Her very existence did nothing but anger him, for the sight of her constantly reminded him of his lost career and the disillusionment to which ideals could be brought.

But if she thought he were a martyr to be comforted, she was very wrong. His whitewash had come off. Now he would show her his other side. Or rather, he would show her very little of himself at all. He would establish the girls at Ravenscroft and then return to London to resume his bachelor life.

Bella, it seemed, had no thought of martyrdom. She expressed anger and indignation, and then the calm assumption that of course this damage was not permanent.

"You'll stand again, as Lord Palmerston advises. On the whole this may be a good thing. You've already created an enormous impression on the public, I shouldn't be surprised if in two years they don't come to think of you as a hero. And this will give you time to really study politics. After all, one shouldn't take up so important a career on an impulse. Don't you agree?"

Guy agreed with nothing. He was speechless at her impertinence. She, a little nobody, sitting calmly at her embroidery as if she had lived in this style all her life, daring to give him advice, and behaving as if the great sacrifice of his marriage were her due!

"I should be obliged, my dear Isabella, if you would keep your opinions to yourself. They don't interest me. Anyway, they are entirely wrong."

Her eyelids fell. She seemed to be taking great care over a stitch in her embroidery.

"You still blame Lally and me," she said in a low voice.

"Of course I don't blame you. You were fate, Nemesis if you like, but that was hardly your fault. I was the one to be a fool."

121

"For saving us? For marrying me? For obeying your good instincts? For making all those grand gestures? If you regret all that where are we? What has been accomplished?"

Her face was lifted now, and no longer calm. The quick colour had flooded her cheeks, her eyes had darkened to that curious golden tinge that he had never seen in the eyes of any well-bred woman. Her little pert nose was lifted as high as his mother ever lifted her much more aristocratic one. She was behaving once more as his equal. And the unforgivable thing was that he wanted to make love to her violently, at that moment, not caring that it was mid-afternoon, and somone likely to come in at any moment.

But he had determined not to give in to that weakness again. He could not treat his wife like a street girl, nor, contrarily, this woman as a wife.

"You can't answer me," she said sadly.

"Oh, yes, I can. We're exactly where we were when I explained to you what our marriage would be."

"Except that now you don't have a career to compensate for it. So you're always going to blame me and Lally. But as I've said before, it's your mother who's to blame. If she'd had the courage to take your side from the beginning, supported you instead of turning her back on you at the opera, and made her friends rally to you, it would have turned the scales. But she chose not to, and that was just the extra thing that made the world turn against you. So you blame me instead, and that isn't fair."

"I'm amazed at your impertinence!"

"No, no, what you can't believe is the truth."

"You're illogical, like all women. My mother, indeed!"

"Even now, I believe it isn't too late to make amends, if she would," Bella persisted. "If she made it public that she has become reconciled to me as your wife it would make a great difference."

"She hasn't a nature that is easily reconciled," Guy said shortly.

"Oh, I know that. She wanted you to make a better match. Some dull débutante. I believe she's only sulking at not getting her own way."

"*You* dare to say that!"

The scorn in his voice made Bella's colour flame.

"Yes, and I refuse to apologize. Perhaps you deserve a dull wife, but at least you haven't got one." She met his gaze with angry defiance. "If you had married Lally you would very soon have got tired of her vapours. And the empty chatter of a débutante—"

"You can scarcely know what débutantes chatter about," he interrupted.

"I think I'm not too unintelligent to guess." Bella had flung her sewing aside and was standing. "Believe me, you haven't made such a bad bargain. The situation is—" He had turned away sharply, and didn't seem to have heard the break in her voice. His answer came over his shoulder, flatly, bleakly.

"Unremediable," he said.

"No, no," she whispered. "Don't let us hate each other."

But he had gone, banging the door behind him, and she could tell him no more.

She had done very badly. Instead of comforting him for his lost ambitions, she had quarrelled with him. She had tried at the beginning to be wise, but he had resented the words he would have gladly accepted from Caroline. That was what had made her angry. He wanted her speechless and invisible, not a wife at all but a nonentity. He hadn't begun to know her.

Nor had his mother.

Bella put on her bonnet and cloak and asked Doughty to get her a cab. She sat in the hall tapping her feet impatiently while waiting for it to come.

Her husband came out of the library and saw her.

"Where are you going?"

Did he think she intended to vanish out of his life? She had to disappoint him.

"To get Tottie. She was to be prepared to come today, before we left for the country."

"Tottie? Oh, the deaf and dumb girl."

"She is only dumb, not deaf. It should please you to have someone who can't answer back." The childish retort escaped her before she could prevent it.

"I hardly expect a servant to do that."

"You hardly expect your wife to, either."

"No. Frankly I don't."

The now frequent feeling of sickness was coming over her again. She swallowed, praying she could conquer it. She had planned to tell him her news this afternoon, not knowing of the unfortunate interview with the Prime Minister. But she couldn't tell him, in this mood. She doubted now if she could ever tell him quietly and happily, as she had planned.

But if only he would kiss her, her lips would stop trembling.

"I don't think you would care for a wife who has no opinions of her own."

"How can you possibly know my tastes?" he said coldly, finally.

Doughty was coming in to say that a cab was waiting. His old rheumy eyes looked curiously from his master to his new mistress. At least, if Bella were not the débutante she had talked of, she knew one didn't exhibit one's quarrels to servants.

She sprang up. "Then I must go. Goodbye, my love. I won't be above an hour." She lifted her face innocently for her husband's kiss. She knew it was a trick, not to deceive Doughty, but to have his lips on hers, after all. And although he merely touched her cheek, the treacherous excitement shot through her again, making her forget her anger and her sickness and leaving her with scarcely strength to walk out of the house.

She gave the cabman the address on the Chelsea Embankment, one she had acquainted herself with some time ago, climbed into the cab and, as the door shut on her, as weakly as Lally, dissolved into tears.

There were no signs of her tears, however, when the cab stopped at the tall red brick house overlooking the muddy river. She alighted, and asked the driver to wait, as she would be only ten or fifteen minutes. After that, he was to take her to Wigmore Street.

The white door, surmounted by its beautiful Georgian fan of glass, was opened by a stiff elderly maid in a very correctly starched cap and apron. She didn't know who Bella was, and obviously impressed by her rich appearance—Bella did not intend her mother-in-law to be dressed more grandly than herself—respectfully asked her to come in while she ascertained if her mistress were at home.

"What name shall I say, madam?"

"Mrs. Guy Raven," Bella answered, carelessly removing her gloves to display her wedding ring. "Tell my mother-in-law I'm sorry to arrive unannounced, but it's important I see her."

The maid was flustered now. She left Bella in the hall as she hurried up the stairs. Bella sat composedly in one of the carved and very uncomfortable chairs. Her heart was beating rapidly. She realized she was looking forward to this encounter.

She didn't dream for a moment that Mrs. Raven would refuse to see her.

A sudden yapping of dogs came from upstairs. A door closed. The elderly maid came hurrying downstairs, more than ever discomposed.

"I'm sorry, madam, my mistress isn't at all well. She says she can't see callers. She asked me to see that you have a cab."

Bella sat very upright, unmoving.

"I don't think your mistress could have understood. It's quite vital that I see her. Tell her so, pray."

"But, madam—"

The poor faded creature was terrified of Mrs. Raven, as everyone seemed to be.

"Just tell her," said Bella gently. "I mean to stay here until you do."

There was nothing for it but to return upstairs. The woman did so, with a backward glance at Bella that expressed resentment, but also a reluctant respect.

This time there was the sound of that now familiar overbearing high-pitched voice. The words were intended, Bella realized, for her ears.

"Doesn't she understand the English language, Martha? Didn't you tell her I was ill? In any case, she must know I don't receive women off the streets. Well, go along, woman, go along."

Bella rose. Before the pitiably embarrassed Martha was halfway down the stairs, she had begun to mount them.

"I'm so sorry, Martha. You shouldn't have had to do so difficult an errand. I'll do it myself."

"Madam! You mustn't! Didn't you hear—"

"I hear what I choose to hear, just as my mother-in-law does." Bella swept on up the stairs and reached the door at the top. Without knocking, she flung it open. Then she stood within it and made an elaborate curtsey to the little upright figure in the chair by the fire.

"Good evening, Mrs. Raven," she said. "I'm sorry you're indisposed. I promise not to disturb you for more than a few minutes."

Mrs. Raven had got to her feet; two poodle puppies scattered from her lap, yapping excitedly.

"How *dare* you!" she hissed. "You hussy! Bursting in

here with no manners—" She poked angrily with her stick at the yapping dogs. "Be quiet! Be quiet! Hannah! Where are you? Show this—person out."

The meek Hannah, even more intimidated than Martha, made a movement towards Bella, but was defeated by the impossibility of the task. A lady could not be shown out if she refused to go.

"Forgive my bad manners, Mrs. Raven, but I can't go until I've said what I must. You won't know what has happened to my husband today. He has been asked by the Prime Minister to postpone his political career."

"Ha! I guessed as much! And serve him right!"

"I don't think you mean that, Mrs. Raven. I think you love your son very much, and would like to help him. I know that if you intervened for him, showed the world that you were on his side—"

She was interrupted by Mrs. Raven's outraged voice, "On *his* side! You mean on your side, you conscienceless fortune hunter! Have you no pride?"

"No," said Bella, and realized with wonder that she was speaking the truth. "Not where the good of my husband is concerned. I would have thought a mother would feel the same."

Mrs. Raven swung her stick dangerously. Her face was mottled with rage.

"How dare you tell me how a mother feels! Seeing you and your sister parading at the opera, dressed up like strumpets, wearing *my* diamonds—oh, yes, mine, until my son went mad—and you dare to tell me how a mother should feel. All I ask is that you stay out of my sight. The damage is done. But I, an old woman, expect peace. Now go."

"Mrs. Raven—"

"Hush! You won't get round me with any mealy-mouthed talk. If you must know, I feel only pity for you. It can't be very amusing living with a man who will already have begun to hate you."

"Hate—" It was one thing to suspect it herself, but quite another to hear it put into words. A stone was in her heart, weighing it down. She had lost her fine anger.

"I'm glad to see you have some vestige of feeling," Mrs. Raven observed dryly. "I'd advise you to conquer it. You didn't marry into a forgiving family. But that's your mistake. Now I ask you again to go. We have nothing more to say."

Hannah was holding the door open and urging Bella out. She was on the threshold before the momentary black misery lifted and she recovered her wits.

"Mrs. Raven—"

The door had slammed in her face. There was the unmistakable sound of a key turning in the lock.

Nothing could have roused her fury more. To be locked out! And that old woman talked to her of manners!

She banged on the door, not caring now if the whole street heard her.

"If you lock me out, you lock your grandson out, too. Don't you want to see your grandson?"

There was a moment of complete silence. Bella leaned her hot forehead against the door, reflecting miserably that this was a fine way to tell her news, shouting it out to a hostile silence. But perhaps it was fitting. It was the way, after all, in which the baby had been conceived, in hostility and without love.

She whipped up her defiance.

"If you want to see him, Mrs. Raven, you must be the one to come to me. I shan't come to you again."

After a long silence the answer came, "I am afraid your cab driver is getting tired of waiting."

13

BELLA SAID LEVELLY, "WILL YOU please ask Davis to stop?"

Guy looked at her in surprise. "What's the matter, my dear?"

Lally leaned forward. "Bella, are you ill? You look very pale."

Bella took a deep breath and controlled her mounting sickness. For a moment the landscape stopped tilting, and she could see the newly-budded trees and the green fields. She had expected to enjoy the twenty-mile journey into Hertfordshire, but the rocking of the carriage, and the closeness, with the four of them in so small a space was too much for her. She sat in rigid silence while Guy tapped on the

127

window and asked Davis to stop the horses, then tumbled out hastily, ignoring Guy's proffered help.

"Turn your back!" she gasped. "Please!"

When the spasm was over and she was able to lift her head and gratefully breathe the sweet air, she was aware of her husband's critical gaze.

"You didn't tell me you were a bad traveller."

"I'm not, usually. I think I must have caught a chill. But I'm quite recovered now. Shall we go on?"

He had his hand on her arm, delaying her return to the stuffy carriage.

"Are you going to have a baby?"

"Yes. Yes, if you must know."

"If I must know! I should imagine it's my business, as well as yours. A fine time you choose to tell me, on the roadside in the middle of a journey."

"I hadn't meant it to be like this," she pleaded. The air was so sweet after the tainted London mist, the country so beautiful. And Guy standing there hatless, the wind lifting his dark gold hair, looked so handsome, it would really have been a romantic place after all in which to tell her news. Except that the horses were fidgeting, and Lally was looking out anxiously, and there was Tottie crouched in her corner, not once daring to lift her head, through which who knew what terrors were racing. There was no trace of tenderness in Guy's face. He looked instead as if he had been unfairly deceived, as if, indeed, she had become pregnant only to annoy him.

But of course his first thought would be of the child and the wife he had lost. That was natural. He perhaps had a horror of childbirth. It would be nice to think his stern expression was caused by anxiety for the ordeal ahead of her.

"I would have told you yesterday, only you had had the upset of your meeting with Lord Palmerston. So I intended waiting until we were at Ravenscroft."

"You needn't have subjected yourself to this journey at such a time."

She seized on his concern, and exclaimed light-heartedly,

"Poof! This is nothing. Papa used to say the more tasks a woman did, the better. Besides, I did ask Doctor Bushey's advice, and he assured me it would be perfectly safe. There's no danger of harming the baby. Truly."

Guy glanced towards Davis on the box who was staring rigidly ahead.

"Well, now you have broadcast your news, perhaps we can continue on our way."

He hadn't expressed pleasure, but after his first reaction of stiff shock, he had behaved quite courteously. He would quickly grow used to the idea and like it, Bella told herself optimistically. What man wouldn't want a son, even under these circumstances. She would promise not to be like that poor delicate Caroline and keep everyone on tenterhooks for months beforehand. And surely, when the baby was born, Guy could not go on hating its mother.

"Bella, are you really—I mean, are you recovered now?" Lally's face was quivering with excitement. Lally at least, with her passion for babies, would not let this one arrive unwelcomed.

Bella squeezed her hand gratefully, and said blithely, "I am, as well as I shall be for quite some time. You must help me with my sewing, Lally. I'm afraid we're going to be poor company for some time," she added to her husband.

But he was suddenly lost in thought, and gave no more sign of hearing her happy chatter than Tottie did. Tottie hadn't lifted her head, but Bella did think she caught a flicker of her eyes, and once she let the little pink tip of her tongue run round her lips. Poor Tottie, in her neat dark poplin dress and shawl and shiny new buttoned boots, would soon realize that she was not going to her doom. She would grow interested in the arrival of the baby. It really seemed that the baby might solve a lot of problems. Bella herself was almost able to forget her two humiliations, the way she couldn't stop herself turning to fire at her husband's touch, and the way his mother had turned her out, like some sort of vermin.

She had been a little scared and not very pleased when Doctor Bushey had confirmed her suspicions about her pregnancy. But now she was glad. The baby would change everything.

Lally exclaimed in admiration at the first glimpse of the long white house lying in a green hollow round the curve of the drive. It was not large like some of the great country houses, but Bella saw at once that it had great elegance. Guy's grandfather must have been a man of taste. Perhaps, in the arid dusty heat of India he had dreamed of this cool oasis, green lawns, yew trees, the glimmer of water, and the cool, white pillared house.

Lally's wide eyes indicated that she thought the whole

thing a dream, but Bella clung to reality. It was true that she was going to be mistress of this mansion, and her baby would be born here, but she knew she would never truly belong until she and Guy had established some genuine contact, friendship at least. She refused to go on being considered a usurper.

Actually there was more to overcome than her husband's hostility. The first shock was to find that half the servants had left, influenced, it seemed, by the elderly housekeeper who had been greatly devoted to both Guy's mother and his first wife.

"Why wasn't I informed?" Guy asked, his brows tight.

Broome, the butler, replied that it had happened with great suddenness, and there had been time only to find a substitute housekeeper. He hoped to replace the maids, the boot-boy and the under-gardeners shortly.

He introduced the new housekeeper, a Mrs. Walter. She was a neat person, middle-aged, with grey-streaked black hair drawn tightly back from a long sallow face. She scarcely lifted her eyes to look at Bella, which was a pleasant change from the rude staring to which Bella had become accustomed. She curtseyed and her mouth was prim.

Broome, like Doughty in London, was elderly, a fringe of white whiskers framing his chin. He looked at his new mistress quite frankly, but with respect. Bella liked him at once. Mrs. Walter was not so easy to know.

Although she was dropping with fatigue from the long journey Bella refused to rest until she had seen the house. She took Guy's arm and insisted that he show her every room. Lally and Tottie were sent upstairs with Mrs. Walter while they walked alone through the sunny rooms.

The sun was the first thing Bella noticed, streaming through all the long windows, filling the rooms with golden light. Here was none of the claustrophobic gloom that people nowadays loved. The curtains were drawn back, the furnishings were in delightful colours, gold, crimson and turquoise. The Indian influence predominated in the carpets, the bronze ornaments, the yellow silk curtains, and the cabinets full of old India china. There were English things, too, fine old mahogany and walnut, Chippendale chairs and mirrors, but the general effect was of tropical gaiety.

Bella found it utterly delightful.

"How could one be gloomy in a place like this?"

"I told you you would like it. I believe your reply was

that you refused to become a gardener like Cousin Henrietta."

Bella giggled, very youthfully.

"In this garden, I may be tempted."

"Not until after your baby is born."

She was glad for his concern, but wished he had referred to the baby as theirs, not hers alone. She bit her lip, refusing to let her thoughts grow carping.

"You are pleased about the baby?" She caught his arm. "Tell me."

"My dear Isabella, I couldn't honestly say I was pleased about anything in the present situation. I don't think you would expect me to be. But if the child amuses you, I am glad."

"*Amuses* me! Is that all you can say about your son! That he is to be a toy to keep me distracted, and therefore less of a burden to you!"

He frowned wearily.

"Please! Do you want me to be less than honest? Very well, then," he bent to kiss her brow, "I will look forward to the child, too."

Bella turned away, blinking back tears. The lovely rooms, the sunlight, the feeling of light and warmth and happiness, was ruined by her husband's utter indifference about a child that was to be hers, and not Caroline's. She believed he wouldn't even care if this one also failed to live and its mother, too.

She would make him care!

Upstairs, the only room that interested her was the master-bedroom. Strangely enough, this was the one gloomy room in the house. It was not that it didn't get plenty of light, but simply that the decorations were too subdued, all greens and blues that gave a curious under-water effect. Not that they were not modern. They looked as if they had been done quite recently, and of course they would have been. By Caroline. No doubt she fancied the cool subtlety of the blending of colours. But to Bella the effect was extremely depressing. She resolved to make alterations as soon as she could do so.

Guy's reluctance to linger in the room was marked. He said he would leave her, as she would no doubt want to rest after the long journey.

"But there's so much more to see. The other bedrooms, the garden." Bella found herself as reluctant as he to be in this room alone.

"You have all the summer in which to see everything."

That was a reasonable remark. But all at once Bella was not in a reasonable state. This cool submarine room was doing strange things to her.

She tugged fretfully at the bed hangings.

"I shall have these changed to a more cheerful colour. I have a great dislike for green."

"I would prefer it if you didn't."

She was uncertain, looking at his suddenly ravaged face. The knowledge came to her that this must be the room not only where he had loved Caroline but where she had died. For a moment her courage deserted her. There was too much to fight.

There were plenty of bedrooms in the house. She would choose another. This one could be closed, left to gather dust and cobwebs, like an old tomb.

But no, that would only preserve the unwelcome ghost. And she herself would remain an intruder. In this room Guy must learn to know his new wife.

So she ignored his private torment and said reflectively, regarding the bed hangings, "Yellow, I think. And white curtains at the windows. And the walls with a crimson and gold design. You won't believe the difference. Let me amuse myself in this way."

His wintry eyes met hers. She knew he read exactly what was in her mind and was astonished at her lack of tact. But some madness had seized her. If she couldn't take him in her arms, cradling that tormented face against her breasts, then she must stir him to anger, anything rather than this morbid remembering.

"You would find my scheme very much to your liking when it is complete. A turkey carpet, I think. So warm."

"Don't waste your time trying to change me, Isabella."

She deliberately misunderstood him and cried gaily, "Not you! The room! The bed, those silly spindly chairs which I am sure would collapse if you sat on them, everything. Oh, I promise not to change other things in the house. But this room where I will spend a great deal of time, surely that's my domain."

His frozen face drove her to add, crazily, "I won't sleep in the bed where your wife died!"

"I forbid you to touch a thing," he said, and turned on his heel and left.

But I will touch everything! If your first wife was allowed

132

to decorate her bedroom why shouldn't your second have equal rights? Bella kicked childishly at one of the spindly chairs hoping one of its elegant legs would break off.

A tap at the door stopped her angry muttering. She hastily smoothed her hair and put her hands to her hot cheeks, summoning back the dignity she had lost. At her bidding the housekeeper, Mrs. Walter, appeared.

The woman stood meekly, her hands clasped over her apron, her eyes resting anxiously on Bella's face.

"Is everything in order, madam? Can I be of help to you?"

Bella saw that the woman fortunately was more concerned with making a good impression than in noticing her new mistress's discomposure. Sadly, she found herself appreciating civility after her husband's harsh treatment.

"Thank you, Mrs. Walter, but Tottie will unpack for me."

It was only a flash in her mind that this woman seemed a little too servile. That wouldn't be true, for Mrs. Walter, gathering confidence, was already expressing an opinion.

"Please don't think me forward, madam, but your sister tells me the girl you brought with you is to be your maid. She seems so young and untrained, and besides not being able to speak. Please forgive me, madam, for presuming like this—I am sure you have performed the kindest action— but I would be so happy to find you a capable maid while the child learns."

"The child is learning, Mrs. Walter. I am teaching her."

"I realize that, madam. It's most kind of madam. But supposing a grand toilette is required—"

Bella's eyes darkened. She remembered the occasion of her one and only grand toilette.

"Tottie will manage very well, Mrs. Walter. I want her with me. We won't speak of it again."

The woman's eyes were downcast, hiding their expression.

"As madam wishes."

A suspicion came into Bella's head. "Perhaps you had someone in mind?"

"Oh, no, madam. But I have experience in engaging maids."

"Of course. I am sure you have the highest credentials. It was fortunate you were able to come to us at practically a moment's notice. What was your last position?"

"It was in London, madam. With Lady Merriweather of Eaton Square. But the fogs didn't agree with me. I had to come to the country. I'd given my notice when I saw Broome's advertisement, so it was lucky I could come immediately. That's how it was, madam. I'd like to say I'm very happy to be here."

"Well, it seems fortunate for us, too," said Bella briskly, and wondered if Lady Merriweather were missing her neat, quiet, and observant housekeeper, and what had been the true circumstances of Mrs. Walter's departure. For she doubted that Broome, in his thankfulness to get a decent respectable person at such short notice, had asked many questions.

But Mrs. Walter seemed to have fallen on her feet, too. She had done well enough for herself, without getting her niece, or whatever young woman she had in mind, into the house as well. For all her meekness, she didn't lack initiative.

When she had gone Lally came bursting in.

"Oh, Bella, is it really true about the baby?"

Bella nodded, and Lally flung her arms round her, the ready tears filling her eyes.

"You should have told me! You should never have set out on that long journey without even telling Mr. Raven."

"You must learn to call him Guy, Lally."

"Yes. I suppose so. But he still frightens me. I know I'm silly, with this lovely place and all. But I just can't think how we can be here. Us, Bella! We're only used to living in a cottage. I keep being afraid there's a trick in it all." She hurried on, ignoring Bella's disapproval. "You must admit Mr. Raven's heart isn't with us. And that Mrs. Walter—"

"Snooping Susie!"

Lally's changeable little face sparkled with laughter.

"Is that what you call her? It suits her admirably. You think she's not noticing things, but she is, under her eyelids. She stared at poor Tottie." Lally clasped her arms round herself apprehensively. "There will be all the other strangers here to stare at us."

"There'll only be the servants, Lally."

"Yes. Only servants," said Lally uncertainly, and suddenly, the shadow of Seven Dials seemed to be there. It hadn't bothered Bella at all while they stayed in Knightsbridge, she had pushed the murky evil-smelling city streets out of her mind, but here, many miles away in the safety of the peaceful country, the shadow was as sharp and clear as a thundercloud.

"They won't like us. They'll think we should be one of them," Lally went on.

"They'll do nothing of the kind. I dare you to let them do so."

"I do so hate people staring," Lally muttered.

"Oh, for goodness sake, be more cheerful," Bella said briskly. "You'll love being here. And you are looking forward to the baby, aren't you?"

"Oh, yes, the baby!" Again Lally's face brightened. "I can hardly believe that. I can hardly wait. You will let me help care for it, won't you, Bella?"

"Of course I will, goose."

"And it won't die?"

"I don't intend going through all this discomfort just to have a child that dies."

Lally began to giggle. "You're so outspoken, Bella, really. How you stand up to Mr. Ra—Guy, I'll never know. Tell me—is he kind to you?"

"He's as all husbands are," said Bella, shrugging indifferently. "I'm going to do this room over. I told Guy I didn't care for green as a colour."

"Already!" Lally squeaked.

"It must be done at once."

"Because it was Caroline's?" Lally looked soberly at her sister. "How brave you are, Bella. I should just have said I liked green and been miserable. But I suppose with the baby coming, Mr. Raven won't refuse you anything. Oh, isn't it exciting! It will make him forget Caroline, and perhaps I'll forget that poor little angel in the snow. I don't dream so much of it now. Only when I'm very tired. Bella—Noah couldn't find us here, could he?"

"Lally, once and for all, Noah is in Newgate prison. And even if he weren't, he couldn't do anything to us now. We're safe. Mr. Raven has made us safe. You should be grateful to him, not afraid of him. And now, where's Tottie?"

"I told her to unpack for me, but every time she heard a footstep she wanted to hide."

Bella sighed. "Really, you and Tottie are a fine pair. And now I've got to make her a good maid or Mrs. Walter will laugh at me."

"Mrs. Walter?"

"She's already told me she could find someone better."

The quick apprehension was in Lally's face.

"I told you she stared."

"Oh, for goodness sake, she only wants to get a good position for a relation, I should think. Don't fret. I can manage Mrs. Walter."

But so far she hadn't been able to manage Tottie, who had quite disappeared, and was discovered at last crouching in the corner of the large wardrobe in Lally's room.

"Tottie, for goodness sake, come out at once."

The girl crept out shamefacedly, her shoulders drooping, her head bent.

Bella lifted her chin.

"Look at me, Tottie!"

Tottie obeyed, her dark eyes still as wary as a wild creature's.

"Now do I look the kind of person who would allow anything bad to happen to you? Or does my sister look unkind? I know this house is big and strange, but it's beautiful. You're a very lucky girl to be here. Whatever are you afraid of? That someone will eat you?"

Lally giggled obligingly. The merest twitch passed over Tottie's dull face. But Bella recognized it for what it was. The child had almost smiled. It must be something she had forgotten how to do long long ago.

She swallowed the foolish lump in her throat, and made herself speak briskly,

"Now finish Miss Eulalie's unpacking, then come at once to me. I want a change of clothes put out, and my hair brushed. Do you know, Lally, now I'm expecting a baby I find the most soothing thing of all having my hair brushed. Tottie has a very nice touch. But she must learn to be quicker about her work."

Then the small miracle happened. Tottie came to life. Nodding vigorously, and going down on her knees, she began tumbling the remainder of the articles out of Lally's bag. Her little head, with its tufted, straw-coloured hair still short from its drastic clipping by Doctor Bushey, was tousled and would have to be covered neatly with a cap, her dress was rumpled already, and her reddened hands clumsy. But all her actions suddenly spoke of willingness and hope. Bella knew the battle to win her trust was over and won. Trainable or not, Tottie was going to be a loyal servant.

If she could tame a wild creature like Tottie, surely she need not fail too badly with other people.

14

some intelligible sound from Tottie when Guy paid his first
visit to the disputed green and blue bedroom. It was Sunday morning, three days after their arrival at Ravenscroft.
During the days Guy had been courteous and thoughtful,
showing Bella the gardens, strolling with her down the long
shadowed yew walk where even the quarrelling of the rooks
seemed muted, displaying the rose garden and the kitchen
garden, and the slope of the lawn that led to the gently
flowing river, the water as green as the willows that bent
over it.

There was a ballroom and an orangery, a croquet lawn
and an archery. Bella had to cling again to reality. She could
scarcely believe that an ill-considered acquaintance made on
the London coach could have led to her becoming the
mistress of this beautiful estate. She began to catch Lally's fear
that they would both have to wake up. There must be a
trick in all of this.

The only flaw was the lonely nights in the hated bedroom. But these she could endure at present. She had resolved to be patient. She didn't think her husband a too
patient man. Her baby had not yet begun to spoil her figure.
Guy must notice soon that it was charming. She couldn't
believe that he would hate her forever.

"Open your mouth wider, Tottie. That's better. Now say
o-oh, o-ooh."

Tottie's familiar grunt, the only sound she ever made,
was cut off at Guy's entrance. She shrank back, hanging
her head.

"Good morning, my love," Bella said brightly. "I was just
giving Tottie her daily lesson in speech. Tottie, you may
go now."

"Have you made any progress?" Guy asked, as the girl
hurriedly retreated.

"Not yet. But it's too soon to form an opinion."

"How do you know she could ever speak?"

"She must have been able to, to understand everything
we say. Words are familiar to her. Doctor Bushey says this.

Her development has been arrested and her vocal cords paralysed by her dreadful experience. He says she is also older than she appears, at least sixteen or seventeen. If ever she is to recover it will be here, in this peaceful place."

"Perhaps. You're optimistic, I think. But I didn't come to discuss Tottie. I want you to be ready to go to church at eleven o'clock."

"Of course," Bella said placidly. "Lally, too?"

"It would be wise."

"Wise? I had hoped to go to church to worship, not to be shown off to the villagers."

Would she never learn to control her tongue? Now the friendliness had gone out of his face.

"For whatever reason, you will come."

It was only while entering and leaving the church that people had the opportunity to stare. During the service Bella, Lally and Guy sat in the boxed-in pew, its walls too high for the rest of the congregation to see over. The villagers from the little village of Underwood, and the servants, Broome, Mrs. Walter, two maids, and the shrinking Tottie, sat at the back of the church. Mrs. Walter was being kind to Tottie after all, and today had taken her under her wing, seeing that she had a posy of flowers to carry with her clean handkerchief and her prayer book, and shepherding her safely into the church.

It was a beautiful little church. Bella felt herself in a placid enough mood to enjoy its peace, and it was only when they stood to sing the first hymn that she saw the Raven pew was directly opposite the neat, square, painfully-new tablet set in the wall to the memory of Caroline Charlotte Raven, aged twenty-two years, also her son, stillborn.

Guy stood with his head held high, his profile calm and austere. Although Bella watched him surreptitiously for the whole of the service she never once saw him turn his head to the ghost on his other side.

It was left to Bella to have the tightened throat and pricking eyelids. Poor Caroline gone from the bright day. And lucky, lucky Bella to be alive.

Her mingled pity and exultation enabled Bella to walk with easy dignity out of the church after the service, smiling a little at the frankly-staring villagers, responding graciously to the vicar's welcome. She hoped that she was behaving as her husband wished. It was so wonderful to come out into the spring sunshine, to smell the may flowers and the lime

138

blossom. They would return home as they had come, by the short cut across the path through the fields that led to the long yew walk and the house. Already she was enjoying the thought of the stroll in the sunlight.

She was happy, she realized. She had so much. She would never complain about anything again.

The next morning Guy left for London, and refused to say when he would be back, if ever.

Once more it was Lally who took Bella's mind off herself. It really seemed as if Lally would never again be able to face the world with ease. Even going to church had proved to be a tremendous ordeal. She hadn't been conscious of anything the vicar had said, but only of the people staring. She had been so sure that they were not all innocent and friendly. An enemy could lurk behind the bluest and gentlest of eyes. Didn't Bella remember how innocent Aunt Aggie had seemed?

She had nightmares again that night, and the next day refused to leave her room. She felt safe only within those four walls. It took three days to coax her to go into the garden, and another week before she could be persuaded to accompany Bella to the village. Indeed, then it was only when Bella said she wanted to shop for materials with which to make baby clothes that Lally consented to go.

This outing, accomplished without any untoward event, seemed to restore Lally's confidence, and after that she became quite cheerful, sewing the tiny garments with her exquisite stitching. One would have thought it was her own baby for which she was preparing.

Guy, it seemed, had left instructions with Broome and Mrs. Walter that they were not to engage any more staff. He would attend to the matter himself.

A few days after his departure a letter arrived for Bella. She made herself crush down any expectancy that its contents would express affection. It was as well she did so for the letter was scarcely more than a note which advised that two servants, a young woman and a boy, named Molly Hancock and Joseph Smith respectively, would be arriving by the London coach the following day. Perhaps Bella would be good enough to arrange for them to be met at the coach stop in the village.

The brief chilly note ended, "I hope you and your sister are well."

Mrs. Walter, in spite of her meek air, somehow managed

to express disapproval of the new arrivals, particularly the girl. Molly had no idea how to set about cleaning a room or laying a table and must have lied to the master about her credentials. However, Mrs. Walter said with resignation, she would personally supervise the girl's work and keep her out of trouble with Broome. The lad was a strong young fellow and would be useful for carrying scuttles of coal and other heavy work.

Bella was intensely curious about these two young people. She suspected that they had both been in some kind of trouble and that Guy, in spite of his intention to go back to the idle life of a rich man, was still making investigations among the poor.

It wasn't difficult to get Joseph's story from him. For all his large frame he was little more than a bag of bones. He had been attempting to support a sick mother and five young brothers and sisters by running errands or begging for jobs at the doors of rich houses. But mostly he had been driven off because of his rags and his unkempt appearance.

"I seemed to fritten them mostly," he said cheerfully. "They'd throw up their hands and bang the door in me face."

But somehow he had managed until it seemed as if his mother was dying. Then he had begun to steal. It was mostly food, a string of sausages snatched from a butcher's, an orange from a coster's barrow, a loaf of bread, once a blanket hung out to dry in a back garden.

He had got caught for stealing a bun out of a bakeshop the day his mother died.

"They buried her in the new plague cemetery," he said. That was the thing that lay heavily on his mind, a far worse grief than his brothers and sisters being sent to an orphanage and himself to court. "She didn't have the plague. She shouldn't have to lay there among the plague."

Joseph said he thought he was fifteen.

Bella asked him how it had happened he wasn't sent to prison, and he said that was because of the master.

"He promised to see I kept out of trouble. Then he told me that he'd give his word I wouldn't do nothing bad so now I'd have to give mine to him. It was a new experiment, kind of."

"So of course you gave your word," said Bella.

The boy looked at her with his great hollowed eyes.

"I'd die as soon as let him down," he said.

Molly Hancock was another matter. She was a pretty creature with melting dark eyes and pouting lips. At first she would say nothing at all about her past, but finally, it was Lally in whom she confided. She had discovered Lally's intense interest in Bella's coming baby, and one day it had slipped from her that she, too, had had a baby. That was why she had been dismissed from the dressmaker's where she had worked.

"Old Miss Fairbrother, you should of seen her face. You'd of thought babies were some kind of foreign animal."

Of course, Molly explained, hers hadn't got a father, at least not one who would take responsibility. So she had had it in a charity home, a nightmare place, she said, and left it there to get adopted or put in an orphanage.

Lally was horrified. How could she bear to part with the baby? Molly tossed her head and said it was an ugly little thing. Anyway, wasn't it better that one should starve instead of two?

"Starve?" said Lally.

"How was I to get another job with a brat in my arms? I couldn't even have gone on the streets."

"You didn't do that!" Lally gasped.

"I would have if it hadn't been for that old doctor."

"Doctor Bushey?"

"Yes. He got me this place. I had to go and see Mr. Raven first and he said I could come down here. I'd rather have stayed in London, all the same. It's awful quiet in the country."

"It's safer," said Lally, with a shiver.

"Safer?"

"Terrible things happen in London. Look at what happened to you, having to part with your baby." Lally stopped her sewing to ponder on the terror in the world. "And us. My sister and me. If it hadn't been for Mr. Raven— Tell me," Lally knew she shouldn't be talking like this to a servant, but it was such a relief to air her feelings, "what did you think of Mr. Raven?"

Molly's eyes glinted.

"He was ever so handsome. I wouldn't mind being in the country so much if he was here." Seeing Lally's shocked expression she added, "You know what I mean. A house isn't alive without its master."

Lally repeated this conversation, or most of it, to Bella. Bella had to approve again her husband's good intentions, but she was afraid they might have been wasted on a lively piece like Molly Hancock. All the same, Molly was a cheerful good-natured creature, and she wasn't likely to repeat

141

her lapse at Ravenscroft where the only men were old Broome, the gawky Joseph, and two gardeners, both elderly. Lally had taken a fancy to her, and, when Molly was with her, seemed to throw off her fear of meeting strangers or being stared at. In Molly's company she ventured again into the village on shopping expeditions.

Bella was glad to see Lally so much brighter, but she felt lonelier than ever herself.

She had written to Guy telling him that Molly and Joseph had settled down, and that she fully approved what he had done. No answer came for three weeks. Then there was a brief note saying that he hoped all was well. She was to communicate with him if anything worried her. He hoped her health remained good. He was afraid he would be detained in London for most of the summer. That was all. She had to remind herself that he hadn't lied to her. He had told her at the beginning how their marriage would be.

All the same, Cousin Henrietta's letter some weeks later made bitter reading.

"My dear Isabella,
"I expected better of you. Haven't you learnt how to keep your husband at home? I hear disturbing rumours about his behaviour in London. They are disturbing, or I hardly need to tell you I wouldn't behave like a busybody and pass this news on. I think myself he is doing this deliberately from some peculiar kind of cussedness which runs in the family; since he has to suffer from that wicked gossip in the press he will prove it true. He must be stopped before he entirely ruins all prospect of a career or happiness. If you can't give him love, child, and God knows that can't be given at will, give him friendship. He needs true friends. I don't know how you can get him out of London, but get him out. Use your instinct."

Bella's first instinct, and not one she was proud of, was to sit down and weep. Her next was much more creative. She rang for Mrs. Walter and asked for one of the guest-rooms to be prepared for her temporary occupation. She was planning to have the master-bedroom redecorated.

So Guy could console himself with cheap women, could he? That was what Cousin Henrietta's letter had been meant to convey to her. Caroline's ghost didn't intrude when his surroundings were some over-decorated boudoir and the arms

142

about him strange ones. Therefore, every trace of Caroline should be removed from this house. The morbid blue and green furnishings should go. Bella had obeyed his order not to touch them until now. But no longer. In future, if the room reminded him of anyone, it would be of his present wife, Isabella.

This was not the act of friendship Cousin Henrietta begged. But it was the way her instinct worked.

Those shameless women in London! Bella could scarcely control her fury at the thought of them. She kept calm only by plunging herself into activity, ordering the carriage every day and driving into the neighbouring towns to look at brocades, wallpapers, carpets. Workmen were hired. The transformation began.

When it was completed three weeks later she sent the bills to Guy, with an apology that tradesmen nowadays always seemed to cost more than anticipated, but she was sure he would be as delighted as she was with the result. "After all," she wrote unabashedly, "it is important to have surroundings to one's taste when one has to spend a good deal of time in bed. Unfortunately, the doctor has ordered me to do this as my health," she stole a look at her blooming face in the mirror, "is not at present what it should be."

Which emotion would bring him back? Anger with her for her disobedience and extravagance? Or anxiety for the safety of his coming child?

Would his imagination show him a picture of her lying in the big bed with its new drapes, "48 yards Italian brocade, cutting, sewing and hanging . . ."

At least he would be reminded sharply of her existence.

But she had no opportunity, after all, to see if her ruse would succeed. For something else happened.

Lally had gone with Molly on one of their expeditions to the village. After they had completed their shopping they went, as usual, to have tea at Mrs. Bunt's tearooms. Mrs. Bunt served hot scones with whipped cream which Molly particularly liked. Lally enjoyed giving her this small pleasure, but enjoyed more sitting in the cosy low-ceilinged room with its dark rafters and gleaming copper and brass. Curiously enough, she didn't feel stared at here. The two girls always had the table in the darkest corner where they could watch people coming in and scarcely be noticed themselves.

It was a very simple diversion, and Molly thought Lally a

143

bit simple to find it so absorbing. What did she care who groups of people off the London coach which stopped at the inn next door were? Passers-by, people you would never see again. Lally made up their histories, pondered where they had come from, discussed their clothes. Daft, Molly thought. She herself would rather be in the inn parlour, hoping for a glimpse of the men at the bar. She had struck up a close friendship with a young man, Tom Field.

But today there was someone sitting at their corner table, a little round teacosy of a woman wrapped in a woolly shawl, with a neat black bonnet trimmed with cherries framing her plump pink and white face.

Seeing her there Lally exclaimed first in annoyance, then, as her eyes accustomed themselves to the gloom, she gripped Molly's arm so hard that Molly cried, "Ouch! What's the matter, miss?"

"It's Aunt Aggie!" Lally said in a strangled whisper. "Oh, dear God, it's Aunt Aggie!" She dragged at Molly. "We must fly. Quickly!"

Molly stood her ground. She wasn't flying from anybody, least of all a harmless, plump, elderly woman. Besides, people were beginning to look now, and it was embarrassing.

She said sensibly, "If that's your aunt, you ought to speak to her, miss. Come on."

Lally gasped and looked as if she would faint, and at that moment the old lady, who wore spectacles and seemed to be short-sighted, saw them.

"Is something wrong with the young lady?" she asked in a concerned voice.

"I think she's mistaking you for someone else," Molly said, for if Lally thought this woman her aunt, the woman obviously hadn't the slightest recollection of her niece.

"You're Aunt Aggie!" Lally managed to say at last. "You must be."

The old lady shook her head.

"I'm sorry to disappoint you, my dear. I've never heard of your Aunt Aggie. Not that I wouldn't mind having a pretty niece like you. I'm a lonely old widow."

The soft insinuating voice was the same. And yet how could it be? Aunt Aggie was in jail. Lally's head spun.

"Perhaps you'd do me the honour of taking tea with me, anyway," said the old woman.

Molly made a move forward, but Lally was in a panic. "No, no, no!" she cried. "It isn't safe!" She literally ran

144

out of the room into the street, followed by Molly who now made no effort to hide her dudgeon.

"You did make us look fools, miss. Running away like that from a nice old lady."

"She isn't a nice old lady, she's a monster! Let us go home quickly. I must tell Bella."

Bella didn't know what to make of it. She had to admit a shaft of fear touched her as she listened to Lally's incoherent story, but it was obvious that Molly had the true state of affairs. The old lady must have borne a remarkable resemblance to Aunt Aggie, that was all. After all, she had denied recognition of Lally. It must have been pure chance that she had sat at their table. She could never have done it deliberately to be sure of catching the girls' notice, for how could she know they usually sat there? She was probably a coach traveller passing through the village.

To satisfy herself, Bella immediately paid a visit to Mrs. Bunt. Needless to say, Mrs. Bunt was agog with curiosity as to what had caused Lally's strange behaviour.

"Looked as if she'd seen a ghost, poor child. And it was only the lady from Southampton breaking her journey. Coach travel didn't agree with her, she said. She had to go by easy stages."

"My sister thought she was someone we once knew," Bella murmured. "It gave her a shock to find she was speaking to a stranger. The lady's name—what did you say it was?"

"That I can't tell you, Mrs. Raven. She was a widow on a visit to her daughter in Twickenham. A pleasant-spoken body. She's staying at The Feathers."

A pleasant-spoken body . . . That description fitted Aunt Aggie exactly.

Bella knew there was only one thing to do and that was to go to The Feathers and interview the mysterious old woman.

This was not at all difficult, for the lady in question was sitting alone in the inn parlour.

Bella's heart gave a great jump. She did look remarkably like Aunt Aggie, the round body in the neat dark dress with its voluminous skirts, the short plump neck and the upswept grey hair beneath the frilled cap were an exact replica. But when the woman turned her head the resemblance ended. For one thing, she had clear penetrating eyes that needed no spectacles. (Lally must have imagined the spectacles beneath the bonnet in the dim corner of Mrs. Bunt's

145

tearoom.) And her expression was not bland like Aunt Aggie's, but petulant and forbidding.

The truth was, a great many stout elderly women looked alike, and poor Lally's fear-clouded eyes had led her to wrong conclusions.

For this definitely was not Aunt Aggie.

"I think you were the lady having tea at Mrs. Bunt's this afternoon," Bella said. "I came to apologize for my sister's behaviour. She mistook you for someone else."

The woman nodded affably.

"That's very civil of you, my dear. I was quite distressed for your sister. She seemed to sustain a shock."

"She's in poor health."

"That was very evident. She seemed afraid I would do her some harm. Dear me, a simple old woman like me! I would consult a doctor about her."

"Yes, I intend to."

"Has she had some shock recently?"

"I'm afraid so."

"Tch! Tch!" Bella's heart stood still. The voice and the expression were Aunt Aggie's exactly. Yet she was looking into a perfectly strange face.

"Such a pretty child. You must take good care of her . . ."

The whole thing was a remarkable coincidence, and a highly unfortunate one, for, in spite of Bella's assurance, Lally could not be convinced that the innocent stranger hadn't been Aunt Aggie. Hadn't she even worn the familiar cherry-trimmed bonnet? Bella hadn't seen the lady's bonnet. But cherries were not an unfamiliar trimming on bonnets. That proved nothing.

Nevertheless, Lally shut herself in her room again and refused to have the curtains drawn back even at midday. Like a pale flower she wilted in the gloom, starting at every sound.

"She's heard about your baby, Bella," she kept saying. "That's why she's come."

15

THE NEXT DAY—OR NIGHT—

Molly disappeared.

Mrs. Walter discovered her absence when she went up to

the servants' rooms in the attics to find out why Molly hadn't come down to help with the breakfast.

Her bed hadn't been slept in and her outdoor things were gone.

She came at once to report to Bella who was still in bed. At the urgent knocking on her door Bella started up in absurd anticipation that it might be Guy. Mrs. Walter's knock was usually much more discreet.

But the woman seemed to have caught something of Lally's uneasiness. She kept saying, "Where can the girl have got to? Out all night. It isn't right, madam."

Bella had never thought Molly a pillar of virtue, but she was a kind-hearted girl, and had been particularly understanding with Lally. It would be a pity if she had to be dismissed.

"She hasn't taken all her things, surely?"

"No, madam. But she hadn't much of anything. She was wearing her good dress and petticoats and outdoor boots. Her bonnet and shawl have gone. If she was running away, I don't suppose she'd set much store on the trifles left. I don't like saying it, madam, but if she was running off with a man, he'd no doubt be promising her better than she had. She wouldn't want to be bothering with her old things."

All that Mrs. Walter said made good sense. Molly was flighty, easy-going. She had a weakness for men. She even had a friend in the village, Lally had said. Someone she had talked to in the inn. If she didn't come back before the morning was over, it was the most likely thing in the world that she had run off with him. It was quite unreasonable of Bella to think that Molly's disappearance was a significant happening so soon after Lally imagining she had seen Aunt Aggie.

Yet she did not think so. She gave orders that Lally was not to be told of this new event, then sent Broome to the village to make discreet inquiries as to whether Molly had been seen there last evening.

Broome came back to report that Molly hadn't been seen at all. Indeed, the young man she had favoured, Tom Field, had waited all evening for her to meet him as she had promised to do. When she hadn't come, he had gone home in disgust. He vowed he would have nothing more to do with her. She had roving eyes, he said. He had always noticed her casting sly glances at the travellers by coach.

147

She'd be easy enough to pick up. Look for her in London, he said.

The elderly widow who had spent a night at the inn had continued her journey to Twickenham. This Broome had discovered, as Bella had asked him to. She had been travelling alone.

Bella forced herself to think coolly and logically. Molly had found life too dull in the country, and had run off the first opportunity that had offered. A letter would have to be written to Guy telling him to be more careful about the kind of servant he engaged. In the meantime Mrs. Walter had better find someone to take Molly's place.

Bella made this last decision deliberately. Mrs. Walter was proving a splendid housekeeper, unobtrusive and efficient. But Bella had never quite got over her faint distrust of the woman, and Lally disliked her. Now let her prove her honesty by the kind of girl she engaged.

Surprisingly enough, she did, that very day. The farmer who supplied the big house with milk and eggs had a daughter needing a position. Her name was Norah, she was just sixteen, a pleasant, fresh-faced country girl full of eagerness and good intentions.

Bella liked her immediately. She decided at once that Norah was the kind of girl she would like to look after her baby. And she would get on with Tottie. Tottie had been in awe of the sophisticated Molly, which wasn't surprising, since Molly considered her quite daft. But Norah would be sympathetic and kind. Bella was so satisfied with the arrangement that she began to think Molly's flight providential, and almost didn't notice the look of sly satisfaction on Mrs. Walter's face. It was a very fleeting look. It vanished at once. Bella was annoyed that it even perturbed her.

That seemed to be the end of the matter, except for Lally having to be told that Molly had gone. Bella waited until the following day, to make quite sure the errant girl didn't intend returning. Then she went to Lally and broke the news.

Lally gave a great gasp and exclaimed, "Aunt Aggie's got her!"

"Oh, Lally, how can you be so stupid!" The whole dreary story would have to be gone over again. "Aunt Aggie's locked up in jail. That wasn't her you saw. And Molly's run off with a man. She's a bad girl, I'm afraid. And Lally dear, you mustn't sit here in the dark. I'm going to draw the curtains back. It's a lovely day and you should be out in the garden. Let us take a walk before lunch. The doctor said I was to take a little exercise every day."

If she hoped a reference to her condition would rouse Lally, she was wrong, for the girl hunched closer into her chair. With her shawl drawn tightly round her thin shoulders she looked like an old woman, the gloom of the curtained room making her fair hair silver. Her hair was dishevelled, Bella noticed, and she was dressed carelessly, some buttons undone in her bodice and her skirts crumpled. It wasn't like Lally to be careless of her appearance. Her nervousness had worried Bella for a long time, but this strangely apathetic condition was much more disturbing. She needed rousing now, not soothing.

"Lally, do tidy yourself. I'll send Tottie to brush your hair and help you change your dress. Put on the sprigged lawn. It's so pretty."

Lally spoke slowly, in a slurred voice, as if she were half asleep.

"Molly will be in that bedroom now. Do you remember the blue bows on the curtains? We thought Aunt Aggie must be nice because she bothered about bows on the curtains for her lodgers. I expect Molly thinks she's nice, too." Lally started up, her eyes suddenly imploring. "Bella, she must be warned."

"Lally, once and for all—" Bella stopped as the peremptory knock came on the door. Not Mrs. Walter's knock, not Tottie's, not— But it was!

"May I come in, Isabella?"

Guy's voice was as peremptory as his knock. He didn't wait to be bidden to enter. He was standing in front of them dressed in riding clothes, and looking dusty and worn, as if he had galloped hard all the way from London.

Bella's heart beat in her throat. She had a longing to run into his arms, to lift her face to be kissed, to tell him he looked thinner but otherwise exactly as she remembered him.

She stood quite still and said in a faint voice, "You came? Are you very angry?"

"Who wouldn't be? What's this new trouble? Is it manufactured or real?"

"I assure you—the bills are quite real."

"The bills?" He looked as if he didn't know what she was talking about.

"For the materials and the work. There was a lot of work."

He stared at her in disbelief.

"Do you seriously think I've ridden since dawn because of a handful of bills?"

"Then what—"

"The morning newspapers. I suppose you haven't seen them. We have headlines again. I'm accused of abducting another young woman. Tell me, what is all this? Where is that wretched girl?"

So it was Molly about whom he had come. Bella couldn't begin to wonder how the news had reached the morning papers. She was too deflated. He seemed indifferent to her disobedience, even to her having laid her hands on the sacred work of Caroline. Indeed, it seemed that it was only the silly feather-brained Molly who was responsible for her ever setting eyes on her husband again.

"I haven't any idea where the girl is," she said shortly, "And I simply don't understand how the papers have got hold of the story".

"I know where she is," said Lally.

"Lally—"

"She's with Aunt Aggie."

Guy made an impatient gesture. "Is she on that again?"

Bella nodded and said in a low voice, "She has been ever since she thought she saw Aunt Aggie in the village. There was a woman who resembled her, but she was just someone on a visit to her daughter in Twickenham. It was only coincidence that Molly disappeared the night she stayed in the village."

Guy was frowning in bewilderment.

"I never heard anything so improbable. The old b—I mean, Mrs. Proudfoot, is in Newgate, so how could she be in the village? Although I must say—"

Bella's heart missed a beat. Surely he wasn't going to fan that little flame of fear that never quite left her.

"What is it, Guy?"

"The newspapers were on to this story with suspicious quickness. Did you report Molly's absence to the police?"

"No, I didn't, though everyone in the village would be talking. The story was no secret. Mrs. Walter says you can't reform the kind of girl Molly is. Perhaps your good intentions were a mistake."

"It certainly seems so. I'll have to take old Bushey to task for this. He convinced me the girl only needed a new start. Though I think we ought to be sure Molly has run off with a man before we condemn her."

"And if she hasn't?" Bella breathed the words.

"Then we must make every effort to find her, if only to save the dregs of my own reputation." Guy smiled wryly. "It's being hinted now that I might be indulging in a little of the white slave traffic myself. You and your sister have disappeared from the scene, and now a servant girl."

"Guy! How appalling!"

"Hiding behind Aunt Aggie's ample skirts, eh? But the thing can bear looking into." Guy's keen eyes were on Lally. "What's wrong with her?"

"She's upset about all this."

"Is that all? Just upset?"

He had noticed Lally's strange vacancy, her dishevelled appearance. Bella put a protective arm round her sister's shoulders.

"That's all. You know how sensitive she is."

"And you, my love? I must say, for someone who has been advised to rest in bed, you look remarkably well."

Bella flushed. "I can only tell you what the doctor said."

"Then he must think husbands shouldn't be worried by their wives' delicate state of health. He said in his letter to me that your condition couldn't be improved on."

"He wrote to you! Why?"

"I imagine in answer to my letter to him. I did take the trouble to assure myself that you were not in any imminent danger."

Bella met his ironic gaze. She thought dolefully that she had meant to be reclining in bed when he arrived, wearing her new wrapper with the swansdown trimming, and looking fragile and in need of cherishing. Instead she stood here, flushed and plump and abounding in health. And Doctor Frobisher, for whom she had developed a prejudice because he had also been Caroline's doctor, had given away her foolish ruse.

But Guy had bothered to inquire about her. She supposed her small flicker of joy about that was legitimate.

"It would be too much to expect a man to understand how a woman feels," she said defensively.

"I expect it would. Well, let us get all the bad things over at once. Let me see what your efforts at interior decorating have achieved."

It was odd how her confidence in the room ebbed away when he stood at her side. Had so much red been wise? She had thought it so warm and comforting. Was the wallpaper with its cabbage roses a little overpowering? Should there have been fewer velvet drapes over mantelpiece, tables and stools? And the beautiful golden brocade bed curtains looped back—were they a little bizarre?

Guy suddenly shouted with laughter.

"It's like an Eastern bazaar."

"You don't like it?" Bella's voice was edged with ice. That laughter hurt more than his anger would have done.

"Can you sleep among so much grandeur?"

"It had to be *warm*!" Bella burst out.

"Well, now you've practically lit a fire."

She realized that he was determined not to take her changes too seriously, in case he let his guard break down in front of her again. He would find the room amusingly preposterous, nothing else. In that way he made her harmless.

Harmless! She would show him.

"Doesn't it compare favourably with the rooms you have been visiting in London?"

For a long minute their gaze locked.

"So you too join the scandal-mongers," he said at last. His colour had heightened. "I believe you're as mad as your sister."

Long afterwards a candle flared beside her bed.

"Why didn't you come down to dinner?"

Bella wanted to bury herself deep in the pillows, unwilling to face even the frail light of the candle. Why must he choose this time to come, when she had been weeping for hours, and then, worn out, had not been able to endure ever having her hair brushed. She had let Tottie undress her and had tumbled into bed, aching-eyed and wan. The weeks and months of strain had culminated in that torrent of tears. She had felt unable to face life any more. It was all too much, the anxiety about Lally, the nameless threat that seemed to hang over them all the time, the baby her husband didn't care about growing heavy and tiresome within her, and last of all, Guy's accusation that she was mad. As mad as poor darling Lally.

"Are you ill?" the voice at her bedside persisted.

"No," she muttered into the pillow.

"Are you sulking?"

That roused her momentarily, and she turned, pushing back her heavy hair from her tear-stained face.

152

"I'm not a child!"

"But you've been crying."

"Is that—so extraordinary?"

"Only that I've never seen you cry before."

He sat on the side of the bed and looked down at her.

"What is it you cried for? Something I said? Or the state Lally is in?"

His voice was quite gentle and he had stopped calling Lally Eulalie, as if he accepted her at last. All the same his attitude resembled that of a kind uncle. Bella thought she preferred his hostility. But at least in this mood he could be talked to.

"You called me mad, too," she said.

"You provoked me."

"Do you really think Lally—out of her senses?"

"She doesn't improve, does she?"

"No," Bella had to agree. "Every time she gets a new fright she's worse. It's as if someone knows they can do this to her, and takes pleasure in it. Just as the news about Molly is already in the newspapers so that it will do you harm. Guy—" unconsciously she had taken his hand and was holding it tightly, "do you think Noah can be carrying out his threat already?"

"From Newgate prison? That would be an impossibility."

"He wouldn't want to wait a whole year," Bella said instinctively. "Yes, I suppose it is an impossible idea. We'll find out where Molly is, and all will be well. If only Lally would get better. I've asked Norah to sleep with her tonight."

"Norah?"

"She's a nice reliable girl. Mrs. Walter found her to take Molly's place. Later I want her to be the baby's nurse. And Tottie—" Bella was growing more animated, "you'd be surprised. Actually, I think Joseph has taken a fancy to her. Or else he's good at protecting people the way he did his poor sick mother. I've seen him smiling at her, and there's nothing like a man's interest to perk up a girl. Though they're neither of them more than elderly children, poor things." Bella caught Guy's expression and said apologetically, "I'm chattering. We should be talking about more serious things."

He stood up.

"In the morning."

"Are you returning to London—immediately?"

"To make certain inquiries. But not for long."

Her heart leaped. She had the courage to say, "I'm sorry if I distressed you about this room."

"Distressed me? I think you overestimate your abilities."

"No!" she said passionately. "I'm flesh and blood. Feel me! Feel my hand, my arm."

His kindly mood had gone. His eyes glinted steel.

"Let that poor ghost go, Guy. Only you keep her here."

"You're shameless!"

"I have to be! You can go to other women. Why not me? If I were a woman in the street—"

His fingers cut into her wrist.

"You're my wife."

"Your *wife!*"

"According to our agreement."

"Unwanted, unloved," she said bitterly.

"You should have thought of that when you begged to take your sister's place."

"You would rather have poor Lally without her wits!"

"I would infinitely rather have neither of you," he said brutally, and turning abruptly left the room.

Bella lay back against the pillows. An occasional dry sob escaped her. Why couldn't she be tranquil, disciplined? Why couldn't she enjoy being treated like a tearful child? All this emotion was bad for the baby.

But she couldn't help it. The truth had come to her inexorably in the last few minutes. He might never stop hating and resenting her for being his wife, but she loved him. She loved him terribly and forlornly and forever.

Early in the morning a different crisis was precipitated. Lally was found wandering downstairs in her nightgown. She didn't seem to know where she was, and when Mrs. Walter tried to take her back to her room she thought she was being attacked, and screamed that she would not be put aboard a ship, or buried in the snow. Doctor Frobisher had to be sent for post-haste. He prescribed sedatives, but viewed the situation with the utmost gravity.

"I'm afraid she'll have to be taken away for a time," he told Bella. "I know of a very reputable home that takes cases like this. There's no use my concealing facts, Mrs. Raven. Your sister's mind is temporarily unhinged."

"Don't send her away!" Bella begged. "Guy! Poor Lally! I can't bear to have her sent away."

"Is there any alternative?" Guy asked the doctor.

154

"You could have a reliable woman to look after her, I suppose. Someone who can be trusted never to leave her. I'd much prefer that she was in a proper establishment for this kind of illness."

"Surrounded by others worse than herself?" Bella cried. "Then she'd never get better."

"I'll find a suitable woman when I return to London," said Guy. He didn't speak to Bella but to Doctor Frobisher, who hummed and hawed, and said that he could only give advice. Nevertheless, if that was the way they preferred it, he would take his leave. The patient had better be kept under sedatives until the nurse arrived.

"Thank you, Guy," said Bella fervently. "That was good of you. I know Lally will get better when the baby comes. That's what she's waiting for."

"You'll keep her away from the baby," Guy said sharply.

In spite of her gratitude, Bella's quick temper flared.

"As if Lally would hurt my baby! She'll be as gentle as an angel."

"How can you tell, with this obsession she has about infants? She must be watched all the time."

Obsession—it was not a nice word. It was what the scurrilous papers said Guy had for young women in distress. . . .

"This woman who is to watch Lally—she had better be elderly, or middle-aged at least. And plain."

Guy's voice was hard. "Why?"

"You know very well there wouldn't have been anything to base a scandal on if that wretched Molly hadn't been pretty. I suppose there might not have been any scandal at all if Lally and I had been homely."

She wasn't crying now, so he didn't have to be gentle. He could give her that long cool rakish look, that might very well justify the stories circulated about him, and say,

"Oh, indeed! For then it's most unlikely I would have come to your help. But I saw you leaning out of the window, beauty in distress."

"Guy, don't joke!"

"Why? Must we be deadly serious for the rest of our lives? Or must we speak the unpalatable truth as we did last night? Anyway, you wouldn't want your sister frightened out of her remaining wits by some old crone. Would you?"

16

THE WRINKLED MONKEYISH FACE
looked up at Guy questioningly and with servility. Finely
dressed gentlemen like this seldom visited Newgate prison.

"Did you want to visit the prisoners, sir?"

"No. I'm merely inquiring about their welfare."

"Oh, they're well, sir. Very well. Not a trace of jail fever."

"They haven't attempted to escape?"

"Ha ha! Ha ha ha! They may have attempted, sir, but
they haven't succeeded."

"And they're due to be released when?"

"On the twelfth of December, sir. Nicely in time for
Christmas. The old lady may go earlier for good conduct.
She's been quite an example, clean, tidy, helpful to others.
Has a Bible reading every evening to those who will listen."

"That doesn't surprise me," said Guy distastefully.

"You know her, sir? Did you think her wrongfully accused?"

"I accused her," said Guy harshly. "Her sentence was too
light by ten years. Thank you and good day."

His next visit was to the house in Seven Dials.

He went on foot so as not to arouse too much notice. For
all that, the ragged children and women in doorways, brought
out by the warm summer day, stared at the fine gentleman
venturing into their territory. He soon had a clutch of skinny
barefoot children, like a flock of moulting chickens, at his
heels. The sun had not only brought out the inhabitants but
the smells of the narrow airless streets. The dust underfoot
reeked. A child whose entire clothing seemed to be a torn
newspaper thrust a skeleton claw at him. He peered into
the matted curtain of hair to see if it were a boy or a
girl and failed to decide.

This blighted street was England, he thought. Just as
much England as the smooth rich lawns and sweet air of
Ravenscroft. No wonder vice flourished and crafty op-
portunists like Mrs. Proudfoot and her villainous son bat-
tened on the weakness and desperation of misery.

Aunt Aggie's modest house with its soot-grimed bricks certainly looked empty, its windows closed and the lace cur-

tains drawn. Nevertheless, Guy rapped on the low door and impatiently motioned to the clustering urchins to be quiet while he listened. Was that a shuffling footstep inside?

An old woman stuck her head out of a window opposite. Her frizzed hair was like grey lichen.

"There's no one home there. They be in prison." She cackled maliciously. "Serve the old 'ooman right, with her stuck-up airs."

"Does no one live here now?" Guy asked.

" 's' all locked up. There be nobody there. In spite of what my old man says."

"What does he say?"

"Swears he saw a light two, three nights ago. I tell him it come out of a pint mug." The old crone with her broken teeth cackled again. "Who's to light a candle, I ask him? They's in prison, where they ought to be."

"Did anyone else see this light, or hear anything?"

"Naw. Not my old man neither. We sees nothin' and hears nothin' at nights. 's' only way."

Guy nodded. It was the only way. But he wasn't satisfied. He tossed the persistent children some coins and left them scuffling and fighting in the dust.

By a little reconnoitering he found he could reach the backyard of the house from a narrow and particularly evil-smelling alley. There didn't seem to be anybody about. He vaulted the tumble-down wall easily and found himself in the tiny yard. There was no snow now. The sour black earth kicked up in a fine dust. The small excavation where the baby had lain was still exposed. A broken-handled shovel lay nearby. Someone had broken the kitchen window. The gaping hole made it easy to peer into the bleak strip of room where Tottie had had her uneasy domain. Something scuttered and rustled. A rat probably. These old houses so near the Fleet river crawled with rats.

But a rat couldn't have lit a candle.

Guy found that by reaching through the hole in the window-pane he could turn the lock and push up the window. He smiled wryly as he stepped into the dubious room. He wasn't dressed for breaking into empty houses.

The place was familiar enough to him after his first visit there. He remembered the little parlour, its antimacassars and bobbled velvet covered now with a filter of dust. Without the warmth of firelight and lamplight and Aunt Aggie

157

herself, whose cosiness couldn't be denied, it was a dreary little room, smelling musty and damp.

The stairs creaked with a painful protest beneath his weight. He wasn't going to search the whole house. His main objective was the bedroom at the top. The last time he had seen it, Lally had been sprawled in her deep sleep across the bed, and the girl who was now so improbably his wife had been shaking her sister and lifting her own distraught face to her rescuers. It seemed strange now to find the room completely empty. He scarcely knew what he had expected to find. Strewn garments? A dishevelled bed? Signs of a struggle?

There were certainly marks in the dust on the dressing-table, but they could have been made by rats. There was also a little water filmed with dust in the washbasin. Beyond that, nothing.

He had never believed Lally's fantasy about Aunt Aggie in the village, and even less had he thought the missing Molly a victim of these people who could just possibly have tentacles stretching out from Newgate prison. He had felt impelled to explore these possibilities and although he hadn't believed in them he felt a curious lift of spirits to find himself right. He hadn't realized that Noah's threat had weighed on him.

All the same, there were strange aspects. The speed with which the newspapers had had the story of Molly's disappearance, as if they had been fed with private information, and this surely not from Sir Henry Shields, who was no longer his rival. There was a personal touch to this new persecution which disturbed him.

But this drab little house was innocent. Or was it? Guy's eyes caught a dark gleam in a corner of the kitchen. For a moment he thought it a drop of blood. He stooped to pick up the object. It was an artificial cherry such as a woman might wear on her bonnet. One side was pitted with tiny teeth-marks, which had obviously been made by a rat. The rat would have carried its disappointing trophy here from where it had been dropped.

Who wore a bonnet trimmed with a cluster of cherries?

Mrs. Proudfoot? Isabella or her sister? Molly? Or one of the faceless stream of young women whom he was certain had passed through this house?

How was he to know? But the small object lying in the palm of his hand was almost free of dust. It seemed very unlikely it had lain there all the months Aunt Aggie had been in prison.

Guy was glad to find Doctor Bushey at home. There was a great deal to talk about.

The doctor was inclined to view Molly's disappearance with nothing but indignation.

"The ungrateful wretch! Now there I thought was a young woman anxious to turn over a new leaf. She had a chance to become respectable, get herself a husband, perhaps. But she's thrown it all away. Well, you can never tell. You have to give them a chance. I'm sorry I let you in for this new trouble. But it'll blow over."

"I wonder."

"Eh? You think it's not all cut and dried?"

"I'm not sure. Two hours ago I'd have agreed with you. But since then I've found this."

He exhibited the cherry and described how he had found it. He said, "I'm going to the police. I want this girl's disappearance thoroughly investigated. I know it's a hundred chances to one she has gone off with a man, she was apt to make friendships easily, I'm told. But the one odd chance she hasn't must be investigated. You see, if it should prove true, this can happen again. From my house. A war of attrition, so to speak."

Doctor Bushey regarded Guy with astonishment.

"My boy, what you're suggesting is fantastic."

"Don't you come across fantastic happenings every day in your round?"

"Oh, aye. That's human nature. But you're endowing this old woman with diabolical powers. Do you think she projected herself from Newgate into the village of Underwood as a sort of apparition? Or more likely, though still improbable, that she had a double? And if she had, and if Molly were lured away by some rich promises, would they do something so foolish as to take her to that same house?"

"It might be their only headquarters—I mean, they might not have had time to advise their contact from the ship due in port of a new address. In any case, that street, as you must realize, tells no tales."

"Fantastic!" muttered Doctor Bushey.

"I expect you're right. I expect the whole thing's on my nerves. On top of it all, my wretched sister-in-law seems to have gone out of her mind. That won't surprise you, perhaps."

"I'm very sorry to hear it. She has an unstable personality. It's her method of escape from reality."

"Who wouldn't escape from reality. Poverty, disease, death." Guy was thinking of the children with the grey, ancient faces, the desiccated hands.

Doctor Bushey shot him a shrewd glance. "At least you made the right choice when you married."

Guy's mouth twisted.

"You think so?"

"Good heavens, boy, would you have wanted an hysteric the mother of your child? I warrant Isabella isn't out of her mind."

"Far from it. At least, not in the same way."

"You haven't really seen her yet, have you?" the doctor murmured, his eyes bland.

"Seen her! I am supposed to be the father of her child!"

Doctor Bushey began to chuckle maddeningly.

"Why, I believe she tricked you! Did she trick you, boy?"

"If you ask me," Guy said, his temper rising, "I've been tricked all round. Caroline dead, my mother alienated, my career gone, married to a shrew!"

"And able to see only an inch in front of you. Poor boy, poor boy! Let's have some brandy. It won't give you long sight, you've got to develop that yourself, but it might help to clear the way slightly."

"Oh, stop your damned riddles! I can manage my own affairs. When the child's born I shall come back to London permanently." Guy took the proffered glass, his eyes still smouldering. "And I'll get a bill through Parliament on slum clearance if it kills me."

"In the meantime?" Doctor Bushey prodded.

"In the meantime I need a woman, someone with some nursing experience, to take care of this mad creature I have foisted on me. She'll have to be watched all the time. My wife doesn't seem to realize the danger of letting her near the baby. She'll most likely smother it when she thinks she's only showing it affection."

Doctor Bushey nodded gravely.

"I see you understand her condition. She has a fixation on infants since her unfortunate experience. You're quite right, she shouldn't be left alone with the child. But certainly let her share it a little."

"Oh, my wife will see to that, you can be sure."

"Your wife shows a warm devotion to her sister. Well,

then, we must find a suitable woman. I'd suggest someone young and kind to appeal to Miss Lally."

"That's exactly my own idea."

"But not Miss Isabella's?"

"My wife is suspicious of everyone, even, if you can believe it, of Caroline."

"Women!" said Doctor Bushey shaking his head. "Unpredictable creatures! Have another brandy, my boy. And did you know your mother has been ill?"

"How should I? She refuses to see me."

"You mustn't take women entirely at their word. They don't expect you to. Anyway," Doctor Bushey twirled the liquid in his glass. "She's well on the way to recovery now. She had a slight lung infection. Nothing more."

His mother's illness may have been slight, but it was enough to send Guy hurrying to visit her. He only half expected to be admitted, and was surprised when he was bidden to her bedroom. Perhaps her illness had softened her attitude, although it did not appear so by her outward appearance. Propped against pillows, a ridiculously befrilled cap obscuring almost everything but her sharp nose and the inquisitive glitter of her eyes, she gave no sign of pleasure at her son's visit.

"You come with your tail between your legs, I hope," she said in her rasping voice. "A fine mess you've made of your life. What's this new scandal about a housemaid?"

"The scandal is in the minds of news-mongers. How are you, Mamma? I'm sorry to see you ill. Why wasn't I informed?"

"Because I wasn't dying. I have absolutely no intention of sending for you except to attend my deathbed."

Guy's lips twitched. He was feeling a great deal better already. He had hated the breach with his mother. She was the most exasperating person in the world, but an incomparable wit-sharpener. He was in need of having his wits sharpened.

"Then I'm glad I came while you can still hold a conversation. What does Doctor Bushey say?"

"What does that old fool ever say? Rest, physic, a melancholy reminder of one's age. I have had a small chill, nothing more. I'm getting rid of my nurse next week. I never did need the woman. Hannah could have managed very well."

"Your nurse? What's she like? Old? Young?"

"Good gracious, boy, what's that to do with you? Have you

161

an obsession about servant girls? What did happen to this silly creature at Ravenscroft? Did she run away to you, or from you?"

"My God, Mamma, if you were a man I'd call you out for that."

Mrs. Raven sighed deeply. A tinge of colour had come into her parchment cheeks.

"Thank heaven, this impossible wife hasn't made you lose your spirit."

"Did you think she could?"

"I'd have denied you were my son if that had happened. But you're breeding from her!"

"So you know that, too."

"Of course I know it. The girl came and shouted the news at me like some gipsy shouting her wares."

"Hardly, Mamma," Guy murmured, but he was suddenly amused, seeing Bella with her blazing eyes and her indignation. And remembering with sudden violence the way her body had showed through her thin nightgown that night. That memory had been deliberately crushed for a long time.

"She's healthy?" Mrs. Raven's voice was casual, intended to disguise anxiety.

"Extremely."

"Then why the interest in my nurse?"

"A woman's required for the sister. She's had some kind of a breakdown. The doctor recommended a nursing home, but Isabella prefers her to remain at home."

"You mean she's out of her mind? Then I'd get rid of her. Immediately. But I suppose you can refuse your wife nothing in her condition."

His mother's sarcasm stung. "She has little enough!" he retorted.

"Little enough! A rich husband, a mansion, a child. And you call that little enough. How does she assess her possessions, this nobody from the gutter?"

"She has a half-witted sister and a dumb maidservant. Otherwise, nothing but enemies."

"Faugh! Melodrama!"

"She needs friends," Guy heard himself saying. It was his mother's implacable antagonism that made him defend his wife. "There seems to be some kind of conspiracy. I don't think I imagine it. That servant girl disappearing . . . I admit I engaged her hastily and perhaps too trustingly. That comes from old Bushey's sentimentality. But from now on I intend to exercise the greatest care. That's why I asked about your nurse. Would she be a suitable woman?"

"I'm glad to hear you've learnt your lesson about picking up people off the street. The poor aren't all deserving. Nor are they unfortunate innocents. You'll find that missing girl completely corrupted—if she ever turns up again. I hope for your sake she doesn't. But Miss Thompson isn't that type. Doctor Bushey knew better than to foist any of his converts on to me. She's a genteel person, has pleasant manners. Interview her, if you like. She can give you her own references." Mrs. Raven's colour was parchment again, her eyelids drooping.

"You're tired, Mamma. I'll leave you. Will you come down to Ravenscroft to convalesce?"

The befrilled head sank deeper into the soft pillow. Only the old lady's nose was visible.

"And forgive that little upstart for wearing the Raven diamonds. Her chin in the air—imagining herself a queen! And I expected not to turn my back! Forget! Forgive!" The rasping voice was only a mutter in the snowy pillow. "I've never heard the words."

17

SO MISS CLARA THOMPSON ARrived at Ravenscroft. She had smooth dark hair parted in the middle and drawn down primly over her ears, black cherry eyes and a small curved mouth that seemed to be always smiling. She was smiling into Guy's eyes as he handed her out of the carriage—he had brought her down from London himself—and she continued to smile, but in a subtly different way, at Bella when they met.

This was no flighty Molly nor yet a young woman who had been in distressed circumstances. For Miss Thompson had a rounded well-nourished look about her, as if she had never been hungry or afraid or in need of help. Guy said little about her except that she had been nursing his mother and had frequently nursed cases for Doctor Bushey.

"That silly old man!" Bella exclaimed unfairly. "His heart's too soft for his head."

"But my mother's isn't."

Bella had to agree to that, although she added that Mrs. Raven would hardly put herself out to send someone whom she and Lally would like.

"Don't you like Miss Thompson?" Guy asked patiently.

What was it she didn't like about the woman? She was soft-voiced, clever with Lally who had to be coaxed and humoured. Although she took her meals with Guy and Bella she didn't obtrude, speaking only when spoken to and then with impeccable politeness. She must have known Bella's history—who didn't?—but there was no sign of scorn or patronage in her manner.

Yet all the time there was something, a subtle confidence, almost a veiled amusement. And she got on too well with the other servants, even Mrs. Walter who might have been expected to feel some rivalry. It seemed odd that she should set out so deliberately to be liked, as if it mattered that old Broome or the awkward tongue-tied Joseph should be her admirers.

That was, she got on with all the servants except Tottie.

But perhaps she felt that Tottie was too unimportant and minuscule to bother about. And harmless because of her lack of speech?

That thought only came to Bella after she noticed Tottie try to shrink out of sight when Miss Thompson came into the room. It was months now since Tottie had reverted to that old instinctive fear. Was it fear or rather just an enormous shyness in the presence of someone so brisk and confident as Miss Thompson. Bella didn't know. She had never been able to persuade any intelligible sound from Tottie's lips, but it did seem that the girl was increasing her efforts to make herself understood, even in her happy good-morning bob and mumble with which she greeted Bella each morning. Her face had grown round and rosy and her starved flat child's body had softened into a definite shape beneath her neat poplin gowns. She blushed easily, and sometimes unmistakably giggled. She had learned to launder and iron even to Mrs. Walter's satisfaction, and her now chubby and healthy hands had become adept at twisting Bella's hair into fashionable styles. It was nice to have someone so quiet and willing and adoring. It was nice to be adored, Bella added honestly to herself. It wasn't an emotion she had much of in this house.

But Tottie definitely wasn't the same girl since Miss Thompson's arrival.

When Bella suggested this to Guy she thought she caught a flicker of some deeper interest in his eye before he said easily,

"Pooh! She's shy about being teased. We caught her making daisy chains with Joseph in the orchard."

"We?"

"I met Miss Thompson strolling in the garden last evening."

"Oh," said Bella, remembering quite distinctly what Miss Thompson had worn at dinner last night, a grey silk gown, perfectly suitable for someone in her position, but with a fichu of very beautiful lace that could hardly have been bought out of her wages as a nurse. She had touched it and said that it had belonged to her grandmother, making Bella inevitably conjure up the picture of some aristocratic old lady with plenty of servants of her own. Which no doubt was exactly what Miss Thompson had intended her to think, and perhaps it was true. Although Bella was more inclined to think the lace had been the gift of some grateful patient. Or perhaps something the sly creature had helped herself to while a patient lay dying.

Her thoughts were uncharitable, but she meant them to be so. She and Lally had sat in the drawing-room after dinner last night, she with a piece of embroidery that bored her unendurably, Lally with knitting that lay idle in fingers no longer able to work with precision. The evenings were always like this, long, monotonous, the light never seeming quite to die. It was only fair that Miss Thompson should have a little relief from her care of Lally. And Bella herself had grown too cumbersome to walk far.

But it would have been more thoughtful of Guy to entertain his wife and sister-in-law than to walk in the garden with Miss Thompson. Bella found herself unable to believe that their meeting had been accidental. She had thought that Guy was staying at Ravenscroft only to await the birth of the baby. But then she had seen him lighting Miss Thompson's candle at night and handing it to her with a courteous little bow, twice they had been laughing together in the drawing-room before dinner. Once he had drawn back a little too abruptly when Bella had come into the room.

And Miss Thompson's black cherry eyes had a secret gleam. She seemed to take especial care with her appearance.

"You never did tell me about Miss Thompson's background," Bella said to Guy.

"Didn't I? I'm sure I did. I told you she is alone in the

world, like you and Eulalie. Her parents are dead and her only brother was killed in the fighting at Sebastopol. She decided to emulate Miss Nightingale in a nursing career, but to do it at home where she feels nurses are needed just as much as they are in theatres of war."

"Why hasn't she married?"

Guy gave her his cool glance.

"I've hardly presumed to inquire into her private affairs."

"She's good-looking. She must have had opportunities. Is she too ambitious?"

"My love, aren't you being a little carping? Miss Thompson is doing the job she came here to do. Your sister likes her and is much more docile with her. Isn't that the beginning and end of the matter? We don't have to inquire into her ambitions or emotions. They're her affair."

"They're not if they lead to trouble as Molly's did."

"Oh, come, my dear, Miss Thompson isn't the kind to have assignations in the village with yokels like Tom Field."

No, thought Bella. Miss Thompson cast her net for bigger fish. The master of the house, no less. A careful toilette, strolls in the dusky garden, whispers over lit candles . . .

Or was her mind growing unhinged like Lally's, so that she turned every trifle into a dark shadow, a significant happening.

Even the cherry off Aunt Aggie's bonnet. But it was Guy who had thought that significant. He had asked her if Molly had had a bonnet trimmed with artificial cherries, and she had said no, that was Aunt Aggie.

How could she forget? Both she and Lally had admired the nodding luscious bunch of them on Aunt Aggie's bonnet in the coach that very first day. And later Lally had insisted that the woman in the teashop had had cherries on her bonnet. which had seemed to Lally irrefutable confirmation that she had been Aunt Aggie. But Doctor Frobisher said that must have been an hallucination. Lally had thought the woman Aunt Aggie. So she had dressed her as her mind remembered her.

Guy had thought the information important enough to have the police pay a special visit to the house in Seven Dials and search the cupboards and wardrobes to find the cherry-trimmed bonnet. But it hadn't been there. And Aunt Aggie hadn't worn it to prison. She had sat in the dock in a humble black bonnet trimmed with nothing more frivolous than a few jet beads.

So where was the famous cherry-trimmed creation? Had the rats eaten it all except one last cherry?

And where was Molly? Guy's influence in the county had caused a widespread police search which so far had yielded no clues whatever. The girl had disappeared without trace.

Then something did turn up. A small boy had picked up a mesh reticule such as ladies wore on their wrists in the evenings. It had been run over by the wheels of a vehicle and ground into the mud. The boy had found it contained, together with a handkerchief and a muddied scrap of paper, a shilling, so he had kept the shilling and hidden the purse. The visit of the police, a routine one they were making to each cottage in the vicinity, had scared the child and he had confessed his discovery.

The muddied scrap of paper was found to be a note. It said, "Instead of coming to The Feathers tonight meet me at crossroads, same time. Have made arrangements. T."

The initial T of course indicated Tom. Tom Field. And there was no doubt that that was how Molly had interpreted it. When Tom was interviewed he admitted that he and Molly had talked of running off, but they had never fixed it finally, and how could the note be his since he couldn't read or write?

So Molly had obviously been lured into a trap. Someone had been at the crossroads that night with a vehicle of some kind, and she had been spirited away. To where?

How had Molly got the note? No one knew. Perhaps it had been slipped into her hand that afternoon when she had been in the village with Lally. Nobody knew anything. All the servants at Ravenscroft were questioned. Tottie was the only one who had no answers but then poor Tottie couldn't speak. All that happened was that she got back her look of slack-mouthed stupidity which Bella knew was caused by terror. Bella understood the terror well enough, for she was beginning to feel it herself.

The safe world had vanished. It never had been safe. The shadow of Seven Dials was back, and overpoweringly threatening. No one could be trusted.

That night Bella had one of Lally's nightmares about the dead baby. She thought she had it in her arms, its tiny frozen face against her breast. She woke screaming, and Guy came hurrying it from the adjoining bedroom.

"What is it? Are you ill? Is the baby coming?"

The shreds of terror were still round her and she couldn't even take satisfaction in his very evident concern.

"Do they have designs on my baby?" she whispered. "I'm so afraid."

"You've had a nightmare," said Guy in relief.

The wavering candle flame seemed only to accentuate the shadows. Bella's arm still felt curiously the weight of that weightless infant.

"Lally said they would come for it."

"Lally's mad."

"She has intuitions which are true. She knew they'd never forgive us for digging up that baby—not letting it stay hidden. They'll bury mine instead."

"What nonsense! What utter nonsense! Do I have to remind you again that they're in prison?"

"They'll be out soon."

"Not until December."

"For Christmas. Do you think they'll have Christmas dinner in the parlour? There'll be the fire burning and the lamp lit and the curtains drawn. It's a very cosy room. And the cradle on the hearth. I can't see that room without the cradle on the hearth, although I know it won't be there. Oh, Guy!" her voice held entreaty, "I'm talking like Lally."

"You've had a nightmare. I'll ring for Norah to make you a hot drink."

"Our baby will be exactly eight weeks old then."

"When?"

"When they come out of prison."

"Stop thinking of it. You're perfectly safe." In the dim light Guy's face had grim lines. "I'll see that you're safe."

"Guy, Molly must be found."

"She will be found. Don't doubt it."

Guy was right, Molly was found, though not until six weeks later and then in a not unexpected fashion. A young woman arrested in Piccadilly for being drunk and disorderly gave her name as Molly Hancock, and recognizing that she might be the missing maidservant from Ravenscroft, the police sent for Guy to identify her.

He not only identified Molly, but Molly, brazen and impertinent, identified him as the gentleman who had kidnapped her that night at the crossroads.

Nothing would shake her from that story. Although it was pointed out to her that Guy had been in London that

168

night, she swore he had been the gentleman in the carriage waiting at the crossroads.

She said she had thought at first it was Tom Field, who had written her the letter, and had begun to climb in eagerly. Then she realized she had been mistaken, and dropped her reticule in the ensuing struggle.

But Mr. Raven, she said, staring boldly at Guy, had been too strong and had overpowered her. She admitted that after the initial struggle she had gone willingly enough.

"But he soon got tired of me," she complained. "He turned me out without a penny. It's through him I had to go on the streets."

Guy could scarcely believe the change in the neat and self-respecting young woman whom he had sent down to Ravenscroft. Molly's hair was tangled and lank, her gown dirty, her face hectically flushed, and with that look of almost frenzied boldness. He had no notion of what she had gone through since her departure from Ravenscroft but he did guess now that beneath her brazen demeanour she was terrified. Scared to death.

The young police inspector, scenting duplicity, questioned the girl remorselessly.

If Mr. Raven had her in this house in the country why should he use such elaborate means to abduct her?

He'd hardly keep her side by side with his wife, would he, said Molly insolently. He wanted her to himself, hidden away, secret. He took her to a house near the river. No, she didn't think she could identify it again. It was dark when she arrived and dark the night she left. She knew it was near the river because she could smell the mud when the tide went out, and hear foghorns. She thought the two rooms in which she was confined, the outside door always locked, were rented from a woman who lived downstairs. The windows faced a brick wall. She couldn't look out to see where she was, nor was there any way to escape.

If she had wanted to, she added slyly.

Mr. Raven's wife was in a certain condition and it was well known that that was a time for husbands to be unfaithful. She gave this information gratuitously. In any case, everyone knew what sort of a marriage it was. Mr. Raven had been caught in his own snare that time.

Here Guy interrupted the girl's bitter invective.

"Some one has made you say all this, haven't they?" He spoke quite gently. "I don't know what you've been threatened with. But these people aren't all powerful. You're quite safe now. Just tell the truth and you'll be protected."

The girl looked at him with her sunken sullen eyes.

"I am telling the truth. Every word of what I said is true. I'll swear it to my dying day."

Bella said, with dry lips, "What are you going to do now?"

"What can I do? It's my word against hers, and unfortunately, with the sort of popularity I'm enjoying at present, the world prefers to believe the girl."

"It's outrageous!"

Guy gave a wry smile.

"Thank you, my dear, for believing me. You have little enough reason to."

"That little slut! She's quite without conscience."

"No. She's frightened. That's all."

They were all frightened—except perhaps Guy who was looking quite calm and unruffled and pretending that this new persecution was trifling and would be forgotten in a day. Perhaps it would be. But what would happen next?

"Guy, that old woman was visiting her daughter in Twickenham. That's near the river, isn't it?"

"What old woman?"

"The one Lally thought was Aunt Aggie. Though she wasn't, of course. But Molly did say the house was near the river."

"Molly has been rehearsed in a story that is nothing but a malicious fabrication. There was no house, no river, no foghorns."

"Then it was the house in Seven Dials," Bella said, in a whisper. She added helplessly, "Poor Molly. No wonder she's frightened."

18

IN EXACTLY HER OLD SANE VOICE
Lally said, "I think you ought to know, Bella, I saw Mr. Raven kissing Miss Thompson last night."

Bella had intended never to speak sharply to poor Lally again. But her retort leaped out. "Don't be absurd! You must have dreamed it. You know you're always having nightmares."

Lally shook her head slowly. Her eyes were wide, serious, alarmingly sober. "It wasn't a dream, Bella. It was just before we went upstairs. Mr. Raven lit a candle from the hall stand, and then as he handed it to Miss Thompson he kissed her on the cheek. She stood and stared. She looked quite embarrassed. But pleased."

By enormous self-control Bella kept her voice calm.

"I expect you did dream it, Lally dear. But if you didn't Miss Thompson will have to go."

"She looked pleased," Lally repeated.

A little later her slow wits reminded her what Bella had said.

"Don't send her away, Bella. I wouldn't have told you if I thought you would send her away. She's kind to me. She doesn't scold. Last night—"

"What about last night?"

Lally frowned, her lovely eyes going blank.

"I can't remember. I find it so hard to remember things."

"You said Miss Thompson had been kissing my husband."

"No, no I didn't. It wasn't like that. It was him kissing her. He was holding the candle crooked, spilling grease. Bella! Bella, don't look so angry! I don't like you looking angry! After all, it's nice that people should be kind and loving." Lally turned her large imploring eyes on Bella. "Don't send her away. She doesn't stare at me. She says 'What a baby you are!' and helps me dress, and doesn't laugh when I can't do up the buttons. I don't know why I can no longer do up buttons. And my knitting gets into such a snarl. Look! Why is it so snarled?"

Bella gently took the knitting away from Lally's clumsy and fumbling fingers.

"I'll untangle it, love. I expect you're tired."

"You won't send Miss Thompson away, will you, Bella?"

What could she do? Lally was making encouraging progress, Doctor Frobisher said. One couldn't risk her having a relapse.

"Not if you insist."

"Oh, thank you, Bella. You're so good to me." Lally, with her swift changes of mood, suddenly began to titter. "After all, Mr. Raven has a weakness for women, hasn't he? Remember, he wanted to marry both of us."

Bella soberly studied her reflection in the mirror in her bedroom. Not even a crinoline concealed her condition now. She was as big as an elephant. It wasn't to be wondered at that Guy sought more attractive companionship. She would bide her time until the baby was born and she had got back her slim figure. Then that sneaking cat Clara Thompson would get her deserts.

At least Guy was staying at Ravenscroft, and even if it seemed much more likely that Miss Thompson, rather than his coming child, kept him there, Bella was infinitely glad to have him. The fear that hung over her like a shadow, growing a little darker with each falling rose and yellowing leaf remained in control while he was near. But one day he would laugh at her fancies and go back to London and it would be winter, and Aunt Aggie and Noah would be free.

It must be her condition that made her so easy a prey to her imagination. She had faced things blithely enough before. It was the long dull days of waiting. She hated inactivity and the harmless indoor pursuits with which ladies passed their time bored her to distraction. Letter writing—she had no one to write to. Embroidery—she hadn't the patience for it, nor for sewing the minute garments for her baby. Lally, when she was in one of her good moods, and Norah, were so much better at the cross stitching and the tiny embroidered flowers on bibs and bonnets. Pressing flowers in an album or painting in water-colours she regarded as quite useless occupations. There really seemed to be nothing to do except sit at the window and watch the autumn mists turning the air smoky blue beneath the trees in the park, and count the leaves falling.

Besides, from this vantage point, she could see Guy when he rode back from some activity of his own. He was perfectly polite to her nowadays, they hadn't quarrelled for a long time, but he never told her where he was going or what he was doing. There was no more news of the treacherous Molly in London, poor Molly who had come to a bad end. That sharp short scandal had blown over and Guy's name, mercifully, was no longer in the newspapers. Indeed, the last few weeks had been remarkably peaceful with Guy as courteous to her as if she were a visiting cousin or the sister of a friend, and Lally improving encouragingly.

But it was a spurious peace. For Miss Thompson, for all her appearance of being constantly attentive to Lally, watched the window, too, and more often than not happened to be crossing the hall, or just about to go upstairs, when Guy came in. Or she would shiver at dinner because she had left her shawl in the drawing-room, and Guy would fetch it, draping it over her white shoulders. Bella's self-control was strained to breaking point. For Lally's sake she somehow kept her temper. Also, she knew it would be a weakness to have Miss Thompson dismissed from jealousy. It would only accentuate all those stories about her husband's vulnerability for women. Miss Thompson must be found out in some other misdemeanour.

But all her wisdom was discarded the day she heard Mrs. Walter and Miss Thompson whispering together.

They must have thought she was still in the morning-room with Lally. They wouldn't know that she had grown so intolerably restless she had to walk about the house, since the early mist had turned to drizzle and it was too wet to stroll in the garden. She had crossed the ballroom, and wandered through the orangery, and was about to enter the drawing-room when she heard the low voices.

"You'd better be careful, my girl. Don't lose your head." That was Mrs. Walter, brusque and unsentimental. Mrs. Walter had never been over-friendly with Miss Thompson, probably because she resented her superiority.

"I'm not losing my head."

"What makes you think he'll fall in love with you? He's as cold and calculating as the devil."

"He wasn't always, I'm told."

"You're thinking of his first wife. That's why he's as he is now. I don't see why you think you can change him if his new wife can't."

"Her!" Miss Thompson gave an intolerable snicker. "You know *her* story. Naturally he wouldn't love her."

"No, nor anyone else. Not even his lights of love."

"I have no intention of being his light of love."

There was a hiss of indrawn breath.

"Save us, you wouldn't—"

Miss Thompson gave a little trill of laughter. The blood bursting in her head, Bella flung open the door. There was a whisk of skirts as Mrs. Walter moved swiftly to gather up fallen rose petals from a polished table, muttering something about careless maids. Miss Thompson didn't move. She lifted her little pointed chin and looked inquiringly at Bella.

"Oh dear, is Miss Eulalie needing me? I'm so sorry, I'll go at once."

She had gone, composedly, before Bella could speak. She seemed quite unashamed, almost glad that Bella might have overheard that outrageous conversation.

"Mrs. Walter," Bella said icily, "I don't approve of servants gossiping."

She had never seen Mrs. Walter in any state but her prim docile one. Even now, after the briefest flicker of fury in her eyes, she had herself in hand, and said quietly, "If you're referring to me and Miss Thompson, madam, we weren't gossiping. I was merely attempting to give Miss Thompson some advice on a foolish attachment she has formed."

Was the woman being insolent? It didn't seem so, but how could one read beneath her servility?

"Miss Thompson's moral life doesn't come within your duties, Mrs. Walter. I'd advise you to get on with your legitimate tasks. You may go."

After that it was a matter of waiting until the evening when Guy came in. She could have ordered Miss Thompson to pack her bags and be out of the house before Guy returned. She was pretty certain if she did that the woman would find some means of communicating with him, and making herself out to be the injured innocent. No, she must somehow provoke Miss Thompson into admitting her ambitious plan to Guy himself.

What would she say? "I think Miss Thompson is planning to run off with you, my love. . ." "I think Miss Thompson is waiting for me to die in childbirth. . ."

At least the dinner-table conversation would be enlivened tonight, she thought grimly. No more inventing polite comments to break the long silences. No more pretending she found Miss Thompson's replies interesting.

The afternoon must be spent preparing Lally for the shock of Miss Thompson's departure.

It was true that Lally was so much better she didn't require constant supervision. But by some freak of fate a storm blew up that afternoon and Lally hated storms. The wild wind and the sudden showers of leaves and the black clouds bringing dusk far too early filled the house with uneasiness. Doors banged and curtains billowed. A great cloud of smoke and soot came down the chimney in the morning-room, so they had to retire to the drawing-room where a fresh fire was lit. But the lamps were not enough to brighten the long room, and Lally, crouched over the fire, abruptly reverted to one of her worst moods.

174

"It's going to snow, Bella. Where will you hide the baby?"

"Lally dearest, the baby hasn't come yet."

"But it has! I saw it in the cradle. It was so tiny . . ." Lally began to walk about the room in distress, as if she no longer recognized her surroundings. Then suddenly, with her nose pressed against the window, she cried loudly, "Bella, there's Noah! Look! Over there under the copper beech!"

Bella flew to the window, unable to stop herself. Sure enough, in the premature dusk, she could make out a figure under the great spreading beech tree. For a moment it looked a wild sinister figure, wearing a cloak billowing in the breeze. But almost immediately she burst out laughing, saying that it was Joseph sheltering from a shower, a sack wrapped round his cowering shoulders.

At that moment Miss Thompson came in, and Lally exclaimed in exactly Bella's tone of asperity, "Don't be silly, Bella. He intends you to think he's Joseph. But he's Noah. Isn't he, Miss Thompson?"

"No!" cried Miss Thompson, her hand at her throat.

Bella looked at her curiously.

"Do you know Noah, too?"

"No, no, of course I don't. It's only that Miss Eulalie's talked so much about him. I felt startled——"

She was startled enough for the colour to have left her face. But she recovered quickly when she saw that the sheltering figure was indeed Joseph.

"I was foolish. It couldn't have been the terrible Noah. Come, Miss Eulalie——"

"I think you'd better take her to her room," said Bella. "Give her some of her sedative. The storm's upset her."

"Yes, Mrs. Raven. I will, at once. But what about you, Mrs. Raven?"

All at once, she seemed very anxious to please. But no doubt she was thinking of the episode that morning, not of the fright she had just had. . .

The wind was still battering against the walls when they sat down to dinner, the three of them. In spite of the well built house, somehow the draughts came in, and the candle flames in branching silver candlesticks flickered constantly. Miss Thompson, no doubt deliberately, was wearing her plainest gown, and for once looked dowdy and pale. She kept her eyes downcast, not responding even to Guy's attentiveness. There was no doubt she had had a fright. The last thing she would want would be to be dismissed.

So much for that, thought Bella, and opened her mouth to speak.

Her words were unrehearsed and surprised even herself.

"Don't worry Miss Thompson, Guy. She had a bad fright this afternoon. She thought she saw Noah on the lawn sheltering under the copper beech."

"Noah?" said Guy sharply, looking at Miss Thompson. "Do you know our archfiend, too? My wife and her sister constantly think they are being persecuted, by his ghost presumably, since he himself is still in prison. But I didn't know you subscribed to this fantasy."

"It's only that Miss Eulalie talks of him a great deal." Miss Thompson's voice was low and calm but she didn't look up and she was still very pale. "From her description of him, I hope never to set eyes on him."

"Oh, he's quite a good-looking fellow in his way," Guy said easily. "I can imagine some women admiring that black visage."

"Not Miss Thompson," said Bella. "She admires an entirely different type of man. Don't you, Miss Thompson?"

She hardly knew what response to expect from that remark, certainly not the quick intimate glance that passed between Miss Thompson and Guy. For a moment it was as if she were not there. Or did they think her blind? Couldn't she interpret the adoring light in that shameless creature's eyes, and the tenderness—a tenderness he had never shown to her—in her husband's?

In the next moment they were both looking at her, two pairs of eyes, polite, disinterested, as if she were no more than a shadow and deserved as little notice.

"What were you about to say, my love?" Guy inquired courteously.

The sheer blatancy of it was beyond endurance. Bella was on her feet and hardly knowing what she did, leaned forward to snatch a candle from the candlestick.

"I wouldn't dream of boring you with my trivial remarks. Continue your conversation with Miss Thompson. She knows a better and quicker way to ruin your career than I ever did. I am going upstairs."

"Bella—"

The intimate shortened version of her name caught her ear as she flung round to go. She couldn't help turning back, and it was then that the candle, held in her violently trembling hand, caught the ruffled lace of her gown. She screamed as the hot flame scorched her face. A violent pain shot through her body. She seemed to be consumed with fire. She was aware of falling, then of being held tightly, swaddled in something, and the room going dark.

When it grew light again there seemed to be a great many faces bending over her. She could hear Guy's voice from a long way off, "Not burnt, thank God! We got the flames out in time. But the doctor had better be sent for."

Bella tried to speak. She wanted to say that she must be burnt badly, otherwise why should this pain be wrenching her. She saw Miss Thompson's pale face bending too close, the black eyes full of triumph. Miss Thompson would have liked to see her burnt to charred ash. Even the baby— Oh, it was the baby giving her the pain. . .

Someone was lifting her. She could smell scorched clothing, and through that the faint pleasant eau de cologne her husband used. She had so longed to be held like this in his arms, and now it was spoilt by the pain and her faintness and shock. Everything was always spoilt . . .

She must have fainted again, for somehow she was in bed and the lamp lit at her side. Now it was Mrs. Walter's face bending over her, and beyond it Norah's frightened one.

"Don't leave her—with him," she muttered.

"Who, madam? Who are you talking about?"

She shuddered as a new wave of pain poured over her. She was gripping something. A hand. Guy's hand. It must be, for now his face was there, shadowed, grim. Her enemy. Why had he smothered the flames when he like Miss Thompson must hope that she would die? He had sworn to her that he would never love again, that dead Caroline had his heart for ever. But that was before he had known how susceptible he could be to black cherry eyes and a secret smile.

Poor Guy, she suddenly thought. It wasn't his fault that she and Lally were round his neck like millstones. She must summon up enough magnanimity to set him free. Now, before she died . . .

"I shall do—exactly the same again—if you look at her like you did." Again her words bore no relation to her intentions. But she doubted if he had heard. His face remained there, just as lined and grim. Suddenly she remembered how he had looked at her the night she had asked him to marry her instead of Lally. He had wondered then if he could find her desirable. But there had been too much to overcome, his dead love, his feeling of being trapped, his resentment. Even the baby was an accident, a mistake he was determined not to repeat. Now there was nothing between them but their gripped hands, wet with perspiration.

"Are you always going to hate me? Will you never have any regard for me?" Her words were cut off by the pain, inexorable now, beyond bearing. The light faded. She was dimly conscious of a flurry of movement. Her clinging fingers were wrenched open and left empty. Someone far away said, "Of course I have regard for you."

Or did she imagine that?

"Now, Mrs. Raven, grip this. Scream as loud as you like. The little one's chosen a fine stormy night. There now. Thank you, Mrs. Walter. Oh, shock, certainly. For once all those fiddling faddling clothes women wear were a blessing. There seem to be no burns. And your prompt action, Mr. Raven. I think you'd better leave us now. Mrs. Walter and I—"

"No!" shrieked Bella. "Don't let her touch my baby!"

"Decidedly shock," came Doctor Frobisher's voice from far far away. "Pity. Unfortunate. Now, my dear . . ."

19

OH DEAR, MADAM, YOU SCREAMED and said I wasn't to touch your baby!" Mrs. Walter, fussing by the bedside, was almost human, her long face creased in the beginnings of a benevolent smile.

Bella stirred sleepily, reluctant to come back from oblivion. Then a little pang of pleasure struck her as she remembered the snuffling, whimpering bundle that had been laid in her arms, and the blissful end of pain.

"My baby—"

"The sweetest little girl, madam."

"I promised him a boy. I always disappoint—" She stopped abruptly, on guard again.

"If you mean the master, madam, he's ever so pleased with his little daughter."

My husband has very good manners, Bella thought. Except when he forgets me altogether and gazes across the candlelight into another pair of eyes . . .

"I'll tell the nurse you're awake, madam."

"Nurse?"

"Oh dear, yes, Doctor Frobisher sent for one in a great hurry. You gave us all a fright, madam. But all's well that ends well."

Bella looked into Mrs. Walter's familiar dour face, unreadable as always, although it did seem that the woman had been moved to a little warmth by the arrival of the baby.

"And by the way, madam, if I may say something."

"Go on, Mrs. Walter."

"I think you misunderstood what you overheard between me and Miss Thompson yesterday. She's a designing creature, but the gentleman she's interested in is a stranger to you. Begging your pardon for taking this liberty, madam—"

Could she have heard wrongly? Could her suspicions have put imaginary words in Miss Thompson's mouth? Bella longed to believe Mrs. Walter. And really the overheard conversation, and the exchanged glances over the dinner-table last night seemed an awfully long time ago, divided forever by the world of pain and darkness she had since gone through. Just now, the baby, her little daughter, was the only reality.

"We won't discuss the matter, Mrs. Walter. Ask the nurse to bring me my baby. And is Mr. Raven in?"

"He went out riding, madam. I don't think he's back."

But he had seen her immediately after the baby's birth. She remembered him standing at her bedside just before exhaustion overcame her and she slept. It wasn't to be expected that he would linger indoors until she woke again. Nor should she imagine that he would be thinking too bitterly that the wrong people died in childbirth, the wrong ones lived . . .

She hoped the nurse, with her kind strange face, would think her tears were from joy as the baby was put in her arms.

"Has my sister seen the baby?" she asked.

"Only for a minute, Mrs. Raven. It was done to calm her. She was very upset last night. She kept saying it was snowing, I don't know why, because the storm had died down long since. But seeing the baby seemed to quieten her, poor soul."

"Bring her in now," said Bella.

"Oh, but, Mrs. Raven, the doctor said—"

"Never mind the doctor. I can see my own sister, surely."

Lally came in hesitantly, her huge eyes dominating her

little so-white face. But when she saw Bella lying with the small bundle in her arms her uncertainty left her and she flew to the bedside.

"Oh, Bella, it's alive."

"Of course it's alive. What did you think?"

"It's a girl. Does Mr. Raven mind?"

"Of course he doesn't mind. To tell the truth he was only concerned that I was all right."

Lally's eyes were shining. "Then he really does love you?"

Bella's arm tightened round the baby.

"A man always loves the mother of his child. It's only natural."

"I suppose so," said Lally humbly. "Bella—couldn't we take off the shawl and look at her properly."

"To see if she has the right number of fingers and toes?" Bella laughed but she was just as curious as Lally. Together they unwound the swaddled clothing to expose the pink crumpled face and the tiny new hands and feet.

"I think she's like Papa," Lally said.

Bella traced the shadow of honey-coloured eyebrows.

"Her eyes are blue. She's like her father."

"Is she? Oh, imagine—"

"Imagine what?"

"Why, she'll have all the things we never had. Carriages and jewels and balls. She's born to it. Isn't it strange. If we'd never met Aunt Aggie, we'd never be here now with this sweetest little treasure."

The baby stirred against her, and Bella gave a little half sob. It was perfectly true what Lally said, the baby was a tiny precarious blessing, snatched from disaster.

Lally's apprehension was never far away.

"Bella, we must guard her. Aunt Aggie and Noah mustn't find out about her."

"Hush, Lally! None of that talk!" To banish the shadow from Lally's eyes Bella went on quickly, "I've already decided her name."

"Oh, yes! What is it?"

"After Mamma, of course. Kate. Kate Eulalie."

Lally clasped her hands ecstatically.

"After me, too?"

"Yes. And I think Henrietta for a third name, because Cousin Henrietta was kind."

"Does Mr. Raven agree?"

180

"It's my right to chose my daughter's name. If it had been a son, it would be different."

"She's just ours," Lally crooned.

"Well," came Guy's voice from the door. "Baby worship already, I see."

The two heads, Lally's fair one and Bella's dark one, sprang apart.

"Oh, Mr. Raven, Bella has named the baby. Kate Eulalie! You did say that, Bella, didn't you? The baby was to be named after me?" Guy's presence had disturbed Lally and already she was fluttering and uncertain, fearful.

"Yes, I did say it, Lally," Bella answered.

"I think Miss Thompson is looking for you," said Guy to Lally.

"Oh dear, is she? I must go." But Lally's nervousness was overcome by her longing. She darted back to the bedside, her face avid. "Bella, can I hold the baby? Just for a minute?"

"Of course you can." Bella began to lift the baby, but Guy's hand on Lally's shoulder made her stiffen and gasp.

"No," he said.

"Oh, Guy—"

Bella's protest was too late, for Lally's vulnerable face had crumpled into desolation. She ran out of the room, crying.

"Did you need to do that?" Bella exclaimed. "She wouldn't have hurt the baby."

"She might have crushed it. Smothered it. She's unbalanced. Good heavens, don't you know it already?"

Bella tried not to think of Lally's face, avid with longing, her hungry hands. "She wouldn't have done anything while we watched."

"How can you tell? Mad people act in a moment."

"Mad?" Bella's voice faltered. "But she's so much better."

"Not if she still sees Noah in the garden."

"That was Joseph. It was an understandable mistake. Miss Thompson was mistaken, as well."

"How could Miss Thompson be mistaken when she's never seen Noah in her life?"

"She could be frightened on seeing him for the first time, couldn't she? I was, and so was Lally. Miss Thompson certainly looked frightened. And while we're on the subject of Miss Thompson, she'll have to go."

"Oh! Why?"

"I don't trust her," said Bella briefly.

"You don't trust her! But, my dear child, don't you see

how good she's been for your sister? The improvement you mention is entirely due to Miss Thompson."

"Then Lally must go on improving without her. And don't ask me to explain the reason for my not trusting her."

"If you're referring to that ridiculous scene you made at dinner last night, I think the less said about it the better."

Bella looked at the stranger with the glittering eyes standing at the foot of the bed. She tried to speak calmly, and could not.

"Do you think I will sit meekly while you make sheep's eyes at that woman? You're my husband—no matter what the circumstances, you're my husband. I simply won't endure it. And the woman has ambitions, you don't know what ambitions. I overheard her and Mrs. Walter talking. Mrs. Walter tries to excuse Miss Thompson now, but I know better. She must go."

"No!"

The baby, perhaps even at such a tender age sensing its mother's distress, began to wail. Bella clucked at it distractedly. She longed for the peace of a few minutes ago when she and Lally had pored over their miraculous treasure. But there would never be peace when Guy Raven was near, nor could she give her full attention to anyone else, even her newborn child.

"She shall stay for exactly as long as she's needed," Guy went on. "I understand you want Norah to be the child's nurse. So who does that leave to watch your sister? Tottie, perhaps? And how do you know what moment Eulalie will pick the baby up and love it to death?"

"Oh, Guy! You make her sound like a monster!"

"And so she could be, all unwittingly. Miss Thompson understands. I'm afraid you'll have to be grateful to Miss Thompson, whatever confused interpretation you put on her actions."

Bella blinked rapidly. She wasn't going to have her tears mingle with the baby's. She would never admit the good sense of Guy's argument. It was too high a price to pay for sense. And yet—if anything happened to little Kate, if Lally's obsessive love or her instinct for over-protecting, harmed the baby, she would have to blame her own selfishness for the rest of her life.

Beneath the blankets, she ran her hand over her flattened stomach. In a few days she would get up, she would be able to wear her prettier dresses, no longer hampered by pregnancy she could match Clara Thompson any day.

"You only want to keep her here," she muttered.

"I make no secret of that. The child is mine, too. I would remind you. She has my eyes."

"You'd noticed that?" Bella said involuntarily.

"They're certainly not yours. She's no little wildcat."

"Me?"

"Last night, without a doubt."

He was speaking with amusement now, and almost with gentleness, because he had got his own way. Miss Thompson would still move softly about the house, turning up miraculously at the right place to have a whispered conversation, exchange an intimate glance, call "Good night" in her low caressing voice.

It was outrageous and unendurable. It was marriage. That was what Cousin Henrietta would say.

"You don't mind that she isn't a boy?"

"That was an unavoidable mistake. Perhaps not a mistake." He put his finger beneath the baby's chin. "She's very sweet. I have something for you."

He took from his pocket a small morocco box and opened it. The diamonds blazed and sparkled.

"Ear-rings to match your necklace," he said in his formal voice. "I had the design copied exactly."

"They're for me!" Bella couldn't keep the pleasure out of her voice.

He smiled. "I thought you didn't care for diamonds."

"These are different."

"I defy you to recognize the technical difference."

"Oh, technical—what is that?" Bella's fingers lingered over the gems. She knew that they were the conventional gift of a rich husband to his wife after she had borne him a child, but there was still that vital difference between them and the necklace. They were entirely hers. In years to come they would be labelled "Isabella Raven's ear-rings, given to her by her husband on the occasion of the birth of their first child." Nothing could alter that. Caroline's shadowy fingers were not on these. Nor would Clara Thompson's or any other woman's be. They were uniquely hers. They didn't represent wealth or opulence, but a small bright moment of happiness. Hers alone.

"Do you like the baby, Tottie?"

Tottie nodded violently, her rosy face one broad, delighted smile.

"You will help Norah to care for her, won't you? She has to be cared for very well. You'll come to me at once if you ever see anything that worries you, won't you?"

Involuntarily Tottie glanced out of the window. Bella followed her glance, reading her thoughts. The November mists had begun and it grew dark far too early. It would be very easy for anyone to lurk in the garden unseen. Soon it would be December, and if Lally thought she saw Noah, Bella could no longer reassure her by insisting that he was safely behind bars.

Little Kate had been borne into a world of obscure menace. She was surrounded by adoring servants, even to old Broome who hopefully waggled his long white moustache for her, young Norah was proving a gifted nurse and Joseph would have stood on his head for "the babby" if she would smile for him. Tottie liked nothing better than to be allowed to rock the cradle, even Mrs. Walter was not above a little baby talk.

Yet Bella could never completely relax. Guy's orders that Lally was never to be left alone with the baby seemed justified, for although mostly she was touchingly gentle and loving, she had a few wild moments when she was convinced Kate was that other frail infant whose life had flickered out so quickly, and she would cry that Kate must be hidden before Noah came up with the coffin. Any sudden footstep would throw her into that nightmare, and Miss Thompson would hurry her from the nursery and lock her in her own room until the mood passed.

This was a danger that could be controlled. The other one, the one Guy scarcely listened to or recognized, existed in the foggy garden, the dark evenings, the creepers that gave access to windows for some strong agile climber. Noah and Aunt Aggie had a debt to be satisfied. They would be content with nothing less than Guy's ruin, and her own lasting hurt.

Perhaps she had caught something of Lally's haunted imagination, but Bella was convinced little Kate would be their target.

With Lally's health ruined, her own happiness shattered and Guy without a career or a reputation, perhaps they would be satisfied.

Those things must never be allowed to happen.

Bella begged Guy to go back to London. She felt safer in the Knightsbridge house. The noisy bustle of the great city, the cabs and the drays and barrows, the shouting newsboys and vendors of other wares, the chattering, screaming, vociferous populace drowned other sounds. She wouldn't start at the rustle of a leaf blown against the window, the bark of a dog or even the innocent melancholy hooting of the white owls.

Guy laughed at her fears.

"I had never imagined you to be the nervous type. I thought you left that to your sister. London is no place for a young baby, especially in the winter. The air is almost unbreathable. We shall stay here over Christmas. Besides, didn't I tell you, Cousin Henrietta is coming."

"Cousin Henrietta!" Bella was pleased. "No, you didn't tell me. You tell me nothing."

"I'm sorry. The letter only arrived this morning. She wants to attend the christening. I believe she made us this promise before the baby was ever thought of."

"The baby was never thought of," Bella said coldly. "Cousin Henrietta has a better memory than you."

His face darkened. She knew that he hated to be reminded of that night, the disastrous visit to the opera, and then she, unexpected and shameless, in her nightgown. He had meant to punish her forever for being his wife, and had never meant to be trapped, seduced by his own wife! No wonder the memory rankled. His pride was so enormous and so stupid. There would be successors to Miss Thompson, she supposed wearily. She clenched her hands, feeling utterly defeated. And yet she was sure he already loved the baby.

"And your mother?" she went on, making her voice cool and polite.

"My mother doesn't care to travel in the cold weather."

"Is she *never* going to see her grandchild?" Bella burst out. "Really, as a stubborn stiff-necked family, you must have no equal. I tremble to think what my daughter has inherited."

"My temper and yours, my love," Guy said. He seemed suddenly cheerful. "I agree that she's to be pitied. I expect London will rock with scandals in about seventeen years' time. But you'll be tolerably used to them by then, I daresay. In the meantime, shall we plan Kate's christening for Christmas day? And it's customary to have a servants' party in the evening. I'd like you to arrange that. Cousin Henrietta

185

will help. Well—will all that keep your mind off the melancholy country?"

"I'd be happier if we were in London," Bella said stubbornly.

"Oh, forget this melodramatic nonsense. The Proudfoots will have too much sense not to keep well away from us in future."

"What about Molly?"

"Molly's digging her own grave."

"But you said—you thought her intimidated by somebody."

Guy frowned. "That all led to nothing, as you know. It's best forgotten."

"Forgotten! With your character deliberately blackened!"

He shrugged.

"What has happened has happened. Be content with things as they are. You probe too much. It isn't feminine."

As always, he had sparked her inflammable temper.

"But you don't want me to be feminine, do you? You give me diamonds as a polite thank you for Kate, and imagine that matter is finished, too. Don't I begin to look presentable again?"

She stood up, holding herself proudly. She knew her dress becoming, and her waist very slim. He could, if he would, put his arms round her now, pull her to him, kiss her until her lips bruised, tell her that all the hating was a lie.

A tap sounded on the door and Miss Thompson came in.

"Oh, I'm sorry," she exclaimed, in pretty confusion. "I thought you were alone, Mrs. Raven."

Guy's hand dropped to his side. It had been reached towards her, Bella could swear. She was cold with anger. She was quite certain Miss Thompson had been listening at the door.

"Perhaps it would be wise to wait until you're bidden to come in, Miss Thompson. If the matter isn't urgent I'll attend to it later."

"No, no, attend to it now, my love," Guy said easily. "I'm off to the stables, anyway. Besides, Miss Thompson doesn't worry you about unimportant matters."

No, thought Bella furiously. She didn't. She would regard the possibility of Bella being in her husband's arms as very important indeed.

20

days before Christmas. It was astonishing how one dumpy dowdy old lady could make the house spring to life, but this was so from the moment she stood among her usual mountain of boxes and bags in the hall.

"Bella, my dear!" She was muffled in a heavy cloak topped by a shawl, her bonnet was pushed awry, her weatherbeaten face sallow and lined from the cold and fatigue of the long journey. But her familiar grating voice was full of warmth. She was suddenly an old and dear friend. "You're looking extraordinarily pretty," she said, eyeing Bella up and down. "Didn't I say maternity would suit you? I'm sure Guy agrees. Now where's the baby? I must see her immediately."

Norah was sent to bring in Kate who was sleep-flushed and adorable. She was put in Cousin Henrietta's arms and the two surveyed one another, with the greatest interest. Finally little Kate's rosebud mouth twitched in one of her early tentative smiles and Cousin Henrietta exclaimed triumphantly, "We approve of one another. How very excellent. Has her grandmother seen her?"

Bella shook her head.

"The old fool. She must be gnashing her teeth. Well, when is the christening, and how are we celebrating Christmas? Have you worn all those extravagant clothes? No, I suppose you haven't, pregnant and buried in the country. Never mind, the opportunities will come. Guy says your sister has gone out of her senses. Poor child, it will pass. The thing is to keep occupied. Take me, I'm never idle for a moment. I can't do much outdoors—it's going to snow, mark my words, the sky's grey goose feathers from here to the Hebrides—but there's plenty to be done making the house look festive. The tree must go in the ballroom. And we shall need holly, fir branches, ribbons—have you plenty of ribbons? Candles? I shall want a strong lad to come with me to cut the holly . . ."

The shadows receded while Cousin Henrietta was there. The house was filled with bustle and gaiety. Even Lally was infected with the general light-heartedness and for the first time since the beginning of her illness was persuaded to go with Bella and Miss Thompson to the village to do Christmas shopping. She refused to go into Mrs. Bunt's to drink hot chocolate against the cold, but she succeeded in making intelligent choices for her gifts, and never once complained that she was being stared at.

At little Kate's christening, too, she looked animated and happy, her childish face framed by her blue velvet bonnet quite adorable. Indeed, it compared more than favourably with Miss Thompson's, for lately Miss Thompson had lost her colour and looked particularly pinched and cold as she stood in the small semicircle listening to the baby being formally named. Bella was almost sorry for her. Being an unloved wife was not an enviable state, but perhaps loving a married man was even less so. For Miss Thompson had no longer that barely-concealed audacity and triumph. For the most part her eyes were downcast, but once she cast a look toward Guy and Bella thought that it looked unhappy and despairing.

For her own part, she took deep pleasure in holding this small creature with the honey-coloured eyebrows who was her daughter. If there was to be nothing else for her, she could make herself content with her baby. Nevertheless, the old uncontrollable excitement was stirring in her again. Would she never stop being optimistic? Just because her husband stood at her side in church, and seemed not to notice Miss Thompson's unhappy glance, did that make him a loving husband, and Miss Thompson a harmless enemy?

As they came out of the church Bella saw that the threatened snow was beginning at last. So far there was only a frosty rime of it on the grass, but the flakes were growing thicker and the wind rising. Bella bundled Cousin Henrietta, who was carrying the baby, into the carriage immediately, and Lally after her. Guy had already announced his intention of walking, leaving the women the carriage. But Miss Thompson seemed to be missing. Bella looked for her impatiently among the little crowd of spectators, then saw her hurrying round the side of the church. In her haste she tripped on a grass-obscured gravestone and almost fell. The shock took the remaining colour out of her face and she was quite white as she approached.

"Am I keeping you, Mrs. Raven? I'm so sorry. I took a short walk, I felt a little faint." Her voice was breathless, as if she hadn't yet recovered. And her eyelids were slightly reddened, whether from tears or the biting wind, Bella couldn't decide. However, she climbed in the carriage without more ado, although, the foolish creature, she couldn't resist a backward and plainly appealing glance at Guy. Bella found herself feeling a new and unwanted emotion for the woman—pity. If she had realized the ordeal it would be for Miss Thompson to watch Guy's child christened she would not have allowed her to come.

But what else could she have expected but pain when she allowed herself to become involved with a married man? She had most deliberately and shamelessly set out to fascinate him. Bella suddenly wondered what Guy's expression was as he stood watching the carriage leave, and she lost her pity for Miss Thompson, huddled in her pretty green cloak. She was too afraid that Guy's face might have been just as despairing.

Back in the house Cousin Henrietta said bluntly, "Get rid of that woman."

"Miss Thompson?"

"Who else? She's sly and scheming."

"I know. I haven't been blind. I've wanted to dismiss her but Guy won't allow it. He says she's too important for Lally."

"She's too important for him, if you ask me. Haven't you learned to manage him yet?"

"I've tried. I always lose my temper."

"If he must have intrigues, he should keep them out of his home. A clever woman—" Cousin Henrietta had to stop as Bella interrupted her heatedly.

"What can you expect from such an extraordinary marriage as ours? Guy has protected Lally and me most honourably and unselfishly. He could have had Lally sent away. What other man wouldn't have? But he allowed her to remain here so long and she was adequately watched—poor Lally! He hasn't refused anything we have wanted. I was quite wickedly extravagant over—some furnishings, and he said hardly a word. He has hated bitterly my being here in Caroline's place. How must he have felt today in the church with my child, instead of hers? Imagine! If he felt it easier to look at Miss Thompson to whom he isn't forever tied, then I don't blame him. And yet you speak as if by being clever I can solve all these things. I can only be as I am, and mostly that's angry and bad-tempered and jealous. I've tried to be meek and patient and bide my time. Some day, I tell myself, he must see me without all that horrid resentment. But will he ever, Cousin Henrietta? Will he ever?"

"Bless me," said Cousin Henrietta, "you love him."

"From the beginning," Bella admitted.

"Then I am a foolish old woman, and perhaps you are doing very well."

"I get frightened," Bella said, with shame. "Not just of Miss Thompson, but of other things. I get like Lally, I'm afraid all this will disappear like a dream, my husband, my beautiful home, little Kate."

Cousin Henrietta gave her a hoot of derision.

"Now what? Do you think that evil couple can still do you harm? Has the country no laws?"

Involuntarily Bella looked out of the window at the darkening day and the falling snow. She couldn't rid herself of the feeling that the snow was a bad omen.

"They're still trying to revenge themselves on Guy, I'm sure. There was Molly—"

"Nonsense, Molly simply wanted to go back on the streets. Some women, once begun on that life, can never stop. They resent help."

"You mean she resented Guy for bringing her here to live respectably?"

"And that foolish idealist, Doctor Bushey, with his head in the clouds."

This was a view that had never occurred to Bella. She suddenly felt much happier.

"It wasn't true what they said of Guy in the newspapers. That was more wicked slander. Do newspapers never stop hating once they begin?"

"If it makes a good story, they'll malign their own mother," Cousin Henrietta said briskly. "That's a sad fact, but I'm sure I'm not going to let it trouble me on Christmas Eve. Are you?"

Bella jumped up, thinking that she would wear her sapphire-coloured velvet and her new ear-rings. Let Miss Thompson feast her eyes on those.

"Certainly not, Cousin Henrietta."

"You're thinking some malice, I can see. Splendid! We shall have a fine party."

Tottie had laid out the sapphire velvet, as she had been told, with Bella's satin slippers and white silk stockings, her gloves, her lace fan, her silver mesh reticule, and her six crisp white petticoats. But when Bella rang for Tottie to come and help her dress, the girl was slow in answering the bell, and then seemed extraordinarily jumpy and nervous.

"Whatever's the matter?" Bella asked impatiently, as her hair was tugged for the tenth time. "Surely you're not scared of the party tonight, Tottie? You couldn't be scared? With everyone here being your friends?"

Tottie's small bright alarmed eyes stared back at her. She moved her lips, desperately trying to say something. Nothing but the familiar unintelligible grunts came forth, but Tottie had never seemed so angry and frustrated with her lack of speech. She kept glancing towards the windows, although the curtains were drawn, and the bedroom, with its glowing fire and lamplight, very cosy.

"Oh, I know," Bella exclaimed. "You're like Lally, you're afraid of the snow. It reminds you of Aunt Aggie's and that terrible cellar where you lived, poor child. It's a wonder you weren't frozen to death. But it isn't cold in this house, is it? So you don't need to be afraid of a little snow. There, that's better. You've done those curls beautifully." The glossy curls, tied with small velvet bows over her ears, and falling in two luxuriant bunches to her shoulders were a credit to Tottie's growing skill, and at last Tottie's stiff little face relaxed into a look of pride.

"Now just hook me into my dress, and then you must run off and get ready yourself. You're to put on your best dress, remember? And your lightest boots so you can dance. Don't look so alarmed, I'm sure Joseph is looking forward to teaching you the polka."

Tottie blushed furiously, and Bella, satisfied that she had banished the child's nervousness, told her to run along, but to send Lally in before she went up to the attics to change.

This injunction wasn't necessary, however, for at that moment Lally came bursting in unceremoniously. She was still in her day dress, and her hair was dishevelled, a sure indication that she was in one of her distressed states.

"Bella, where's Miss Thompson? Why doesn't she come to help me to dress? I've waited and waited." She darted to the window and flung back a curtain to peer out. "Is she lost in the snow?"

"Hasn't she been with you all afternoon?" Bella exclaimed.

"She was there at first." Lally looked uncertain. "Then she told me I must rest if I was to be up late tonight. I didn't want to rest, I wasn't in the least tired, but she was cross about it. She said 'Do as I tell you!' and then we both cried."

"Cried! Miss Thompson cried?"

"She told me not to be a baby, but there were tears in her eyes, and her nose was quite red. I said we were both babies, and she was cross again. She pushed me on to the bed and told me to behave myself and then she went out and I haven't seen her since."

Was that what Tottie had been trying to tell her, that Miss Thompson had gone out, and, like Molly, hadn't come back? Bella crushed down her sudden feeling of apprehension. She tugged back the curtains that Lally had pulled aside, unwilling to look out at the white night.

"Go back to your room, Lally. I'll come presently and help you dress. I expect Miss Thompson's in her own room lying down. Don't you remember, she wasn't feeling well in church this morning?"

"You'll come soon, Bella? You won't leave me all alone?" Like Tottie's, Lally's eyes were bright and alarmed. But fears chased themselves through Lally's head like mice. With the onset of snow, she would be particularly tense, which made it all the more remiss of Miss Thompson to neglect her. If the woman were ill, she should have told somebody.

But the strange thing was, Miss Thompson did not appear to be anywhere in the house. Bella tried not to think of Molly, as Mrs. Walter checked that Miss Thompson's cloak and outdoor boots were gone, but nothing else.

Then Norah reported that immediately after luncheon she had gone into the nursery to find Miss Thompson bending over the baby.

"I asked her what she was doing, ma'am, and she said the baby had been crying. But I didn't believe her. I couldn't, because the little angel was sound asleep."

"Did she say anything else?" Bella asked tensely.

"No, ma'am. Oh, yes, only that she thought she'd go for a walk because she had a headache. And then—" Norah stopped, hanging her head and looking embarrassed.

"Then what?" Bella insisted.

"Well, later, I saw her and the master going towards the yew walk."

Bella's heart jumped and was still.

"All right, Norah. That will be all. But stay with the baby. Don't leave her."

Norah bobbed and withdrew. Bella looked at Mrs. Walter whose long face was carefully expressionless.

"Is Mr. Raven in?"

"Yes, madam. He's in the library."

Guy was sitting at the table in the library, busily writing. He threw down his pen as Bella came in.

"Well, my love! You're very grand."

"Guy, Miss Thompson's disappeared! And you were out walking with her!"

Guy's eyes narrowed. "And what do you think I have done with her? Thrown her in the river? Strangled her?"

"Don't joke, please!"

"Then don't make statements with so much innuendo. If you must know, I walked to the top of the yew walk and back with Miss Thompson. We were both feeling in need of fresh air. Then we came in."

"Both of you?"

"Come, Isabella! I told you I didn't leave her unconscious in the snow."

Bella shivered irrepressibly. She couldn't get over the feeling that he hadn't been surprised by her news. He was too calm.

"Then where can she be? She's not in her room or apparently in the house."

"Are you sure?"

"As sure as anyone can be. Lally's been waiting this last half-hour to be dressed. She must be out because her cloak and boots are gone."

"Then she's gone into the village for something."

"In the snow? And without telling anyone? Did she say anything to you about her intentions?"

He began to frown. "I'm not her confidante, whatever you may think. If you must have those suspicions, keep them to yourself. And I'm sure there's no need to raise a hue and cry. Miss Thompson will be back. She's much too sensible—"

"To share Molly's fate?" Bella said swiftly.

"Exactly."

"Then you were thinking of the possibility of her being kidnapped."

"My dear Isabella, the way you feel about the lady, wouldn't you be glad if such a thing happened?" But for all his facetiousness he was behaving as Lally had done, going to the window to lift the curtain and peer out. "Is Kate all right?" he asked.

"Yes. I've told Norah not to leave her. Then you do think—you are afraid—"

He came towards her and quite unexpectedly lifted her hand and kissed it with a courtly gesture.

"You're looking very charming. Which reminds me, I must go and dress. I think Kate must share the party, since it's her first Christmas. Let's see if she has the party spirit, or simply sleeps like a mole."

The colour that had flown to Bella's cheeks at his kiss retreated.

"Then you do think she must be watched?"

"I merely think it a pity to keep Norah a prisoner upstairs for the entire evening."

"And Miss Thompson?"

"She must make her explanations when she turns up. We can't allow her to wreck our Christmas."

Nevertheless, Bella knew that Guy was disturbed. There was a curious glint in his eyes as if he felt some secret excitement. His sudden formal kiss, so uncharacteristic of him, had been meant to allay her suspicions.

But what suspicions? He had walked with Miss Thompson briefly and come home, for here he was to prove it. No one had seen Miss Thompson leave the house a second time, but a little later Broome discovered the orangery door open and the snow blowing in. The young trees would be killed, he fretted. How could anyone be so careless?

A young woman going to a secret assignation might be careless. But an assignation with whom?

Lally suddenly remembered that when she had woken from a nap she had heard someone saying, "No, no, no!" But then she wasn't sure that the voice hadn't been part of a dream. She enjoyed Bella helping her to dress, and for the first time for months took pleasure in what she wore.

"I do think this lilac silk becoming, don't you, Bella? I promise not to spill anything on it, or forget things. Miss Thompson says I'm not nearly so forgetful nowadays. It's so exciting to be going to a party. Will Mama and Papa be there? Oh, no, how could I forget? Dear Mamma's in heaven. There'll be only Papa."

A gust of wind struck the windows, the curtains billowed, and some snowflakes falling down the chimney hissed on the fire. Lally shivered violently.

"O-oh! A goose walked over my grave. Bella, where's the baby?"

"In the nursery with Norah. She's coming to the party."

"Little Kate?" Lally clapped her hands with pleasure. "How perfectly sweet. She'll see the Christmas tree, and the candles lighted."

"She'll sleep in her cradle."

"Then I shan't stir an inch from it. Not an inch."

As Lally happily prattled, Bella had a curious little memory of Miss Thompson hurrying round the church that morning, very white, and more than a little distracted. She was sure now that the woman hadn't been feeling faint, but had been meeting someone. Whom?

Cousin Henrietta, who was most grandly attired in black velvet with a great deal of beautiful old lace, completely agreed with Guy that that tiresome young woman shouldn't be allowed to spoil the party. She pooh-poohed Bella's suggestion that Miss Thompson might have been forcibly persuaded to go on some journey with the comment that no one could force such a strong-minded person to do anything against her will.

"We'll do very nicely without her. I think Eulalie long past the need for a nurse. The girl grows better every day. Of course she's a little forgetful, but no more than I am, I assure you. I shall take her under my wing this evening, so you have no need to fret. Mind you," her old eyes twinkled wickedly, "I shall be as interested as the rest of you in the young woman's story when she returns. You can warn her to see that it's a good one."

"Cousin Henrietta, supposing she doesn't come back?"

"Eh?" For an infinitesimal moment the old lady's eyes flickered. Then she said loudly and enjoyably, "Then good riddance! You shall have your desire and believe it or not, I think Guy would be relieved, too."

Bella found that supposition impossible to believe, for Guy, dressed in evening clothes, was suddenly full of a heartiness she had never seen him display before, and which was quite false. She began to wonder if he knew all the time where Miss Thompson was, and was planning to meet her later. Then reason told her that he was assuming jollity for the sake of the servants. They mustn't suspect that there was any significance to Miss Thompson's absence. The party must go on.

The tree, with all its candles lit, sparkled very prettily. The servants, awkward and self-conscious in their best clothes, took a little thawing, but with the help of steaming rum punch, the music of the two young men engaged to play the piano and the violin, and Cousin Henrietta's raucous leading of Christmas carols, their constraint soon broke down. Baby Kate woke once and waved an uncertain fist at the lights and the people, then slept again, with Lally her devoted guardian. Guy danced a sober polka with Mrs. Walter, then a spirited one with Norah. After that he danced dutifully with each maid in turn, even Tottie who stumbled unhappily, and refused to lose her look of apprehension. But now she was probably only worrying about treading on the master's toe.

And all the time Bella expected the door to be flung open and Miss Thompson to appear, making a calculated dramatic entry, beautiful and aggressive and insolent in her most fetching gown. Or would she stumble in through the orangery door, covered in snow, frozen and exhausted from whatever mysterious errand she had been on. In spite of the noise and merriment, Bella kept thinking of the rest of the house, dark and silent. She kept thinking of the snow brushed away and a face pressed against a window. It was morbid imagining. She quickly drank more of the hot punch, hoping to catch the mood of gaiety. She remembered suddenly the champagne she had drunk on her wedding night, and how melancholy it had made her feel. This was only a servant's party, but it was the first she had shared with her husband as master and mistress. She should be gay. Even Lally had lost her apprehensiveness. Only Tottie and herself were haunted by the shadows. That wretched Miss Thompson! It would be better if she were here shamelessly flirting with Guy. Bella was used to that situation. It was much better than the curious image she had of a bedraggled desperate creature out in the snow.

"I think you need another drink, my love," came Guy's voice. He handed her a steaming glass and said under his breath, "Smile!"

"Oh—I'm sorry. Aren't I doing well?"

"You're looking like the snow queen. Drink that and come and dance."

The warming drink, and then his arms about her changed her mood miraculously. A flood of hot recklessness swept through her. She began to laugh, her head thrown back displaying her long throat, the diamonds glittering from her ears.

"Do you realize, we've been married almost a year and this is the first time we've danced together?"

"Ours isn't an ordinary marriage. Must I tell you again?"

"It's a quite extraordinary one. I have to wear my diamonds to a servants' party. Perhaps you think that fitting!"

"It was a nice gesture towards the servants," Guy replied imperturbably.

"Do they look well?" she asked in a low voice.

"You have pretty ears. I expect you know that."

"Prettier than Clara Thompson's?"

"Please!"

"Do I get the diamonds and she the kisses?"

"Don't let us quarrel. Where are your good manners?"

"I suppose I haven't got any. I was rescued from the streets, remember?"

"Bella!" She could feel the savage grip of his hands on her arms. The pain sent a fierce joy through her. She danced lightly, impeccably, smiling at the other incongruous couples, Broome with Mrs. Walter, Joseph trying to steer poor Tottie, Cousin Henrietta swaying with surprising grace in the arms of Thomas, the head gardener. Guy had complained that she looked like the snow queen. Well, now she did no longer, so surely he must appove.

"Are we to give Kate a brother?" she demanded.

Again his fingers bit into her flesh. She almost cried out. She looked him fully in the eyes, seeing the shine in his, as hard as diamonds. No tenderness, no warmth, and yet suddenly her heart was beating suffocatingly. She was thinking that she would wear her lawn nightgown with the Nottingham lace in spite of the coldness of the night. She would send Tottie away early, and leave only the candle at her bedside alight. She had forgotten Miss Thompson.

21

AT THE END OF THE PARTY GUY stood up to make a special announcement. He said that he intended keeping a book, a "commonplace book" he called it, of events at Ravenscroft, that would interest his wife and himself in later years, and after that their children.

He proposed that everyone present at this party sign their

names. Those who could not write were to make a cross, and he would mark it with their name. The page was headed Christmas 1856, and Guy suggested that the first to sign should be Cousin Henrietta. After that came Bella and himself, and Lally, and following that the servants headed by Mrs. Walter.

There was a great deal of giggling and embarrassment, and some pride among those who could write their names. Tottie was last, poor Tottie who scarcely understood what was happening and had to be persuaded to hold the pen in her hand and make her mark.

Then the party was over. From a little too much of the hot punch Bella was in a pleasantly dazed state. She sent Tottie off to bed, hardly noticing the child's reluctance, as if she were afraid to leave the lighted room and make the journey up to the attics. Kate had been carried up to the nursery without waking, and Lally, too, had tumbled into bed and slept almost at once. Cousin Henrietta, still singing *O, come all ye faithful* in a slightly tipsy voice, had departed to her room, and Miss Thompson was still out in the snow, or wherever she was. Bella found herself suddenly quite indifferent to the whereabouts of that scheming young woman who could so obviously look after herself. Her senses were lulled and drowsy and she cared nothing at this moment for mysteries. Her world was within this warm lighted room, to which presently Guy would come.

She sat waiting for his knock. All other sounds were shut from her ears, the faint moan of the wind, the flutter of the dying fire and from somewhere in the distance the persistent barking of a dog.

But the knock which eventually came wasn't on her bedroom door. It was on the front door directly beneath her windows. A thunderous urgent knocking, followed by the clangour of the bell pulled again and again.

It roused Bella from her dreamy state as completely as if the fire had sparked a live coal at her. She flew to the window to throw back the curtains and peer down.

What she could see was like a scene out of a nightmare. A burly man stood leaning backwards from the weight of his burden, the indescribably rigid form of a woman whose skirts fell in a cumbersome bundle but whose face was thrown back to catch the snowflakes—a face as white as the snow.

It was Miss Thompson.

Swallowing her sickness and trying to gather courage to go downstairs, Bella told herself frantically that it did not need to be Miss Thompson. The poor white face was quite anonymous.

But she knew it was. She knew it had to be. Tragedy had come once more with the falling snow.

Someone had opened the front door and the man had edged his way stiffly into the hall. Bella drew her head in, her face frozen. She threw off the flimsy beribboned wrap in which, a few minutes ago, she had felt suitably attired, and substituted a practical heavy woollen one. But she was still shivering violently as she made her way downstairs. The reluctant dread she felt overcame her so severely as she reached the last steps that she stood a moment unseen staring at the little group, Guy in an elegant quilted silk dressing-gown (had he been about to come to her? she wondered agonizedly), old Broome, stooped and muttering, Mrs. Walter, and the stranger who had laid his burden on the floor.

She couldn't see it from where she stood. The little group seemed to have been affected by paralysis as much as she. A dog suddenly ran in through the open door, and the stranger—no, it was no stranger, it was Norah's father, Mr. Jones, whose farm lay beyond the Ravenscroft woods—roared, "Get out!" His voice was shockingly loud, but it broke the inactivity. Guy said in a hard harsh voice, "Get blankets and brandy!" Little Broome scuttered off to obey, and Mrs. Walter dropped on her knees to chafe the cold hands of the figure on the floor.

"It's no use to do that," said the farmer. "She be gone. It's easy to see."

"Mrs. Walter! Wake Joseph and send him for Doctor Frobisher."

"It be too late," Norah's father repeated. "But I reckon the doctor should see her. I'll fetch him. It's a bad night to send the lad out." He turned back to say what he must already have said before, "She must have been lying there hours. 'Twas my old dog barking that brought me out. I thought it must be a ewe on her back. So I come out with a lantern, and found the poor lady. Right at the end of the yew walk, sir. Just at the edge of the woods. I can show you the spot in the morning."

"Yes," said Guy in his hard emotionless voice. "The police will need to see that."

Mrs. Walter's face was lifted. "The police?" she hissed on an indrawn breath.

"Certainly the police. Hadn't you noticed the poor girl's neck? She's been strangled."

Miss Thompson was walking in the yew walk with the master . . . I saw them, I saw them, I saw them . . .

Norah's voice was screaming in Bella's head. With a soundless cry, as if she too were having the breath strangled out of her, Bella flew to Guy's side. Gripping his arm tightly she made herself look down on the poor ruined face. The black cherry eyes looked back at her. They seemed to start out of the still face in loathing. You've won, Mrs. Raven, they were saying.

What bitter victory had she won? And would it in the end be a victory?

"Bella, my love! You shouldn't be here."

"Why not? Isn't my place at your side? Didn't we say 'for better, for worse'?" But this was worse than anything any bishop or parson, mouthing the marriage service, could have imagined. It was so bad that, strangely, Bella's courage grew out of it.

"We'll find out who did it. We'll settle this thing. We're not going to live the rest of our lives with a menace hanging over us. First Molly, now Miss Thompson, who next? Fetch the police, Mr Jones.

"And cover this poor creature up," she added. "Carry her into the library. She can't lie here in all the drafts."

"Yes. My wife is quite right," said Guy, with sudden briskness. "Can you help me, Broome? She—was only a little thing."

She was only a little thing . . . Was that his epitaph for the young woman he had admired, spoken in a brisk practical voice, as if it might have been a dead bird or some other unfeeling wild creature whom he carried out of the drafts from the front door.

The library door was locked on its secret. None of the maids, especially Tottie, must come on it unawares. Guy took Bella to wait by the replenished fire in the drawing-room until the police came. He insisted on her drinking a stiff brandy, instructing Broome, who stood with the useless blankets in his arms, to have one himself and give one to Mrs. Walter.

Then, when he and Bella were alone, he said without preamble, "You know that I'll be suspected of this crime."

"Yes. I know."

"But you don't believe me guilty?"

"Never say that again!" said Bella in a low passionate voice.

He gave a wry half smile.

"You're very trusting."

"Oh, Mr. Raven! Spare me such idle talk. I know you commit sins. A great many. But strangling unfortunate women isn't one of them."

"Why aren't you in hysterics?" He regarded her under his eyelids.

"Because it would be a waste of time. Now tell me what that foolish girl said to you when you walked with her this afternoon."

"She said—heaven help her—that she had fallen in love with me."

"And you?"

"Me? What could I say but that she had been misled? She had wrongly interpreted certain actions of mine. Women are too susceptible, I fear. She was distressed in church this morning, and this afternoon her emotions carried her away. I said that under the circumstances she had better give in her notice. We came back to the house together—"

"Together?"

"Why, of course we did." His eyes, regarding Bella, hadn't a flicker of warmth. They were simply amazed that a female, a mere servant, had presumed to take his advances seriously. Yet Bella was sure there was more to it. Although she was convinced that he was telling her the truth, as it was on the surface. "If she went out again, it was later. To be quite candid, I wasn't surprised when you told me she had gone. I imagined she had left in a pique, hoping to create a little trouble and mystery. That's all there was to it, I assure you. Do you believe me?"

"I believe you."

He took her hand, just for a moment, then dropped it.

"Then why are you calling me Mr. Raven? When I call you Bella?"

Bella rubbed her cold hands.

"I can think of nothing but her. It's so horrible." After a long silence she added, fearfully, "What will happen now? There will be more headlines. You can scarcely survive these. Is that what they intend?"

"They?"

"The Proudfoots," said Bella tiredly. "Noah and Aunt Aggie."

Guy stared at her silently. Then he gave a loud cracked laugh. "Try telling that to the police. The honest unimaginative police who don't believe in wars of attrition. Much less in curses." He pressed Bella's shoulder briefly. "I'm going to wake Cousin Henrietta. You'll need her."

It was true that she would need Cousin Henrietta, for after the police had questioned Guy for an interminable time they asked him to accompany them to the police station.

Everybody was up now, for all the servants had had to be questioned. The unfortunate thing was that although Norah had seen Guy and Miss Thompson leave the house ("at least I think it was the master—it always was the master with her," she said and then turned scarlet with embarrassment), no one had seen them return. No one could swear that Miss Thompson had ever returned. There was only Lally's evidence that could have been a dream, of Miss Thompson's voice saying "No, no, no!" and the open door of the orangery to suggest that she might have gone out again later, and alone.

Guy was allowed to have an overnight bag packed for him.

"But they won't be keeping you!" Bella exclaimed.

He answered quite calmly, "The law can be very slow. I prefer my own nightshirt to a prison one."

Lally promptly gave a strangled cry and fainted. Guy looked down at Bella on her knees beside her sister.

"I believe there's nothing wrong with that young woman but a constant desire for attention," he said critically.

"She's unconscious!" Bella declared indignantly.

He smiled. He seemed grateful for the familiar diversion of Lally's distress. Broome had come in with his bag, and the police, two of them, burly, red-faced, impossibly stupid in Bella's eyes, were impatient to leave.

"Come along, if you please, sir."

"I shall be back as soon as possible," said Guy.

The fantastic enormity of what was happening left Bella suddenly faint herself.

"But, Guy—"

"We merely have a great many things to discuss and investigate. Isn't that so, sergeant?"

The sergeant grew slightly more human.

"Your husband can help us with inquiries into this shocking affair, ma'am."

"Don't fret," said Guy.

"But he can't be arrested!" Bella whispered, as the men left.

"Of course not," said Cousin Henrietta briskly. "He's not in handcuffs, is he?" But she looked very old, nevertheless. Everyone looked older and sleepless. Lally was sitting up weakly with Tottie holding her hand. Tottie was like an aged monkey, all her youthful colour gone. Mrs. Walter looked feverish, a purplish flush in her cheeks and her eyes over-bright. She was giving orders to the maids in a low abrupt voice. Someone was to make hot chocolate immediately, someone else to sweep the snow from the library floor.

Miss Thompson had left some little time ago . . .

It was midday the next day that the incredible happened. Tottie opened her mouth and spoke an intelligible word. She said in a thick triumphant voice, "Clarrie!"

Bella and Lally had been sitting huddled over the morning-room fire. In spite of the dreadful shock Bella was thankful to see that Lally's condition had not deteriorated and she was talking quite lucidly, although she dwelt intolerably on Guy's behaviour.

"He really did flirt quite shamelessly with that poor creature, Bella. It isn't surprising that she took him seriously."

"He must have had motives," Bella said stiffly.

"Oh, yes, motives. To make another conquest. He's like all men, wanting as much amusement as possible without obligations. Supposing Miss Thompson had suddenly begun to make demands."

"What demands?" Bella said coldly.

"Oh, I don't know, Bella." Lally twisted her hands feverishly. "I can't help wondering—well, Molly had a baby without a father, and there was the poor darling mite at Aunt Aggie's. I never believed its father was a sailor. Some young women are very ignorant and frivolous—" Lally's voice died away as she saw Bella's icy anger.

"Are you suggesting Miss Thompson was ignorant enough or frivolous enough to become—for my husband to—oh, no, I can't even put such a thing into words. I declare, if ever you make such a suggestion again, I'll never speak to you for the rest of my life. I can only think that it's the weak state of your mind that puts such thoughts in your head. You have an obsession about babies. Miss Thompson—that sneaking creature—even though she's dead I must say it. Whatever happened to her is entirely her own fault. Oh, Lally!" Bella's voice rose exasperatedly. "Don't cry! You deserved that scolding for saying such a monstrous thing."

But Lally's reproachful tear-drowned eyes were hard to face, for her wild imagining could make dreadful sense. Guy was a healthy young man and he hadn't been sharing her bed. Nor was he any longer having anonymous adventures in London. His own words about Miss Thompson were seared into her mind. *Heaven help her, she had fallen in love with me . . .*

It was then that Tottie, sitting in the background with some sewing idle in her hands, had produced her strange hoarse word, "Clarrie!"

Bella spun round.

"Tottie! You spoke!"

In spite of her terrible anxiety, she couldn't help excitement and pleasure. They had all tried for so long to coax speech from Tottie's silent lips.

Tottie herself didn't look excited. She still had her look of shrinking alarm, and now that the word was out she was trying passionately to say more.

Mrs. Walter had come in at that moment with a tray.

"I've brought coffee, madam, thinking you might care for some. I've brought it myself because those foolish maids are all thumbs this morning, dropping everything."

"Mrs. Walter! Tottie spoke. Say that word again, Tottie. Now don't get excited. Take a deep breath and try to explain what you meant. Clarrie. Oh—it's somebody's name!"

Tottie nodded violently, her face scarlet with effort.

"A woman's name. Clarrie—Clara—" Bella went white. *"Miss Thompson!"*

Tottie nodded again, and Bella exclaimed excitedly, "But why do you call her Clarrie? Have you heard somebody else do that? Tottie—*who* have you heard call her Clarrie?"

The girl sat rigidly, her mouth open, the words refusing to come. Bella knelt beside her, holding her hot damp hands.

"Now listen, Tottie—" It was surprising how quiet her voice was when her heart was beating so hard that it was difficult to breathe. "Have you seen Miss Thompson before she came to Ravenscroft?"

Tottie nodded again, pleased that Bella was beginning to understand.

"Somewhere where she was called Clarrie? At Aunt Aggie's?"

Lally drew in her breath sharply, and looked as if she

might faint again. Mrs. Walter stood listening irresistibly. Tottie made an emphatic motion of her head, several times, and Bella felt the familiar dread, like a cold stone, in her heart.

"Tottie, was she the niece who had the baby? The one who disappeared?"

"The mother of that poor little angel!" Lally exclaimed.

But Tottie shook her head this time. She was moving her lips again. After several unintelligible sounds the second word came out triumphantly. "Noah." When she found that at last she could say it she said it over and over like an idiot. "Noah, Noah, Noah!"

"Noah's wife!" Bella whispered, with certainty, and didn't need to watch for Tottie's assent.

The picture was falling into place. Tottie's fear, from the beginning, of Miss Thompson, whom she recognized, Miss Thompson's startled exclamation the day Lally had imagined she saw Noah under the copper beech, her deliberate attempt to estrange Guy even more completely from a wife he didn't love, her disappearance at church yesterday which suggested she might have been meeting Noah, her bending over little Kate, obviously debating whether to obey Noah's instructions and kidnap her, then later the distressed whisper Lally had heard, as if the woman were fighting a battle with herself.

In her attempt to make Guy fall in love with her at Noah's injunction in order to create another scandal, she had got burnt herself. She had done what no one had anticipated, she had fallen in love with her prey. This had put her in a terrible dilemma. She must have gone out in the snow to meet Noah as arranged, but without Kate. And Noah's terrible black temper had possessed him . . .

Bella sprang up, saying urgently, "The police must be told this at once. I must go to my husband. Mrs. Walter, help me to get ready."

"But I don't think you can go to the master, madam. He's been taken to London."

"To London! How do you know? Why wasn't I told?"

"I didn't want to upset you more, madam. Mr. Jones brought the news. The matter was too important for the police here. The master was taken to headquarters in London."

"Then that's where I shall go," Bella declared. "Send someone to find out what time the London train stops at Underwood, Mrs. Walter."

She was quite calm now, and full of hope.

"Tottie had better come, too, so that she can tell them what she's just told us. And I shall take the baby."

"Kate?" Lally faltered.

"She has to be fed," Bella said simply. "Anyway, do you think I would let her out of my sight after this? With Noah making his fiendish plans. Tell Norah to get her ready, Mrs. Walter."

"If you would allow me, madam," said Mrs. Walter, "I would like to come with you. You'll need help."

"But I'll have Tottie."

"Tottie! The girl's in such a dither she'll be worse than useless. Is she to hold the baby while you buy train tickets and can she find you a cab in all the hustle and bustle of Waterloo station? If she saw anything to startle her she'd fly to hide. That's her instinct."

"Yes, you're right, Mrs. Walter. She certainly has a habit of hiding in cupboards, or any dark spot. Then perhaps it would be as well if you came. Only don't let us waste time. Order the carriage to take us to the railway station. The snow isn't too deep for the horses, is it? It stopped falling some time ago. And Lally dear, Cousin Henrietta will be here with you. You'll be perfectly all right. I'll give orders for Norah to sleep in your room."

Lally's little face was pinched and fearful.

"Supposing Noah is still here looking for his—for Miss Thompson."

"I have more than a feeling that Noah knows very well what has happened to his Clarrie. He won't be here any more. You'll have to be brave, Lally."

"I can't be! It won't be safe! Nothing's ever safe!"

"Lally, please! Try to be brave!"

But Lally was well embarked on her perpetual nightmare.

"Noah will wait until he sees you leave and then he'll take his revenge on me. Oh, Bella! I can't stay here. Take me with you. Let us remain together."

"Don't you think what Miss Eulalie says might be wisest?" Mrs. Walter put in in her dry, quiet voice. "Leaving her might bring on a relapse. She'll be a prey to her fears. I gather there's a capable housekeeper in the London house."

"Oh, yes. Mrs. Doughty. She would be pleased to see us again."

"Then let us all go. It would be best, madam."

"Perhaps you're right, Mrs. Walter. Very well, we'll all

206

go. How quickly can our bags be packed? And Cousin Henrietta is resting in her room. She must be told."

Fifteen minutes later, when Lally and Bella were both dressed warmly in bonnets and cloaks and stout boots, Mrs. Walter came hurrying downstairs to say that her ladyship was sound asleep and it did seem a pity to wake her, considering the night she had had, and her age.

"Could you just write a note for her, madam, and I'll put it by her bedside."

Bella was too impatient to be on the way to argue. Besides, it was perfectly true that Cousin Henrietta had looked alarmingly exhausted after her sleepless night. She went to her desk and hastily scribbled a note.

"We are going to London at once to see Guy. Tottie has spoken at last and been able to give us valuable information. It will completely exonerate Guy, and finish Noah and that terrible old mother of his forever. Can you imagine, Miss Thompson was Noah's *wife*. It has all been a diabolical plot. I hope we will be back tomorrow, Guy as well. I was reluctant to wake you before we left." She hesitated, and added, "Please, dear Cousin Henrietta, have the fires alight for us tomorrow, and we will begin Christmas all over again."

22

THE FIRST THING BELLA WAS aware of as she climbed out of the train at Waterloo station was the raucous words of the newsboy at the barrier. "Murder charge! Guy Raven charged with murder!"

The words jolted her awake. She realized that she had been in a curiously sleepy dreamlike state ever since Mrs. Walter, in the train, had opened her carpet bag and taken out a bottle and persuaded each of them, Bella, Lally and Tottie, to drink a little. It was blackcurrant wine, just the kind of stimulant they needed after the strain they had all been through. Besides, it was warming in this intense cold.

Bella had obeyed, because she was so tired, and yet must remain alert. The wine was sweet and pleasant-tasting. Lally had enjoyed it, and so had Tottie. After that, since they had the compartment to themselves, Bella had unfastened her gown and fed the baby, and replaced her, drowsy and contented, in her basket. Then everybody had seemed to get drowsy. Except Mrs. Walter who didn't seem to need sleep. She had sat very upright in her corner, her arms folded, her face wearing its habitual prim forbidding expression. Bella was glad now that she had come. She was capable and unshakeable. In her care they would undoubtedly arrive safely at their destination.

Although those horrifying words the newsboy hurled at her gave her a moment of pure terror, she suddenly had a desire to laugh scornfully and shout back that it was all a lie. This was what Noah had wanted, not only to ruin Guy's career and marriage (for what it was), but to get him standing in the dock, accused, facing long imprisonment or death. He would have gone to any lengths to achieve such an event, even to sacrificing his own wife. But he had failed. And now, thinking himself safe, he would be easy to track down.

Carrying the baby, Bella followed Mrs. Walter who had gone off in her capable way to get a cab. It was strange how her legs stumbled, as if they had not wakened with the rest of her body. Lally and Tottie were making slow progress, too, although Lally was trying to hold her head up and not wince away from the idle glances of passers-by. It was a long time since she had faced strangers, and the noisiness and steam and belching smoke of this vast station was confusing enough to one in the best of health.

"Bella," she panted. "Where are we going?"

"To the house in Knightsbridge. Doughty will know, or Doctor Bushey will know, where Guy has been taken. Then I will go there immediately. You and Mrs. Walter and Mrs. Doughty must look after Kate while I am gone."

"Mr. Raven won't let me touch her."

"Lally, you know that isn't true. It was only true at the very beginning when she was so tiny. He thought you might love her too much. But now it's different. You may hold her if you like. I say so."

"Oh, thank you!" Lally said fervently. A little feeble gaiety seized her. "Bella, isn't this different from our first coming to London? We are rich, we have Kate." Uncertainly she added, "If only we were safe."

"We are safe," Bella said impatiently.

"People do stare." Lally was looking round furtively. "I'm sure they all know who we are. Murderers and adulterers."

"Lally, what *are* you saying!"

"That's what it's come to. Oh, not us. But poor Miss

Thompson—loved and murdered. Isn't it true? Look, there's Mrs. Walter beckoning to us. I think she has a cab. Where's Tottie? Bella, Tottie—Oh, there she is. She's so slow. Tottie, why can't you hurry? You're not the only one who's tired. I scarcely know what I'm doing. My eyes won't stay open."

"Come along," said Mrs. Walter, giving her tight smile. "There's room for us all. If you will allow me, madam, I will sit with my back to the driver and hold the baby."

"Have you given him the address?" Bella fussed, rubbing her eyes. Really, they were all in a poor state after their sleepless night. Except Mrs. Walter who was remarkably calm and wide awake.

"Indeed, yes, madam. If you would just hold the baby while I get in. There! All safe." She gave another of her rare grudging smiles, and the driver whipped up his horse which set off at a smart pace.

They were back in London. The cab smelt of wet straw, it was bitterly cold, and outside the streets were freckled with snow. The year between might never have happened. Except that there was Mrs. Walter's long sallow face opposite, not Aunt Aggie's, and Mrs. Walter held little Kate, tangible proof that a great deal had happened since their last arrival in London. And they were not on their way to the slums but to a comfortable house in a fashionable area.

The jolting of the cab increased the girls' drowsiness. Lally's and Tottie's heads lolled together, their heavy eyelids closing. Bella was glad of this, for wide awake, both girls could have got into a state of nervous terror. She herself fought with her sleepiness, and tried to take interest in what she could see through the grimy window. Snow and slush, a sky as grey as pewter, dingy buildings, a mass of vehicles, some hurtling by drawn by high-spirited horses, some moving at a snail's pace. They had crossed the river, and soon should be coming into an area she recognized, the broad Strand and Trafalgar Square, and after that the Mall that led to Buckingham Palace, then turned off to Constitution Hill and Knightsbridge, their destination.

In spite of her determination to keep awake her eyelids did droop and she started up at what seemed a long time later to find they were still jogging along, but that instead of the broad streets of the West End they seemed to have got into a narrow street bordered by small mean houses.

At first she thought she was dreaming. She peered again into the early darkness, seeing the low huddled houses and hearing the cries of ragged children. It was all too dreadfully familiar. She shot an apprehensive glance at Mrs. Walter who was still sitting upright nursing the peacefully sleeping baby, and seeming not at all alarmed by the route the cab-driver was taking.

"Mrs. Walter, I think the man's made a mistake. We're going the wrong way."

Strangely, Mrs. Walter didn't look out of the window to confirm her fears. She just gave a strange half-smile and said in her flat voice, "I think the driver knows where he's going, madam."

"But these streets—they must be a very long way round. The man's cheating. Wait till I tell him so."

She made a move to open the flap behind Mrs. Walter in order to call to the driver. Mrs. Walter's arm barred her.

"The man knows his business, madam."

"He certainly does not. None of these roads lead to Knightsbridge. Even the little I know of London tells me that. Why, we must be miles from the city." The never far absent fear was stirring in Bella again. The little dark streets were so oppressive, so reminiscent of that other evil-smelling street shrouded in darkness and snow where the nightmare existed. "Mrs. Walter, please move aside. I must speak to the driver."

"I think not, madam."

The woman's voice was still polite, but subtly not that of a servant any longer. Her smile had gone, her eyes had a narrowed secretive triumphant look.

"You see, I gave the man his orders, madam. He is taking the way he was bidden."

"You mean—" Even then Bella tried not to believe what she was being told. "You mean we're not going to Knightsbridge."

"No, madam."

"But Mrs. Walter—how dare you do this? I must stop the cab immediately. Driver!"

"I think you won't, madam."

"But I will!" Bella declared vigorously, and dragging open the window at her side she stuck her head out. "Driver! Stop at once! We're going the wrong way."

The man on the box, muffled in a greatcoat and stovepipe hat, slowed his horse to a walk. He turned his head.

"Ma'am? You said something?"

His voice was grotesquely familiar. So was his face. Dark,

210

grinning, evil, it looked down at Bella. The cab driver was Noah.

Bella sank back, breathless and faint.

"It's a plot! You're in it, Mrs. Walter. You! And I trusted you!" She looked frantically at Lally and Tottie, huddled together, deep in slumber. There was no help there.

Mrs. Walter read her thoughts and nodded slowly, smiling her infuriating sour smile.

"It wasn't wise to drink the blackcurrant wine, madam. Such young things, they haven't heads for wine."

"You put something in it," Bella whispered. "What was it? Laudanum?"

"Wine's an overpowering drink, madam."

"I shall put out my head and scream for help," Bella announced tightly.

"I wouldn't do that, madam. Really I wouldn't." An indescribable coarseness had come into Mrs. Walter's voice. "If you was to do so I only have to put my hand over your child's face."

Bella stared in mounting horror. The cab was jolting again as the horse was whipped up.

"A baby smothers easy," said Mrs. Walter.

23

GUY RAVEN SHUT THE BOOK with a bang.

"Does that convince you the case must be reopened?" The Inspector nodded slowly.

"We'll try to locate this young woman. It shouldn't be too difficult. She has a regular beat, I understand. She'll have to be made to talk, of course."

"It's urgent," said Guy.

"I agree with that. Things look black for you, I may say, if it can't be proved that Molly Hancock and Clara Thompson are part of the same plot."

"You've got to lay this crime at Noah Proudfoot's door."

"I hope we can, sir. Now let's just go over this again. Why didn't you suspect sooner that someone in your own household might be involved? Apart from the dead woman, of course."

"Because it was only yesterday that I persuaded Clara Thompson to talk. I'd always had suspicions about her. She'd seemed to arrive in my mother's household out of the blue, and to be remarkably anxious to come to Ravenscroft. She was to nurse my sister-in-law who had had a mental breakdown. Not the most appealing occupation for an attractive young woman. However, it took all this time to get beneath her guard. I had to resort to somewhat despicable means that only bore results yesterday afternoon when she told me that she couldn't go on with what she was doing."

"She had become emotionally involved with you, I gather?" the Inspector said pompously.

Guy bowed his head. "It was a course I had to pursue and I succeeded all too well. Although, even then, I couldn't get the woman to divulge her secrets. She did tell me she had 'had enough'—those were her words—and that she intended starting a new life. But she would like to warn me about traitors in my own household. She was in a state of great emotion. I thought she was being a bit melodramatic. But after she had left the house, for London, I presumed, I took this method of getting specimens of handwriting."

He reopened the book and stabbed his finger at the first signature.

"You agree that there's no mistake. My housekeeper's handwriting exactly corresponds with that in the note to Molly making an assignment at the crossroads."

"It does, it does."

"And of course that explains how the note was delivered to Molly. It was easy enough for Mrs. Walter to slip it to her saying Tom Field had brought it. Probably giving the girl a scolding for receiving notes from young men." Guy sprang up restlessly. "But surely we're wasting time. Can't Noah be apprehended at once?"

"Not without grounds, sir. After all, the Thompson woman didn't at any stage acknowledge any connection with him."

"No. I couldn't get her to do that. But I told you of the episode when my sister-in-law imagined she saw Noah in the garden. The woman gave herself away then. She knew Noah, there was some connection between them."

The Inspector nodded.

"But unfortunately Miss Clara Thompson is now beyond telling us anything. So we'll have to depend on the girl Molly for evidence. Don't be impatient, sir. My men are out. I haven't been wasting time, as you suggest."

"Then I hope your men make haste. I don't think even yet you realize how dangerous this black villain is. He'll strike again, at any moment. I'm worried about my wife and child. I trust I'm free to go home."

"No, sir. That's where you're wrong. So long as you appear to be in custody Noah will hold his hand. You see," the Inspector smiled grimly, "I do believe your story. What's more, I believe the black villain, as you call him, has one object, and that is to get you hanged."

24

THE ROOM WAS EXACTLY THE same, the bobbled red plush curtains drawn against the dark and the inquisitive eyes of neighbours, the lamp lit, the fire burning cosily, the cradle on the hearth, and Aunt Aggie rocking gently in her chair.

"Well, my dears, you've had a long journey. It couldn't be helped. Noah had to drive you about until dark. Wasn't it a stroke of fortune that he happened to see you catching the same London train as he was catching himself? He was only anxious to be of service when he bribed the cabby —handsomely, I can tell you—to borrow his cab. But he couldn't bring you here until after dark because we're so troubled with unmannerly neighbours in this street since we've come home from prison. All our comings and goings are watched as if we were criminals! It's quite distressing. But never fear. You won't be stared at. You'll be up and away before the birds."

She smiled affably, her large pale eyes looking over the top of her spectacles.

"Was it quite a surprise to come here again? But a pleasure, I'm sure. I find it a pleasure to see your pretty faces once more. And you both so richly dressed, too. Such clothes! Such jewels! See what good fortune I brought you!"

"Mrs. Proudfoot, why have you brought us here?"

Once again anger was overcoming Bella's fear. The shock of returning to this house had brought back Tottie's look of animal fear and Lally's blank-eyed apprehension. The two girls crouched on the small sofa, holding hands, dazed and uncomprehending. They were useless, puppets in Aunt Aggie's plump white fingers. Bella had to fight alone. How could she, against so many enemies?

"I don't know what you're planning to do," she went on vehemently, "but you won't succeed. I left a letter for Cousin Henrietta telling her exactly what had happened. She will get the police immediately."

Aunt Aggie put her hand in her apron pocket and drew out a folded sheet of paper.

"Is this the letter, my dear?"

Bella's mouth went dry. "Mrs. Walter didn't leave it!"

"Naturally. She wouldn't be so foolish. Oh, but you don't really know Mrs. Walter, do you?" Aunt Aggie raised her voice calling, "Lily! Come here, will you, my dear."

In a moment Mrs. Walter had appeared. Her long face wore its look of guarded triumph. As Aunt Aggie said, "This is Mrs. Jennings, my dear," Mrs. Walter dropped a mocking curtsey. Aunt Aggie went on, "The lady everyone decided didn't exist. So foolish of them. The only person who didn't exist was Lady Merriweather, her supposed mistress." Aunt Aggie chuckled comfortably. "Your grand husband was careless there, Miss Isabella. He went to such trouble to find out what he could about poor Clarrie, and quite ignored Mrs. Jennings, who is a great deal more clever and trustworthy. Aren't you, Lily, my dear? And I believe you still have those nice positions for these young ladies?"

Mrs. Walter nodded, her mouth hard.

"Ready and waiting. The parties concerned are getting impatient, I may say."

"Yes, we know. They'll be satisfied before morning. Tch, tch, Miss Isabella! You're looking alarmed. I wouldn't hurt you. Not a hair of your pretty head. I have a most sensitive nature. But Noah—he's another matter. He's very upset about Clarrie. He trusted her and it wasn't nice to find she wasn't trustworthy. Indeed, I've never known him so upset, and I fear he hasn't my sensitive nature. He's revengeful. If I know him he won't rest until someone has paid for Clarrie, and everything else."

"You mean he killed his wife because he found her—" Bella couldn't go on.

"Unfaithful," said Aunt Aggie sadly. "Untrustworthy and unfaithful. She refused to do as he told her. Now you as a married woman will understand, Miss Isabella, that it's a wife's duty to obey her husband. She even threatened to leave him, no less! And he still has not recovered in health after that terrible year in prison. Small wonder he—well, no matter. But you may be sure he is clever enough not to have the crime laid at his door."

"My husband is to be accused!"

"And has been," said Aunt Aggie, her sausage curls nodding gently beneath her spotless white cap. "So now there is only the little matter of you and your sister. And Mrs. Jennings is seeing to that."

"You're monstrous!" Bella whispered.

Although Aunt Aggie still smiled blandly, a subtle change had come over her face. Her eyes had turned as cold as stone.

"Monstrous, you say! And who wouldn't be after the year Noah and I have lived through. Stink, squalor, corruption! Rats running over our faces at night. Food not fit for a pig to eat. Lice, fleas. Filthy straw, damp, jail fever. The poor dregs of humanity, the rakings of the gutter, as companions. Ah, if you'd heard the screams, the despair, the dreadful language. Night after night, day after day, and you, Miss Isabella, you and your sister, living in luxury, pampered, petted, never giving a thought to the ones responsible for your blessings. Never a thought for Noah and me. Oh, no. My sister told me that."

"Your sister!"

"She reported faithfully on your doings. She had great amusement from wearing my best bonnet—you will remember the one with the cherries—and frightening Miss Eulalie out of her wits."

"The woman in Mrs. Bunt's teashop!" Bella exclaimed. "Then she *did* lure Molly away."

"That was a trifle. A mere preliminary skirmish. Not a tenth of the debt your husband still has to pay."

"She took her to her house. The house by the river that Molly talked about."

"In Twickenham, my dear. Where I go once a week to get fresh eggs and butter. She has a nice little farm. Only a few acres, but well-tended. Why, you'll remember sampling her eggs yourself. And talking of food, why don't we all have a nice cup of tea? Tottie! Tottie, wake up, girl!"

Tottie started up, her poor little face a mask of terror.

"Go into the kitchen and get out the tea things. Make haste now, or Noah will be up the stairs to hurry you up."

"Mrs. Proudfoot! Tottie isn't your servant any longer."

"You mean, she is too grand, also? I think not. I think not, Miss Isabella."

Tottie slunk out of the door. If Bella had had hopes that she might have the sense to escape out of the kitchen door and try to get help they quickly died. A persistent hammering was coming from the cellar. It indicated Noah's whereabouts, and Bella knew Tottie's meagre courage unequal to defying Noah. She herself didn't dare to leave the room because of the baby asleep in the cradle on the hearth. She had already heard Mrs. Walter's dreadful threat, and she was all too sure that that woman or Aunt Aggie would not hesitate to carry it out.

Besides, with Tottie's departure, Lally had suddenly roused herself and gone down on her knees beside the cradle. Her face was full of the utmost anxiety. One finger very gently touched Kate's chubby cheek.

"It's so small and weak. Aunt Aggie, will it live?"

Aunt Aggie shook her head concernedly, and gave her "Tch! Tch!" Her concern was not for the baby but for Lally.

"Dear me, she thinks it's that other baby. It's true she's lost her wits."

Bella sprang up furiously.

"If she has, it's all due to you! Are you a woman or a fiend? Let us go! Please let us go! We'll go on foot in the snow. Anything! Please let us go!"

The slow bland smile showed Aunt Aggie's black rotting teeth.

"You were thankful enough to shelter under my roof the last time it snowed. Shame on you, my pretty child, where's your gratitude?"

"If my sister and I disappear like this how do you think you can escape suspicion?" Bella cried passionately.

"Now who in the wide world is going to worry about two young women picked up out of the gutter returning to it again? With your grand husband discredited and hanged— oh, hanged, indeed, don't wince, my dear!—who is going to trouble? Certainly not your mother-in-law, eh?" Aunt Aggie chuckled obscenely. "Nature will out, you know. It was proved with Molly. She wanted only to get back on the streets. Why not you and your sister, too? Oh, the world won't fret about you. It doesn't care for upstarts. If Noah and I and Mrs. Jennings can't make up a pretty enough story to explain your disappearance then we're poor creatures, indeed. As dim-witted as your sister."

"And—my baby?" Bella gasped.

"As sweet an infant as you'd ever set eyes on. I'll take care of her, you may be sure. Calm yourself, my dear. Would Aunt Aggie harm an innocent child?"

After a long time Bella managed to say, "Molly will be found and made to tell the truth."

"Molly? Oh dear, oh dear! You don't know about Molly, of course. You'd better come and see for yourself. And Noah's downstairs, too. He'll want to see you. He's hard at work, as you can hear. Bang, bang, bang, from the moment he arrived home. I declare he splits my poor head." She gave a glance at Lally who was sitting on the hearthrug crooning wordlessly to the baby. "Leave her there, poor child. Let her be happy in her world of fancy. She's fortunate, if only she knew it."

The cellar stairs were steep and dark. Bella wanted to refuse to go down them, but a dreadful fascination forced her on. The tap of Noah's hammer ceased as first Aunt Aggie, and then Bella, stumbling after her, reached the cellar.

In the guttering light of two candles, Bella saw him towering in the dank room, his black tousled head all but touching the ceiling. His great hands hung at his side in their familiar posture, she saw that his face was stubbled with a half-grown beard, his eyes red-rimmed.

Yet the only impression that remained in her mind was his teeth gleaming in a grimace that wasn't so much a smile as an expression of derision and triumph.

"So here she is, Ma, the delicate lady of fashion. What has she come to see?"

"Why, your work, of course. Show her your clever work. You didn't know Noah was so handy with carpenter's tools, did you, my dear?"

"It's not exactly a piece of furniture I'm making," Noah said, with his sudden coarse laugh. "Perhaps the lady would like to look closer at it. I'll hold the candle."

The room was damp and chilly enough, but it wasn't that that made Bella freeze with horror. It was the shape of the box that the wavering light showed. A long narrow box made out of rough planks of wood. There was an identical one beside it, obviously finished, for it had the lid on.

They were coffins.

"Not a baby's size this time," Noah said in his indescribably gleeful voice, and behind him his mother gave her cosy chuckle.

"See, isn't Noah versatile! Of course, the wood isn't of the best quality. I'm afraid it's only what they use for paupers and plague victims. But, even so, Noah doesn't spare his workmanship."

Bella was clinging hard to self-possession and sanity.

"You—told me—I would see Molly."

"And so you shall, my dear. So you shall. Show her, Noah."

Noah moved the candle so abruptly that the flame wavered wildly.

"I'll show her."

He tipped the lid of the second box back. Bella's hand went to her mouth, strangling a scream.

She wouldn't scream, she wouldn't faint. That would please these two monsters too much. She would somehow look at Molly's ivory face and remain calm.

"Murder!" she whispered. "You think you can escape with murder?"

"Bless you, you pretty innocent," cried Aunt Aggie. "She isn't dead. She's only asleep. There!" She stooped over the still form. "Feel her heart. She's quite safe. It's only more convenient to have her this way. It stops her tongue from wagging. Doesn't it, Noah? We'd prefer Miss Isabella and Miss Eulalie to be quiet, too, wouldn't we?"

"I'd have them quieter than that," said Noah, with ferocity. "I'd have them as quiet as Clarrie." He swung round on Bella. "Did you know your swell husband wasn't content with you, but he had to have my wife, too? I had to kill her, the bitch. That's women for you. You all deserve to go the same way." He gave a kick at the box he had been hammering, sending it slithering towards Bella. "Get in it and see if it'll fit. There's another for your precious sister. Where's the sister, Ma?"

"With the baby, poor wandering creature."

"Then fetch her. We haven't got all night. We've got to get going. A brougham to fetch and three coffins—I *beg* your pardon, ma'am—" he sketched a low satirical bow to Bella, "three boxes to load, and then the drive to the docks."

"Get the girl," Aunt Aggie said briefly to Mrs. Jennings.

Mrs. Jennings hastened to obey, her skirts rustling up the narrow stairs.

Bella clenched her frozen hands. "My baby?" she managed to say. "Tottie?"

"Now never you fret, my dear. They'll both be cared for.

Tottie will learn to be grateful for the good home she scorned, and as for the baby—a foundling home, perhaps. What do you think, Noah? Is a foundling home too good for Guy Raven's daughter?"

"Well, now, Ma, that will have our consideration." Noah spoke with exaggerated gentility. "Perhaps the dear little mite would be happier in the gutter. One thing's certain, she can't go with her ma. Oh no, that would be no good at all. Unhampered, they likes them. Buxom and healthy and unhampered."

"How can you carry—these things," Bella couldn't bring herself to call the boxes by their grisly name, "on board a ship? You'll be stopped and questioned."

"That's where you're wrong. No one interferes with the dead, especially dead Chinese liking to be buried in their own country. I'll have names put on these. Lee Wang, Lee Hong, Lee Ching. Three brothers. Very sad." Noah gave his great laugh, but it was cut off sharply as Mrs. Walter's voice came hissing down the stairs.

"Mrs. Proudfoot! I believe the girl's gone!"

"Who? Tottie?" Aunt Aggie had darted towards the stairs.

"No. The mad one. You did say you left her with the baby. The baby's gone, too. The cradle's empty."

The stairs shook as Aunt Aggie's ample form catapulted up them. She was followed by Noah who reached the top in three strides.

Left in the cold dark cellar, Bella stood rooted to the floor. She didn't dare to hope. Had Lally miraculously had the sense to take the opportunity to fly? Had Aunt Aggie trusted her weak mental state too much? She had forgotten Lally's obsession about harm coming to the baby, any baby, either Kate or the other long-dead mite. If Lally had snatched up Kate and fled, she would hardly know which infant it was, only that it was alive and must be kept that way.

There was the sound of doors banging. This was followed by a long silence. After an interminable time footsteps came back. Bella heard Noah's furious voice,

"You left her alone! Knowing she could run off!"

"But her senses had gone. She didn't know what went on round her. Mrs. Jennings! You knew that?"

"I must say I didn't expect her to have the spirit, any more than the dumb one."

"Never mind about spirit!" Noah said savagely. "She's gone. She's nowhere in sight and I'm not going knocking on

doors, looking for her. You two muddling fools! You luna-
tics! I'm off!"

"Noah! Where are you going?" For the first time Bella
heard an uncertain quaver in Aunt Aggie's voice. It gave her
an exultant vindictive delight. Darling Lally, flying like that to
save Kate.

"To save my skin. Where do you think?"

"But who's going to take in a crazed creature like that with
a baby and listen to her? She'll be turned out in the snow."

"With her fine clothes? Anyone'll tell she isn't off the
street. And what about the brat, dressed like a lord's daughter? And knowing how the neighbours is full of Christian
charity and love for us! You stay and face them if you like,
and serve you right for muddling fools. But I'm off!"

Aunt Aggie's voice had risen in panic. "What about the
other one with her educated tongue? Are you going to let
her go free?"

"I won't touch her, Ma!" Noah's voice was suddenly vicious. "Not that I don't want to. What I'd give to get my
fingers round her pretty white throat. I'd like to see her without a breath in her body. I'd make her pay for Clarrie. But I
won't swing for her! I've got enough sense for that. Kick her
out in the snow. Let her freeze. If you know what's healthy,
you'll come with me. Only I ain't hanging around waiting.
So make up your mind quick. Are you going to wait to be
strung up, or coming with me?"

After a long moment Aunt Aggie's voice was slow, falter-
ing, the voice of an old woman.

"Where?" she asked.

25

THE LITTLE ERECT FIGURE IN
the elegant bonnet and lavender gown sat before the fire
dandling Kate on her lap. She paid no attention to Bella's
tumultuous entrance. She appeared to be fully engrossed with
the baby, talking and cooing to her, and then laughing with
surprised delight at Kate's tentative response.

Bella's first instinct was to snatch Kate from her. How
dare she think she could behave in such an icily, bitterly
hostile way, and then walk in and take possession of her
grandchild, as if the baby belonged to nobody else.

220

But all at once Bella found she had been too near too many ugly tragic things to have any more hate.

"Her name is Kate," she said. "Do you like her?"

As if just that moment aware of Bella's presence, Mrs. Raven lifted her eyes.

"She resembles her father, although she has my hands. I confess I don't care for the name Kate, but I wasn't consulted so I suppose I must put up with it. Good gracious, child, you're shockingly dishevelled. Let Hannah—where is Hannah? Find her and ask her to attend to you."

"Why did you come here?" asked Bella curiously.

"To defend my son, of course. Why else? I draw the line at murder. Other indiscretions, perhaps, but murder is absurd. I'm very glad the whole nasty affair is cleared up. If you ask me, your sister has been the only one to keep her senses."

"Lally!" Bella said, giving a high-pitched laugh at the absurdity. "Where is Lally, anyway?"

"Here I am!" Lally cried, at that moment flying into the room. "Oh, Bella, how did you escape?"

Bella thought of the interminable time that had elapsed after Noah, Aunt Aggie and Mrs. Walter had fled. The house had been so eerily silent. She had sat in the cellar in the flickering candlelight straining her eyes to hear that Molly still breathed. She had been obsessed with the fear that if she went for help Molly would die. She had told Tottie to fly to open the door immediately anyone came, but Tottie had crouched half-way down the cellar stairs, paralysed with fear. It had been a time when all will had left Bella. She had sat chafing Molly's cold hands, sure only that Lally would send help.

"I saved the baby!" Lally was saying. "Bella, do you hear? I saved the baby!"

"How you can say your sister is crazy when she seems to be the only one who kept her head, I don't know," Mrs. Raven observed, rocking Kate in her arms. "It seems a very unfair and damaging statement to make."

But Bella knew Lally was unaware it was Kate whom she had saved. She thought the other forlorn baby was alive again, and the knowledge seemed to have brought back her sanity. Her face was white and intolerably strained, but it had none of its old wildness. Instead it had a sad sweetness that made Bella put her arms round the slight figure and draw her close.

221

"You were so brave. How can I thank you?"

"I wasn't brave at all. I was scared to death. That's why I took the baby before Noah could get a chance to bury it. I could hear him hammering a coffin, couldn't you?"

"Yes," Bella said, shuddering. "And where did you take the baby, Lally?" Noah and Aunt Aggie hadn't known much about human nature or they would have realized that that sinister sound would have penetrated even Lally's dazed wits.

"To the house across the street. I banged on the door and made the old woman who lived there let me in. She called her husband and said he must go off at once to Bow Street to fetch the police. She said that he was not to stare at me and think I'd made up a tale, he knew well enough queer things went on in that house. So presently the police came, and there was a nice sergeant who said I must take the baby home and wait for you because you wouldn't leave Molly. I didn't know Molly was there. Bella—" the flicker of fear touched Lally's eyes again, "she wasn't dead?"

"No. And she won't die, never fear. But Doctor Bushey says it will take her several hours to wake up."

"Is that all the old fool can do?" Mrs. Raven demanded. "Predict the effects of laudanum on young girls. Why isn't he here seeing that my granddaughter has taken no ill effects from this dreadful affair? Or me, having had not a wink of sleep all night?"

Bella was suddenly almost collapsing from weariness herself. With the greatest effort she said, "Doctor Bushey and Guy have gone with the police to search for the Proudfoots. They may not be back for some time. If you will excuse me, Mrs. Raven, I must tidy myself. I'm scarcely fit to be seen."

"Didn't I tell you to ring for Hannah?"

But Bella had a childish longing for familiar faces and reassurance.

"I would rather have Mrs. Doughty, thank you."

It was curious what a feeling she had of being home at last when she was upstairs in her bedroom with Mrs. Doughty fussing and clucking in her motherly way.

"Dear, dear!" she kept saying. "Dear, dear, dear! And Doughty says the predictions are for a new comet in the sky and terrible storms. What a dreadful world, to be sure. And there was the master fretting in town half the summer. Never going anywhere or seeing anybody."

"He must have had some diversions," Bella said.

"Not a one," Mrs. Doughty lied loyally. "There now,

222

madam, your bath's ready. And what gown will you wear? The wine velvet perhaps? A nice cheerful colour for this bitter weather."

Bella knew the dress had been decided on, so made no protest. In any case, Mrs. Doughty's choice was right. The rich colour took away her wan look. Her eyes were quite bright by the time she had finished dressing and drunk the inevitable hot chocolate. She found she was listening intently for the return of the men.

"Aye, fretted all summer," said Mrs. Doughty, her eyes bright, too, and her nose the colour of Bella's gown.

Yet when, a half-hour later, there was the unmistakable sound of arrivals downstairs, Bella found herself leaving her room slowly, and descending the stairs with dignity.

She was not going to fly into her husband's arms. Oh, no! Though she hadn't known the strength of will-power she possessed to prevent it.

She was aware of Guy standing in the middle of the hall looking up at her. There were two ghosts between them now, she thought, Caroline and Clara Thompson.

She could hear Doctor Bushey's voice telling Mrs. Raven what had happened.

"We caught up with Noah just as he was about to board a steamship bound for the Far East. Presumably the vessel that would have carried the girls away."

"And the old woman? Don't tell me she escaped?"

"No, oh, no. It appears she had fallen on a patch of ice and twisted her ankle. She couldn't keep up with Noah so he callously deserted her. We found her in a public house with her evil companion, Mrs. Jennings, both of them more than a little tipsy. I make a prediction there'll be no Bible readings in Newgate prison this time, judging by the obscenities used. But I won't distress your ears, dear lady."

"My ears can stand a little of my son's voice. Where is he?"

Bella's feet took her down the remaining stairs, almost reluctantly. By the look in her husband's eyes, there didn't seem, at that moment, to be ghosts between them. Or perhaps the way he must be so dazzled with the snow, and exhaustion, he couldn't see them.

"Guy, can't you spare me a moment of your time?" came his mother's querulous voice.

Guy held out his hand.

"Come," he said to Bella.

They stood side by side before the old lady as if Bella were being presented to her for the first time. Mrs. Raven held her head high, looking down her little haughty nose. At last she said,

"I hope now you will begin work on your career again, Guy. The Prime Minister wishes you to. He meant you only to stay in the background temporarily, not to disappear out of sight. And don't keep your wife buried in the country, either. I make no predictions, but it's possible she may be no great hindrance to you. She has a passable appearance, and at least she can fight. If you'd heard her shouting at me once through a locked door—" The old lady's head dipped, her bonnet deliberately hiding her face. She seemed to be intent on the baby. Her shoulders shook very slightly. "I confess I laughed for hours. Never enjoyed anything so much. My son has met his match, I told Hannah."

Guy scowled, dropping Bella's hand.

"Mamma, you're impossible. First you won't speak to us, then you laugh at us."

"Yes, I surprise myself. I must be growing old. What's all that commotion in the hall?"

The commotion was the arrival of Cousin Henrietta. A cab was at the door, and Doughty was unloading the familiar endless number of boxes and bags. Cousin Henrietta, hopelessly dowdy in her sturdy country clothes, took one look at Bella and Guy, murmured, "Thank God!" under her breath, and then turned her bright saturnine gaze on Mrs. Raven.

"Good gracious, Edith, you look very old!"

Mrs. Raven inclined her head. "Thank you, Henrietta. I return the compliment."

"But I see you've made the acquaintance of your grandchild."

"And not before time! Do you agree that she has my hands? Her father's eyes perhaps, but definitely my hands?"

The two bonneted heads bent over Kate. Bella found she had slipped her arm through Guy's, and it was held there, firmly tucked against his side. Neither of them spoke. It was enough, at present, that they could smile together at two sentimental old women. It was Cousin Henrietta who had said that marriages were made on earth, and Bella had never lacked determination or optimism.

Perhaps it was her optimism that made her suddenly so certain the ghosts had departed.